ACKNOWLEDGMENTS

My gratitude goes to John Massey for traveling the road with me; to Beth Kapusta, my first and best reader; to psychotherapists Diane Scally and Elly Roselle for sharing their knowledge and insights across lifetimes; to Margaret Dragu for showing me the inside of club life; and to Bruce Bailey for generously loaning his domiciles. For dedicated location scouting I'm grateful to Lisa Harrison, Chelsea Nash-Wolfe, Barb Webb, Steve Reinke, and Philip von Zweck. No one deserves thanks more than my agents, Samantha Haywood and Kimberly Witherspoon, and William Callahan is also to be acknowledged. As well, my appreciation goes to my editors, Tara Singh, Adrienne Kerr, and Marion Donaldson, and to copy editor Sheila Moody. Last but not least, I'm indebted to Karyn Marcus for the edit that changed everything.

THE SILENT WIFE

A.S.A. HARRISON

LARGE PRINT PRESS
A part of Gale, Cengage Learning

GALE
CENGAGE Learning®

Detroit • New York • San Francisco • New Haven, Conn • Waterville, Maine • London

GALE
CENGAGE Learning®

Copyright © A. S. A. Harrison, 2013.
Large Print Press, a part of Gale, Cengage Learning.

LIBRARY OF CONGRESS CATALOGING-IN-PUBLICATION DATA

Harrison, A. S. A.
  The silent wife / by A. S. A. Harrison. — Large print edition.
    pages ; cm. (Wheeler publishing large print hardcover)
  ISBN-13: 978-1-4104-6544-3 (hardcover)
  ISBN-10: 1-4104-6544-6 (hardcover)
    1. Marriage—Fiction. 2. Domestic fiction. 3. Psychological fiction. 4. Large type books. I. Title.
  PR9199.3.H3465S55 2013b
  813'.54—dc23   2013037189

ISBN 13: 978-1-59413-742-6 (pbk. : alk. paper)
ISBN 10: 1-59413-742-0 (pbk. : alk. paper)

Published in 2014 by arrangement with Penguin Books, a member of Penguin Group (USA) LLC, a Penguin Random House Company.

Printed in the United States of America
1 2 3 4 5   18 17 16 15 14

■ ■ ■ ■

PART ONE:
HER AND HIM

■ ■ ■ ■

1
HER

It's early September. Jodi Brett is in her kitchen, making dinner. Thanks to the open plan of the condo, she has an unobstructed view through the living room to its east-facing windows and beyond to a vista of lake and sky, cast by the evening light in a uniform blue. A thinly drawn line of a darker hue, the horizon, appears very near at hand, almost touchable. She likes this delineating arc, the feeling it gives her of being encircled. The sense of containment is what she loves most about living here, in her aerie on the twenty-seventh floor.

At forty-five, Jodi still sees herself as a young woman. She does not have her eye on the future but lives very much in the moment, keeping her focus on the everyday. She assumes, without having thought about it, that things will go on indefinitely in their imperfect yet entirely acceptable way. In other words, she is deeply unaware that her life is now peaking, that her youthful resilience — which her twenty-year marriage to Todd Gilbert has been slowly eroding — is approaching a final stage of disintegration, that her notions about who she is and how she ought to conduct herself are far less stable than she supposes, given that a few short months are all it will take to make a killer out of her.

If you told her this she would not believe you. Murder is barely a word in her vocabulary, a concept without meaning, the subject of stories in the news having to do with people she doesn't know and will never meet. Domestic violence she finds especially implausible, that everyday friction in a family setting could escalate to such a degree. There are reasons for this incomprehension, even aside from her own habit of self-control: She is no idealist, believes in taking the bad with the good, does not pick fights, and is not easily baited.

The dog, a golden retriever with a silky blond coat, sits at her feet as she works at the cutting board. Every now and then she throws him a slice of raw carrot, which he catches in his mouth and joyfully grinds up with his molars. This vegetable toss is a long-standing predinner ritual, one that she and the dog have enjoyed from the time she brought him home as a roly-poly pup to take Todd's mind off his yearning for progeny, which sprang up, seemingly overnight, around the time he turned forty. She named the dog Freud in anticipation of the fun she could poke at his namesake, the misogynist whom she was forced to take seriously at university. Freud passing gas, Freud eating garbage, Freud chasing his tail. The dog is endlessly good-natured and doesn't mind in the least being an object of fun.

Trimming vegetables and chopping herbs, she throws herself bodily into the work. She likes the intensity of cooking — the readiness of the gas flame, the timer marking off the minutes, the immediacy of the result. She's aware of the silence beyond the kitchen, everything rushing to the point in time when she'll hear his key in the lock, an event that she anticipates with pleasure. She can still feel that making dinner for Todd is an occasion, can still marvel at the stroke of fate that brought him into her life, a matter of rank chance that did not seem to favor a further acquaintance, much less a future of appetizing meals, lovingly prepared.

It came to pass on a rainy morning in spring. Busy with her graduate studies in psychology, waiting tables at night, overworked, exhausted, she was moving house,

13

driving north on State Street in a rental van loaded with her household goods. As she prepared to change lanes from right to left she might have looked over her shoulder or maybe not. She found the van awkward, didn't have a feel for it, and on top of this her windows were fogged and she'd missed her turn at the last set of lights. Given these conditions she might have been distracted — a question that later came to be much discussed between them. When he clipped her driver's-side door and spun her into oncoming traffic, there was a general honking of horns and squealing of brakes, and before she could pull herself together — before she fully realized that her van had come to a standstill and she was perfectly alright — he was screaming at her through her closed window.

"You crazy bitch. What in God's name do you think you're doing? Are you some kind of maniac? Where did you learn to drive? People like you should stay off the road. Are you going to get out of your car or are you just going to sit there like an imbecile?"

His tirade that day in the rain did not give a favorable impression, but a man who's been in a car crash is going to be irate even if it's his own fault, which in this instance it was not, so when he called a few days later

14

to ask her to dinner, she graciously accepted.

He took her to Greektown, where they ate lamb souvlaki washed down with cold retsina. The restaurant was crowded, the tables close together, the lights bright. They found themselves shouting over the din and laughing at their failure to be heard. What conversation they could manage was pared down to succinct phrases like, "The food is good . . . I like it here . . . my windows were fogged . . . if it hadn't happened I would never have met you."

She didn't go out on many bona fide dates. The men she knew from university took her for pizza and beer and counted out their money. They'd meet her at the restaurant scruffy and unshaven, still in the clothes they'd worn to class. Whereas Todd had put on a clean shirt, and he'd picked her up, and they'd driven to the restaurant together — and now he was looking after her, refilling her glass and checking on her comfort level. Sitting across from him, she was pleased with what she saw — the way he casually took up space and his air of being in charge. She liked the homey habit he had of wiping his knife on his bread and that he put down his credit card without looking at the bill.

When they were back in his truck he drove her to his building site in Bucktown, a nineteenth-century mansion that he was reconverting — from rooming house back into single-family dwelling. Guiding her up the crumbling walk he lightly held her elbow.

"Careful now. Watch your step."

It was a Gothic Revival eyesore of decaying brick, flaking paint, and narrow windows, with spiky gables that gave it a menacing upward thrust — a vulgar aberration on a street lined with square-built structures that were fully restored. In place of the front porch there was a ladder to be climbed, and in the entrance hall a massive chandelier lay on its side. The front room, a vaultlike space with an implausibly high ceiling, featured heaps of rubble and dangling wires.

"There used to be a wall here," he said, gesturing. "You can see the footprint."

She looked at the floor with its missing planks.

"When they turned it into a boardinghouse they built a lot of partitions. The way it is now, this is back to the original layout. You can really see how it's going to shape up."

She found it hard to picture any sort of

16

end result. It didn't help that there was no electricity, the only light a pale wash coming from the streetlamps outside. He lit a candle, dripped some of the melting wax into a saucer, and fixed it upright. He was keen to show her around, and they carried the candle through the empty rooms — the would-be kitchen, the long-lost parlor, provisional spaces defined by walls that were down to the lath-work. Upstairs, the rooming house it used to be was more in evidence, the bedroom doors fixed with latches and the walls painted in unlikely colors. The musty smell was strong up here and the atmosphere was eerie with the old wood creaking underfoot and the candle creating ripples of light that cast the two of them as specters on the walls and ceiling.

"It's not a restoration," he said. "It will all be overhauled and modernized. Oak floors, solid-core doors, double-pane windows . . . This will be something that everybody wants, an old house with personality but one that's absolutely solid and up-to-date."

He had taken it on single-handed, he said, learning the trades as he went along. He was doing this instead of university, had borrowed money, was living on credit and optimism. She understood just how stretched he was when she saw the rolled-up sleeping bag in one of the bedrooms, and in the bathroom a razor and a can of foam.

"So what do you think?" he asked, when they were back downstairs.

"I'd like to see it when it's done," she said.

He laughed. "You think I'm in over my head."

"It's ambitious," she conceded.

"You're going to be impressed," he said.

By the time she hears him come in, both lake and sky have receded into a velvety dusk. She switches off the overhead fixture, leaving the valance lights to orchestrate a mellow glow, removes her apron, and licks her fingers to smooth the hair at her temples, a gesture that is pure anticipation, listening all the while to his movements in the foyer. He fusses over the dog, hangs up his jacket, empties his pockets into the cast bronze bowl on the console table. There's a brief silence as he looks through the mail. She arranges a smoked trout on a plate with a fan of crackers.

He's a big man with hair the color of sand, slate-gray eyes, and a whopping charge of vitality. When Todd Gilbert enters a room people wake up. That's what she would say if someone asked her what she loved most about him. Also that he can make her laugh

18

when he wants to, and that unlike a lot of men she knows he's good at multitasking, so that even as he's taking a call on his cell phone he can do up the clasp on her necklace or show her how to use a two-step sommelier corkscrew.

He swipes her forehead with his lips, steps around her, and reaches into the cupboard for the cocktail glasses. "Looks good," he says. "What is it?" Referring to the golden, pastry-encrusted meat, which is out of the oven and resting in the pan.

"Beef Wellington. We've had it before, remember? You like it."

It's his job to make the martinis. As she whisks together a marinade for the vegetables, she's aware of the clatter of ice cubes and the sharp fragrance he makes with his knife, cutting into a lemon. He bumps against her, knocks things over, gets in her way, but she likes having him near, the comforting bulk of him. She takes in the smell of his day, gravitates to his body heat. He's a man whose touch is always warm, a matter of animal significance for someone who is nearly always cold.

Having set her martini in front of her on the counter, he carries his own, along with the trout, to the living room, where he puts up his feet and opens the paper that she's

19

left for him on the coffee table, neatly refolded. She places the French beans and baby carrots in separate steamers and takes the first sip of her drink, liking how the vodka instantly hits her bloodstream and streaks through her limbs. From the sofa he throws out comments on the day's news: the next Olympics, a hike in interest rates, a forecast of rain. When he's swallowed most of the trout and the last of his martini he gets up and opens a bottle of wine while she carves the beef into thick slabs. They take their plates to the table, where they both have a view of the lustrous sky.

"How was your day?" he asks, loading up his fork.

"I saw Bergman," she says.

"Bergman. What did she have to say for herself?" He's shoveling in the beef with steady concentration and speaks without looking up from his plate.

"She reminded me that it's been three years since she made the pudding commercial. I think she had it in mind to pin some of the blame on me."

He knows her clients by the code names she gives them. Since they come and go while he's at work he's never encountered even a single one, but she keeps him up-to-date, and in a sense he's intimate with them all. She doesn't see any harm in this as long as their real names remain secret. Bergman is code for the out-of-work actress whose last job — the fabled pudding commercial — is a distant memory.

"So now it's your fault," he says.

"She gets that it's her desperation that's putting people off, and why haven't I helped her with that, she wants to know. Hell's bells. We've been working on that for weeks."

"I don't know how you put up with it," he says.

"If you could see her you'd understand. She's feisty, a real fighter. She'll never give up, and eventually something will change for her."

"I wouldn't have the patience."

"You would if you cared about them. You know my clients are like my children."

A shadow crosses his face and she understands that the mention of surrogate children has reminded him of the actual children he doesn't have. Reverting to Bergman she says, "I worry about her, though. It's one of those cases where she can't believe in herself if no one will hire her, but no one will hire her because she doesn't believe in herself, and the thing is I don't know if I'm actually helping her. Sometimes I think I should fire myself as her therapist."

"Why don't you?" he says. "If you're not getting anywhere."

"Well, we're not getting *nowhere*. Like I said, she's at least figured out that she's doing this to herself."

"I love this beef," he says. "How did you get the meat inside the pastry?"

As if it were a ship in a bottle, but she knows he isn't joking. For a man who can raise walls and sink foundations, he's surprisingly simpleminded when it comes to cooking.

"It's wrapped," she says. "Think of insulation around a pipe."

But he's staring into space and doesn't appear to register her answer.

He's always been prone to these lapses, though it seems to her that lately they've been more frequent. Here one minute, gone the next, carried along by a river of thought, conjecture, worry, who knows? He could be silently counting backward from a hundred or mentally reciting the names of the presidents. At least she can't fault his mood. For a while now he's been distinctly more cheerful, more like his old self, to the point where she's starting to think that his depression is a thing of the past. At one time she feared that it might be permanent. It went on for so long and not even Freud could snap him out of it. Freud as a puppy, with his goofy antics, was as good as a court jester.

At least he could always fake it at a dinner party — keep the liquor flowing, turn on the bonhomie, make people feel good. Women respond to Todd because he's so ingenuous and openhanded. *Rosalie, you've been drinking from the fountain of youth again. Deirdre, you look good enough to eat.* He gives it up to the men, too, letting them talk about themselves without competing, and he gets people laughing with his mimicry: the East Indian naturopath (*You are taking too much tension . . . you must go slowly slowly*), the Jamaican mechanic (*De car wan tree new tires . . . fly di bonnet, mon*).

He's definitely better now, more alive, ready to laugh even when they're alone, more easygoing and relaxed, less of a worry, more like his old self, the way he was in the early years — although the days are gone when they used to get naked in bed to read the paper and watch the game and share a bowl of cornflakes, the milk carton balanced on the bedpost, sugar spilling out of the Domino bag onto the sheets. Back then they had the freedom of knowing each other barely at all; they were in gleeful possession of a leisurely future with all the doors still open and all the promises still fully redeemable.

"Penny for your thoughts," she says.

His eyelids flutter and he gives her a smile. "This is delicious," he says. He reaches for the half-empty bottle and refills their glasses. "What do you think of this wine?"

He likes to talk about wine. At times, what they are drinking can form the hub of an entire dinner conversation. But now, instead of waiting for her answer, he smacks his palm on the side of his head and says, "I meant to tell you. There's a fishing trip this weekend. Some of the guys are going."

"A fishing trip," she says.

He's polished off his two slabs of beef and is mopping up the juices with a piece of bread. "Leaving Friday after work. Back Sunday."

Todd doesn't go on fishing trips, and as far as she knows neither do any of the guys. She understands immediately — there's no doubt in her mind — that he's using the term "fishing trip" euphemistically.

"Are you going?" she asks.

"I'm thinking about it."

Still working on her meal, she's trying to hurry now. The way she sometimes eats — taking minuscule bites and holding them captive in her mouth — can try his patience, she knows. She swallows a tidbit that's only half chewed and it lodges in her throat, triggering her gag reflex. Gallantly, he leaps up and pounds her on the back as she sputters and heaves. At last, the shred of matter that caused the problem erupts into her hand. Without looking at it she places it on the edge of her plate.

"Let me know what you decide," she says, using her napkin to blot the corners of her eyes. "If you go I might have the carpets cleaned. And make some marmalade."

She doesn't plan on doing either of these things; it's just something to say. She has always counted it a plus that he doesn't lie to her, meaning that he doesn't embroider his accounts of himself with the kind of detail that would turn them into lies. The problem here has nothing to do with his circumlocution. The problem is that he doesn't go away for the weekend, that going away for the weekend is something he's never done before.

"Hey," he says. "I got you a present."

He leaves the room and comes back with a package — a flat rectangle roughly the size of a paperback book, wrapped in brown paper and secured with masking tape. He puts it on the table next to her plate and sits down again. He often gives her presents and she loves this about him, but she loves it less when the presents are meant to placate her.

"What's the occasion?" she asks.

"No occasion."

There's a smile on his face but the atmosphere is crackling. Objects should be flying across the room; heads should be spinning on their stalks. She picks up the package and finds it nearly weightless. The tape peels off easily, and from a sandwich of protective cardboard she extracts a beautiful small picture, a Rajput painting, an original. The scene, blocked out in blues and greens, portrays a woman in a long dress standing in a walled garden. Surrounded by peacocks and a gazelle, adorned with elaborate gold jewelry, she is evidently not plagued by any material worries or worldly concerns. Leafy branches arch protectively over her head, and the grass beneath her feet is a wide green carpet. They study the scene together, comment on the woman's hennaed hands, her little white basket, her lovely figure seen through the voile of her gown. As they take in the fine detail and flat blocks of color, their life unobtrusively returns to normal. He was right to get it for her. His instincts are good.

It's nearing bedtime as she clears the table

and starts on the dishes. He makes a per-functory offer of help, but they both know that it's best if he leaves the cleanup to her and takes the dog for a walk. Not that she's so terribly exacting. Her standards are not unreasonable, but when you wash a roasting pan it should not be greasy when you're done, nor should you wipe the grease off with your dish towel, which you are then going to use on the crystal. This is common sense. He isn't careless when it comes to construction. If he were putting up a shelf he wouldn't set it at an angle so that objects placed on it slid to the floor and broke. He'd pay attention and do the job right, and nobody watching would call him a perfectionist or accuse him of being fussy. Not that she's inclined to complain. It's a known fact that in certain contexts people's great strengths become their epic failings. His impatience with domestic work stems from the fact that his expansive energy overshoots the scale of the tasks to be done. You can see it in the way he fills a room, looming and towering in the limited space, his voice loud, his gestures sweeping. He's a man who belongs outside or on a building site, where his magnitude makes sense. At home, he's often at his best asleep beside her, his bulk in repose and his energy dormant in a kind of comforting absence.

She moves through her lovely rooms, drawing drapes, plumping cushions, straightening pictures, picking lint off the carpet, and generally creating the setting that she wants to wake up to in the morning. It's important to have everything serenely in its place as she begins her day. In the bedroom she turns down the covers and lays out pajamas for him and a nightgown for herself, smoothing the fabric and folding back appendages to make the garments look less like uninhabited bodies. Even so, something about them gives her a turn — the white piping on the dark pajamas, the silky ties on the nightgown. She leaves the room and steps outside onto the balcony. There's a raw wind, and in the moonless night the vista is a bottomless black. She leans into the bristling darkness, indulging a sense of isolation, liking the fact that she can control it — linger till she loses her taste for it and then go back inside. She's grateful for the stability and security of her life, has come to treasure the everyday freedoms, the absence of demands and complications. By forgoing marriage and children she has kept a clean slate, allowed for a sense of spaciousness. There are no regrets. Her nurturing instincts find an outlet with her clients, and in every practical sense she is as married as anyone else. Her friends of course know her as Jodi Brett, but to most people she is Mrs. Gilbert. She likes the name and title; they give her a pedigree of sorts and act as an all-around shorthand, eliminating the need to correct people or make explanations, dispensing with awkward terminology like *life partner* and *significant other.*

In the morning, after he's left for work, she gets up, dresses, and takes the dog along the waterfront to Navy Pier. The sun shimmers in a milky haze, casting a net of silver over the lake. The onshore breeze is pungent, scented with the heady marine aromas of motor oil and fish and rotting wood. At this time of day the pier is like a sleeping giant, its pulse slowed and its breath subdued. There are only the locals — the dog walkers and the joggers — to witness the rocking boats, the slapping water, the abandoned air of the carousel and Ferris wheel, the gulls diving for their breakfast. When she turns back toward the city the skyline appears like a vision surging up along the shore, dramatically lit by the rising sun. She came to Chicago as a student more than twenty years ago and felt immediately at home. She lives here not only physically but temperamentally. After the privations of a small town she was thrilled by the soaring buildings, the crush of people, the lavish variety, and even the dramatic weather. This is where she came of age, forged her identity, learned to thrive as an adult and a professional.

She started her practice the spring she finished school. By then she was living with Todd in a tiny one-bedroom in Lincoln Park. Her first clients were referred by her university contacts, and she saw them in the living room while Todd was at work. Having decided early on, while still an undergrad, that her approach would be eclectic — that she would draw on whatever she had in her repertoire that made the most sense in the situation — she practiced active listening, took a Gestalt approach to dream interpretation, and openly challenged self-defeating attitudes and behaviors. She counseled people to ask more of themselves and take charge of their own well-being. She gave them encouragement and positive feedback. During her first year she discovered how to be patient and bring people along at their own pace. Her greatest asset was her genuine friendliness — she liked her clients and gave them the benefit of the doubt, which put them at ease. They spoke well of her to others, and her practice grew.

For nearly a year she skimmed along nicely, getting her stride, developing skills, gaining confidence. And then one day a client of hers — a young man of fifteen who'd been diagnosed as bipolar, a good boy who did well in school and *seemed* perfectly fine — Sebastian was his name — dark hair, dark eyes, curious, engaged, liked to ask rhetorical questions (Why is there something rather than nothing? How can we know anything for sure?) — this client of hers, young Sebastian, was found dead on the pavement underneath the tenth-floor balcony of his apartment, the apartment where he lived with his parents. When he failed to appear for his regular session she called his home and heard the news from his mother. By the time she found out, he'd been dead for five days.

"Don't blame yourself," his mother was kind enough to say. But he'd jumped on the very day of their last session. She'd seen him in the morning and he'd ended his life not twelve hours later. What had they talked about? Some small problem he was having with his eyes. He'd been seeing things in his peripheral vision, fleeting things that weren't really there.

That's when she enrolled for additional studies at the Adler School, and that's when she started picking and choosing her clients.

She crosses Gateway Park, passes the time of day with a neighbor, and stops at Caffé Rom for a latte to go. While eating her soft-boiled egg and buttered toast she reads the paper. After breakfast she clears away the dishes and then gets out the file on her first client, code name the judge, a gay male lawyer with a wife and children. The judge has certain things in common with her other clients. He's hit a wall in his life and believes or hopes that psychotherapy will help him. He's made a commitment to himself to see it through. And he doesn't bring to the table more than she can handle. This last point she has determined through a screening process. People with self-destructive behaviors are referred elsewhere. She doesn't take addicts, for example, whether it's drugs, alcohol, or gambling, and she rejects anyone who has an eating disorder, has been diagnosed as bipolar or schizophrenic, suffers from chronic depression, or has thought about or attempted suicide. These are people who should be on medication or in rehab.

Her schedule allows for just two clients a day, before lunch. The clients she ends up with, after screening, tend to be stuck, lost, or insecure, the kind of people who find it hard to know what they want and make decisions based on what is expected of them or what they believe is expected of them. They can be tough on themselves — having internalized the judgments of insensitive parents — and at the same time behave in ways that are irresponsible or inappropriate. On the whole they can't get their priorities straight, fail to create personal boundaries, neglect their own best interests, and see themselves as victims.

The spare bedroom, which serves as her consulting room, comfortably holds a desk, a filing cabinet, and a pair of armchairs that face each other on a six-by-eight-foot antique kilim. Between the chairs is a low table that holds her clipboard and pen, a box of Kleenex, a bottle of water, and two glasses. The judge is wearing his usual dark suit with black oxfords and vivid argyle socks, revealed when he sits down and crosses his legs. He's thirty-eight and has sensuous eyes and lips, set in a long face. Taking her place across from him she asks how he's been keeping since she saw him last, a week ago. He talks about his visit to a leather bar and what happened in the alley out back. He goes into detail, maybe hoping to shock her, but sex between consenting adults is not going to do it, and anyway this isn't the first time he's tried her patience with something like this. He's talking fast, changing direction midstream, reliving it, doing his best to draw her in.

"My pants were down around my ankles — imagine if someone had — oh my God did the garbage stink. I focused on that — the garbage — to slow things down — I had to do *something.* He'd been staring at me in the bar. I'd seen him there before but didn't think — I haven't been to that bar in ages."

As the story peters out he watches her slyly, eyes glistening, lips slick with saliva. He'd like it if she laughed and said naughty boy, you're a wicked one, but her job does not involve filling in gaps in the conversation or performing social rescues. He waits, and when she doesn't speak he fidgets and looks at his hands. "So," he says finally. "I'm sorry. I really am. I'm very sorry. I shouldn't have done it." These are words that he can't say to his wife, so he says them to his therapist.

His pattern is denial followed by indulgence followed by a renewed period of denial. The denial stage is cued by statements such as "I love my family and don't want to hurt them." The remorse is genuine, but he can no more give up his gay pursuits than forgo the security blanket of his home life. Both play a part in fulfilling his needs, and both are important to his sense of identity. He pretends to himself that his interest in men is a passing phase and doesn't see that abstinence and guilt are ways he has of charging his batteries for a fully loaded thrill. Like many people who cheat, he likes to self-dramatize. He's more of a queen than he knows.

"You be the judge," she tells him. But he's still a ways from owning up.

Wednesday is cheaters' day. Her next client, Miss Piggy, a coy young woman with chubby cheeks and freckled hands, maintains that having a lover stimulates her appetites and keeps her marriage alive. According to Miss Piggy her husband suspects nothing and would have no right to complain if he did. It's unclear why Miss Piggy is in therapy or what she expects to get out of it. She differs from the judge in her lack of a nagging conscience and the practical way she goes about things — on Monday and Thursday afternoons between shopping for groceries and picking up the kids from school.

Miss Piggy appears to be less conflicted than the judge, but from Jodi's point of view she's a greater challenge. Her anxiety flows beneath the surface in underground streams, rarely bubbling up or creating a disturbance. Tapping into it and bringing it into her field of awareness is not going to be easy. Whereas the judge is simply an open book, a sensitive man who's landed himself in a pickle. Eventually, with or without Jodi's help, the judge's problem will come to a head and work its way out of his life.

In spite of Miss Piggy's belief that her husband is in the dark, Jodi thinks that he probably has his suspicions. There are always signs, as she well knows. For instance, the cheater is frequently distracted or preoccupied; the cheater dislikes being questioned; inexplicable smells cling to the cheater's hair and clothes. The smells can be anything: incense, mildew, grass. Mouthwash. Who uses mouthwash at the end of the day before coming home to bed? A shower can eliminate telltale body odors, but the soap the cheater uses in the hotel bathroom is going to be different from the brand he uses at home. On top of this there are all the usual clues: the stray red or blond hairs, lipstick stains, rumpled clothing, furtive phone calls, unexplained absences, mysterious marks on the body . . . not to mention the curious acquisitions — the

fancy key chain or bottle of aftershave —
that appear out of nowhere, especially on
Valentine's Day.

At least he does his best to be discreet
and as a rule does not advance on her
friends, although there have been times.
There was a couple they used to be chummy
with, people they met on vacation in the
Caribbean and bonded with over margari-
tas and snorkeling lessons. The couple ran a
business selling prefab cottages, and Todd
had nothing but contempt for this. Nonetheless, for several winters running they made
a point of meeting up with this couple at
designated resorts. She suspected that Todd
and Sheila had something going on but put
it out of her mind until the afternoon they
disappeared from the poolside and re-
appeared a while later looking like cats who
had lapped up a big bowl of cream. This
alone she might have overlooked, but then
there were the subtle displacements in
Todd's swimming trunks and the dab of
something gelatinous glistening in his chest
hair.

And yet, none of this matters. It simply
doesn't matter that time and time again he
gives the game away, because he knows and
she knows that he's a cheater, and he knows
that she knows, but the point is that the

pretense, the all-important pretense must be maintained, the illusion that everything is fine and nothing is the matter. As long as the facts are not openly declared, as long as he talks to her in euphemisms and circumlocutions, as long as things are functioning smoothly and a surface calm prevails, they can go on living their lives, it being a known fact that a life well lived amounts to a series of compromises based on the acceptance of those around you with their individual needs and idiosyncrasies, which can't always be tailored to one's liking or constrained to fit conservative social norms. People live their lives, express themselves, and pursue fulfillment in their own ways and in their own time. They are going to make mistakes, exercise poor judgment and bad timing, take wrong turns, develop hurtful habits, and go off on tangents. If she learned anything in school she learned this, courtesy of Albert Ellis, father of the cognitive-behavioral paradigm shift in psychotherapy. Other people are not here to fulfill our needs or meet our expectations, nor will they always treat us well. Failure to accept this will generate feelings of anger and resentment. Peace of mind comes with taking people as they are and emphasizing the positive.

Cheaters prosper; many of them do. And even if they don't they are not going to change, because, as a rule, people don't change — not without strong motivation and sustained effort. Basic personality traits develop early in life and over time become inviolable, hardwired. Most people learn little from experience, rarely think of adjusting their behavior, see problems as emanating from those around them, and keep on doing what they do in spite of everything, for better or worse. A cheater remains a cheater in the same way that an optimist remains an optimist. An optimist is a person who says, after being run over by a drunk driver and having both legs mangled and mortgaging the house to pay the hospital bills: "I was lucky. I could have been killed." To an optimist that kind of statement makes sense. To a cheater it makes sense to be living a double life and talking out of both sides of your mouth at the same time.

In asserting that people don't change, what she means is that they don't change for the better. Whereas changing for the worse, that goes without saying. Life has a way of taking its toll on the person you thought you were. She used to be a nice person, nice through and through, but she can't make that claim anymore. There was the time she tossed his cell phone into the lake, complete with the message from the female caller who addressed him as "Wolfie." The time she put his boxers in the wash with a load of colors. The many times she's seen to it that he misplaces things. She is not proud of these misdemeanors. She would like to think that she's above this kind of behavior, that she accepts him for who he is, that she's not one of those women who feel they are owed something by their men after going into it with open eyes, but she counts her own transgressions as slight compared with the liberties that he freely takes.

Having shown Miss Piggy out, she proceeds to the gym on a lower level of the condominium, where she lifts weights and cycles 10K. Following a lunch of leftover cold vegetables with mayonnaise, she takes a shower and dresses for a round of errands. Before leaving she writes out instructions for Klara, who comes in to clean on Wednesday afternoons. Daily routine is the great balm that keeps her spirits up and holds her life together, warding off the existential fright that can take you by ambush anytime you're dithering or at a loss, reminding you of the magnitude of the void you are sitting on. Keeping busy is the middle-class way —

a practical way and a good way. She enjoys
the busywork of scheduling clients, running
her household, and keeping herself fit and
groomed. She likes things orderly and
predictable and feels secure when her time
is mapped out well in advance. It's a pleasure to flip through her daybook and see
what she has to look forward to: spa visits,
hair appointments, medical checkups, Pi-
lates sessions. She attends nearly all the
events organized by her professional association and signs up for classes in anything
that interests her. Evenings, when she isn't
cooking for Todd, she has dinner with
friends. And then there are the two extended
vacations — one in summer and one in
winter — that she and Todd always enjoy
together.

Driving around in her Audi Coupe, she
puts the windows down and soaks up the
noise and commotion of the city, taking
pleasure in the din and tumult of things going on everywhere: the vendors, street musi-
cians, and outdoor markets — and even the
crowds, sirens, and traffic jams. A teenage
girl with a bunch of balloons dances across
the street. A man in a white apron sits in
full lotus on the steps of a restaurant. She
stops at the framer's with the Rajput painting, picks up a travel book, buys a kitchen

scale to replace her broken one, and on the way home sits down with a frappuccino at her local Starbucks, leaving herself enough time to walk the dog and broil a chop for dinner before attending her class in flower arranging.

2
HIM

He likes getting an early start, and over the years he's pruned his morning routine down to the fundamentals. His shower is cold, which kills the temptation to linger, and his shaving gear consists of canned foam and a safety razor. He dresses in the semidarkness of the bedroom while Jodi and the dog sleep on. Sometimes Jodi will open an eye and say, "Your shirts are back from the laundry" or "Those pants are getting bagged out," to which he replies, "Go back to sleep." He swallows a multiple vitamin with a jigger of orange juice, brushes his teeth from side to side, the wrong but fast way, and thirty minutes after getting out of bed he's in the elevator riding down to the parking garage.

Well before seven he's sitting at his desk on the fourth floor of a four-story building on South Michigan, below Roosevelt. This building — a brick and limestone structure with a flat roof and steel-framed insulated windows that were state of the art when he installed them — was his first large-scale renovation, undertaken after a decade of flipping houses and before the South Loop condominium craze sent property values out of sight. When he first acquired it the building was dead space, and he financed its conversion into office suites with three mortgages and a line of credit, all the while laboring side by side with the workmen he hired. He could have done everything himself, but if his money ran out the banks would foreclose. In this business things like mortgage payments, taxes, and insurance make literal truth of the saying that time is money. The suite he has claimed for himself is a modest one, consisting of two offices, a small reception area, and a washroom. His office is the larger of the two, the one overlooking the street. The decor is modern and spare, with bare surfaces and solar shades — uncluttered with antiques and bric-a-brac as it would be if he'd let Jodi have her way.

He makes his first call of the day to the deli that delivers his breakfast and orders, as always, two BLTs and two large coffees. While he's waiting he takes an old tobacco tin from his desk drawer, pries off the lid, and dumps the contents onto his desktop:

Bugler rolling papers, book of matches, and small baggie containing a handful of dried buds and leaves. During the time he was depressed he found that smoking a little weed first thing could lift him out of his apathy and help him get down to work. He's accustomed now to the ceremony of rolling and lighting up, and he likes the mellow way of easing into his day. He takes his spliff to the window and exhales the smoke into the open air. Not that it's any kind of secret that he likes a toke or two; he just doesn't think that TJG Holdings should smell like a frat house.

It used to be that from his window he had a clear view of the sky, but what he sees now is a small irregular patch of blue floating amid the condos across the street. Better than nothing, and he's not going to knock the boom. Anyway, his attention is focused on the people waiting at the bus stop. A few are standing in the shelter even though the morning is clear and mild and the shelter is littered with trash. He likes it when he can ID some of the regulars: the bopper with the headphones and backpack, the old skinny guy in the baseball cap who chain-smokes, the pregnant woman in the sari and jean jacket. Nearly everyone is focused on the oncoming traffic, straining for a glimpse of the approaching bus. As usual, one or two have stepped off the curb and are standing in the street to get a better view. When the sighting finally occurs the tension visibly dissolves, as if they were one and all of the same mind and body. Reaching for fares, the loose congregation compresses into a restless column. He, of course, spotted the bus when it was blocks away. Sometimes he feels like God up here at his fourth-story window.

The man from the deli brings breakfast to his desk and takes the money that's been left for him under a paperweight. Todd gives him a nod and continues talking to Cliff York on the phone. He's making notes but won't need to refer to them. He has no trouble mentally keeping track of names, dates and figures, times and places, even telephone numbers. The project under discussion, a six-unit apartment house in Jefferson Park, is in the middle stages of completion. Initial obstacles — plans, permits, financing — have been overcome, and all the units have been gutted. He and Cliff, his general contractor, are talking about water pressure. They set a time to meet later in the day to look things over and hear what the plumber has to say.

Tackling his breakfast he finds the toast a

little soggy, but the bacon is crisp. When he's finished both sandwiches and one coffee he gets back on the phone, this time with his real-estate agent, who has found him a potential buyer. This is good news. The apartment house is an interim project. If he has to he'll hold on to it and lease the units, but the game plan is to sell it and use the capital for his next venture, an office building on a grander scale, something that will trump everything he's done so far.

Stephanie arrives at twenty past nine. She takes her time getting sorted and it's half past before she appears in his office with her notepad and files and pulls a chair up to his desk. Stephanie is girlish, a young thirty-five, with bushy hair that she bundles into a ponytail. He always takes an interest in where and how Stephanie is going to place herself, whether directly across from him, where he can see her only from the waist up, or to his right, where she's inclined to cross her legs while resting her forearm on the desktop to take notes. The oval desktop over-hanging a rectangular base allows for plenty of legroom all around, so when she chooses to display her legs, for whatever reason, he counts it as his lucky day. If she's wearing jeans he has a view of her crotch and thighs; if it's a skirt he gets to look at her knees and calves. She doesn't flirt but doesn't seem to notice or care if he watches her cross and recross her legs. Today she's in jeans but takes a seat on the far side of his desk, so he has to make do with the twin peaks that strain against the middle buttons of her blouse. She's not much taller than five feet, which is why the size of her bosom is so impressive.

She's brought in a sheaf of files and a list of things to run by him: pricing on ceiling fans, Web addresses of landscapers, questionable invoices. Anything that is not strictly routine, he wants to know about. He didn't get where he is today by overlooking details or letting his business get away from him. He's only one man and his profit margins are not stupendous, which means that everything counts. He glances at his watch, just so she knows that her late entrance has not been overlooked.

"Nothing from Cliff?" he asks, when it comes down to the invoices.

"Not yet."

"Show it to me when you get it. Last time he listed material costs for something that we supplied ourselves. What was it?"

"Bathroom tile."

"Right. Bathroom tile. And grout. He billed me for the goddamn grout."

She's done the research he asked her to do on toilets and hands him the brochures. "The low-flow models are cheaper than the dual-flush, but they're not reliable," she says.

"What's wrong with them?"

"They don't always flush."

"They have to flush."

"It doesn't always go down."

"Cliff has installed them before."

"You can't chance it," she says. "Not with rental units. You should take a look at the dual-flush options."

He frowns and asks, "How much?"

"It's not too bad. You can get something reliable for five hundred."

"That's three grand for the goddamn toilets. We could go to Home Depot and get toilets for fifty bucks apiece."

"You could, but you won't."

"What else?" he asks.

"You need to think about fridges and stoves. It could take a while for them to ship."

"Get me some quotes. If everything comes from the same supplier we should get a price break."

"How do I know what sizes?"

"Look at the plans."

"I don't have the plans. You took them

49

home with you."

"Get a set from Carol at Vanderburgh. The units aren't all the same."

When she's gathered up her papers and given him a view of her retreating ass, he drifts for a while, listening with one ear to the busy noises coming from her office. His mind is on everything at once, encircling the whole of his world at a sweep, as if it were a baseball field and he were on a home run, flying by the bases, all the while with his eye on the ball. It's come to a point where he savors the constant apprehension, the risk he takes with each small decision, the strain of being overextended, the pressure of betting everything on the current venture. The anxiety he feels is stabilizing in a way, letting him know that he's alive and on track. It's anxiety cut with anticipation, an interest in what comes next, a stake in things unfolding. This is what propels him through his day.

During his depression he lost that forward momentum. In fact, the loss of it was the very thing that was wrong with him. It was time without nuance or modulation, always the same, minute by minute, day by day. He knew nothing of the defeat or futility that people assumed he was feeling. He was simply not there, an absence, an empty space.

He checks the time and makes a call. The sleepy voice that says hello gives him a gratifying jolt, waking up his gonads.

"You're not still in bed."

"Uh-huh."

"Don't you have a class?"

"Not till later."

"Spoiled rotten."

"I hope so."

"What are you wearing?"

"What do you think?"

"Birthday suit."

"Why do you want to know?"

"Why do you think I want to know?"

"Is this official?"

"Off the record."

"I'll need that in writing."

They keep this going for a long while. He pictures her lying in twisted sheets in the cramped bedroom on North Claremont where she shares an apartment with roommates. He went there once, in the early days when there were still places on her body that he hadn't touched. Afterward, in the kitchen, the roommates gathered round and asked a lot of nosy questions — mostly about his age and his wife. After that they started meeting at the Crowne Plaza on

Madison, where the staff is consistently distant and polite.

As he talks to her he's buffeted by feelings that still register as vaguely foreign, making him wonder if he's someone else, not Todd Gilbert but a man who sidled into Todd Gilbert's body during the months when he was absent. In the short span of time that he's known her, she's given him back his life. That's what he owes her, the gift of life, as found in the feelings that make a man human — not just love but greed, lust, desire . . . the whole teeming, disruptive lot. Even his impatience is a gift, the impatience to be with her that dogs him the whole day through. Even his jealousy is a gift. He knows it's her right to be with a younger lover and fears that it's just a matter of time before she figures this out. Painful as it is, he's at least in the land of the living.

Jealousy is new to him; he's used to feeling confident with women. According to Jodi the confidence comes from growing up an only child with a doting mother, a nurse, who stuck to part-time work in spite of money being tight so she could mostly stay at home and look after him — her way of making up for the shortcomings of his father, a public-works employee who drank. When he was still in high school he assumed

52

the role of his mother's provider by learning how to make money and take responsibility, and for this he was much praised, not only by his mother but by his mother's friends and his teachers and the girls he knew. Women like him. They like him because he knows how to look after them. He looks after Natasha, but there's a catch with Natasha. She makes him conscious of his aging body and flagging vitality. Not because of anything she says or does; only because she's young and desirable and insatiable.

He's still on the phone when Stephanie returns with a sheaf of checks for him to sign. He's been pacing and comes to a halt by the window. She puts the checks on his desk and waits. Stephanie, he knows, is well aware of the goings-on between him and Natasha, who came here once looking like she could eat him alive. Stephanie's words. What kind of assistant speaks to her boss like that? And lately, Stephanie has made a point of walking in on their telephone conversations. She leaves him no choice but to end them abruptly, like now. She has a pen in her hand and thrusts it at him as if they were fencing.

Before leaving the office he calls Jodi to say that he won't be home for dinner. It's a courtesy call; she's aware that he's seeing

Dean tonight. But he likes to let her know that he's thinking about her. He's a lucky man and doesn't lose sight of the fact. She's still a knockout with her slender figure and dark hair, and in spite of being a homebody herself, she understands that he can't be spending his evenings sitting around the condo. Some of his friends have to be home for dinner every night. Some can't even go for a beer after work. Luckily, his buddies are vast in number — including virtually everyone he's ever worked with — and many of them are single or divorced, so he can nearly always find a drinking partner. Not that he minds an evening on his own, when it comes to that.

He and Dean Kovacs go all the way back to high school. Dean is his oldest friend and the only one who knew his father. When he speaks of his father as a mean old fuck, Dean knows exactly what he's talking about. Dean is like family, practically a brother. But he's also Natasha's father, and that could be a problem. Or maybe not. It's hard to say how Dean will react when he finds out what's been going on. He'll be shaken up for sure, but once he's had a chance to get used to it, who knows? Maybe they'll have a laugh about it — he can call Dean "Dad" or "Pop," and Dean can tell him to get lost. Ten to one everything will work out fine. At least it's not him who has to break it to Dean. That's Natasha's job. She'll tell him when she thinks the time is right. That's what they've decided.

It's a warm day, and down in the street the heat and grime rise from the pavement like perfume. He loves this city right down to the concrete, loves its sheer physicality, the tonnage of its massive structures, and even more he loves its power and thrust, the religion of its commerce, its proliferating For Sale signs and frontier-style delivery of opportunities. Walking the three blocks south to the private lot where he parks his car, he feels his great good fortune in having landed here now — in this place, in this time.

Instead of heading straight for Jefferson Park he turns west on Roosevelt and makes a stop at Home Depot. If he added up the time he's spent in this store it would come to months of his life. He cares about his interiors, has opinions about things like flooring and lighting. The sum total of the details goes a long way toward making or breaking a project. Cliff would be happy to shop for paint, tiles, carpets, fixtures, and add on his ten percent, but Cliff isn't there when potential buyers walk away because they don't like the color or the finish, and whatever happens Cliff still gets paid.

He leaves the store without buying anything and gets on the expressway, his windows down and *Nevermind* playing on the stereo. The only place he ever attempts to sing is in his car, where the wind in his ears and the drone of the engine mean that even he can't hear himself. He knows the words to all the tracks and belts them out as he picks up speed. The album dates back twenty years to the cocky young man he used to be, infatuated with his own capability and promise. He first met Jodi the year that Nirvana replaced Michael Jackson at the top of the charts, and now each song is like a time machine, taking him back to the sonic boom of his love.

He had his first sight of her on State Street, their wrecked vehicles blocking both eastbound lanes, the traffic behind them at a standstill, horns blaring, people crowding round, rain pouring down, her drenched hair stuck to her face, her soaked T-shirt leaving her as good as naked from the waist up. But even though her breasts were resplendent — small but perfect, with nipples standing up like finials in the pelting rain — what struck him blind was her bearing, how cool and unperturbed she was, how regal and dignified. Not before or since has he come across a woman with half Jodi's class.

At the building site he finds Cliff smoking out front in his dusty coveralls and sagging tool belt. Cliff is a sturdy man who speaks slowly and gives the impression that he's putting down roots on the spot. He's the same age as Todd but has a shaggy salt-and-pepper mustache that adds on ten years. When the plumber pulls up in his van the three of them go inside and stroll through the units. Their conversation centers on pipes and drains and the like, compelling stuff when you are Todd Jeremy Gilbert of TJG Holdings and you are invested up to the eyeballs. The place was near derelict when he bought it, and he had to evict tenants, which he didn't enjoy, but now it's just about starting to look like something. The workmen they encounter as they tour around are taking out old wiring and putting up new beams, though it's not quite the hub of activity that Todd would like it to be. Although he's worked with Cliff for going on two decades, he still has to stay on his case. His overhead — what he pays out every day just to own this property and keep the bank and the municipality off his back — is enough to feed a village in Africa for a year.

On his way back to the city he calls Natasha in the hope that she'll meet him for lunch, but she's already eating a sandwich.

"You're eating a sandwich as we speak?"

"I'm unwrapping it, and I'm about to take a bite."

"Save it and we'll go to Francesca's."

"I can't. I have to get to class."

"Can you meet me after work?"

"I'm babysitting from four to seven."

"I'll come over."

"Not a good idea."

"You know I'm busy later on."

"Let's have lunch tomorrow."

"That means I won't see you today."

"Do you think you'll survive?"

"What kind of sandwich do you have?"

"Salami on rye. From Manny's. With extra mustard."

"Are you sitting down somewhere?"

"I told you. I'm on my way to class."

"You're walking to class right now?"

"I'm walking north on Morgan. I just passed the library. And I'm going to be late if you don't let me off the phone."

"Tell me what you're wearing."

She feigns annoyance but he knows she likes it. She likes the finely tuned attention with its erotic undertones. He pictures her laden backpack, the straps tugging at her shoulders, her perfect teeth sinking through soft bread layered with meat. She's in her senior year and will graduate in the spring with a BA in art history. She hasn't thought about a career; what she would like to do is get married and start a family. Apropos of this she has told him that he'd make an excellent father. He's encouraged by what this implies — that she's not about to dump him for a younger man — but hasn't thought about the future except to admit to himself that what he has with Natasha is different, not what you'd call a fling. A fling to him is like sport, a form of recreation that doesn't encroach on your way of life or cause you to lose your bearings. This, however, is messy, demanding, addictive, and fills him with angst. At times he swears that he's going to go straight, but mostly he feels like a drowning man in love with the surf.

The weekend retreat was her idea. It was she who found the country inn on the Fox River with its seventeen wooded acres, heated pool, and French chef, and it was she who booked the room and talked it up to him. They could go back to bed after breakfast and shower together before dinner. They could walk in the woods and make love in a sunny clearing. As opposed to their usual snacking, done on the sly, they could satisfy their appetites at leisure — and so on and so forth.

"Or would you rather stay at home with Jodi?" she asked.

He wished she would not bring Jodi into it. His life with Jodi belongs to a realm that has nothing to do with her, a parallel universe where things run smoothly and will go on doing so, where blameless years stretch sweetly into the past and comfortably into the future. He once made the mistake of telling Natasha that Jodi in bed was a cold dish of porridge. The idea was not to slight Jodi but to reassure Natasha. He's a generous man whose easy embrace absorbs a world of imperfections, especially when it comes to women. He has a knack for accepting things as they are and working with them. Things about Jodi. Things about Natasha.

One thing he puts up with in Jodi is the fact that she has a string of degrees. Not just a BA like Natasha will have but a doctorate and a couple of master's degrees. He doesn't mind her being brainy — what gets him is the ribbings he has to take from the boys, who like to carry on about Jodi being a cut above him. Not that he ever believed there was any inherent value in having a string of degrees. Getting an education is all about earning power — the threat is that if you don't go to school you'll end up working at McDonald's. It's money not education that's the holy grail in America.

He stops for lunch at a British-style pub and resists the urge to order a beer. When he's back at the office Stephanie hands him the price quotes he asked for and a list of calls he needs to make. He stretches out on the couch to make the calls and after that takes a nap. When he wakes up it's four thirty and he heads for the gym.

Working out is a recent thing. It began as a way to combat his depression when the doctor told him that vigorous exercise would generate endorphins, the body's own analgesics. He didn't feel the endorphins at first and found it difficult to bypass the bar on his way to the gym, but that changed when he met Natasha. Now he works with a trainer and uses the free weights instead of the machines, and he's started wearing wrist wraps and a tank top.

After pushing himself for over an hour he feels recharged and slightly horny. When he's showered and dried off he winds a towel around his waist and gives Natasha a call, even though the crowded locker room

61

makes a private conversation out of the question. As a matter of fact, even his thoughts need to be held in check because he doesn't want his ardor standing up and waving in a room full of naked men.

He lets her say hello three times before he speaks up.

"What are you, a pervert?" she asks.

"That's exactly what I am," he says.

"You know I can see your name and number on my call display."

Next time, he decides, he'll use a pay phone.

When he walks into the lounge at the Drake Hotel after handing off the Porsche to a valet, Dean Kovacs is already there, seated at the bar. The vintage nightclub with its burgundy leather, gleaming wood, and old-world masculine elegance is a comfortable and seductive home away from home. Right now it's packed to bursting with the after-work crowd, the din of voices rising and falling in lyrical waves as he weaves his way across the room, thumps Dean on the back, and takes the vacant stool to his left, which is more like an armchair than a stool.

"Hey, buddy," says Dean, throwing back the last of his draft beer. "I got started without you."

"You old bastard," says Todd. "You're one up on me."

"I've always been one up on you, buddy," says Dean. He waves to the bartender and shows him two fingers.

Dean has been packing on the pounds, and with his full face and double chin has come to resemble a chubby baby. He's wearing a blue summer suit with a wash-and-wear shirt that gapes over his paunch, though nothing worse is revealed than a clean white undershirt. His bunched tie blossoms from the breast pocket of his jacket. For the past twelve years he's been earning his living as a sales executive for a plastics company, a job that he likes well enough.

The bartender puts two pints down in front of them. Todd takes a first long swill and wipes the foam from his lips with the back of his hand. Fatigued from his work-out, he wants only to sit back and passively assimilate the alcohol and the atmosphere. Dean has the heart of a salesman, and all Todd has to do to get him going is ask about returns. "Last time I saw you there was a downswing," he says, baiting the hook. Dean obliges by holding forth on market shares and competitive presence, enabling Todd to relax and listen with one ear. He'd rather hear about products and developments — even plastic has its attractions — but Dean is inspired by targets, quotas, profits, and forecasts.

Todd sees Dean two, maybe three times a year. It's always Dean who calls to set it up, but Todd would take the initiative if Dean didn't. Although they live in different worlds the past makes for a strong bond. They grew up in Ashburn on the southwest side and went to Bogan High and played hockey and got stoned and lost their virginity together. The loss of virginity took place on a double date in an RV belonging to Dean's parents. Give Dean a drink or two and he invariably brings this into the conversation. It's meaningful to Dean that he and Todd shared that seminal experience, that he overheard the vocals of Todd's passage into manhood, and that Todd was there for him in the same way. It's meaningful to Todd as well, but he doesn't want everyone in the bar to know about it. Before it goes too far he asks for menus and gets Dean focused on ordering dinner.

After their burgers they switch from beer to shots, and this is where Dean starts in on the resurrection of his wife, who's been dead for ten years.

"Don't tell me she wasn't the best woman

a man could ever want," says Dean. "A woman who comes along once in a lifetime." He straightens his spine to emphasize his point and nods randomly like one of those bobblehead dolls. "Once," he repeats, rapping his knuckles on the bar. "If he's lucky."

"She was a good woman," Todd agrees.

"That woman was a fucking god*dess,*" says Dean. "I fucking worshipped that woman. You know I did."

He waits for Todd's confirmation, which Todd is happy to give. In Todd's mind there is no contradiction between Dean's present sentiments and the fact that he engaged in multiple affairs while his wife was still alive.

"She knew how much you loved her. Everyone knew."

"That's right," says Dean. "I worshipped that woman. I still do. You know that's true, because if it wasn't true I woulda got married again, which I didn't."

In recent years Dean has had a string of girlfriends, none of them as good as his perfect dead wife and none with any hope of replacing her. It works out well for Dean, who likes the game of pursuit and conquest and the feeling of power it gives him to hold a woman at bay once he has captured her interest.

As Dean downs his shots he progresses

from maudlin to bloody-minded. The crowd has thinned, the roar has dropped to a hum, and Dean's interest is wandering. Dipping and turning in his seat, he spies a young woman of about his daughter's age with cropped black hair and carmine lips and launches into a loud monologue, only ostensibly directed at Todd, about what he would like to do to her and what he would like her to do to him. Seated in the middle distance, engaged in conversation, she is unaware that Dean is targeting her, but other people — most of those within earshot — are turning to look at him.

Todd, in the meantime, has slipped into a world of his own. His sense of a benign essential self — his aura, his largesse — has been swelling and expanding and has now realized something like room-size proportions. In his magnanimity he makes no judgments and excludes no one, neither Dean nor the enemies Dean is busy cultivating. Everyone present is contained in the bubble of Todd's benevolence. This is Todd when he drinks. When Todd drinks he has a silent life as a priest, absolving and redeeming all humanity.

Having lost interest in the red-lipped girl, Dean now turns to the woman on his right at the bar. She's overweight and closer to his own age, and in the murk of his alcohol-infused brain this adds up to a good chance that she'll take an interest in him. The fact that she's engaged in conversation with her escort, who is seated on her other side, fails to register with Dean, who puts his mouth close to her left breast and makes lapping motions with his tongue. She has already taken note of Dean and edged her stool away. Now she gives him a look of disgust and tells him to screw off. Dean picks up on the word *screw* and comes back at her with a proposition, whereupon she and her date — a foxy man in designer glasses — stand up and trade places. This man, who now forms a barrier between Dean and the woman he is pursuing, says nothing to Dean, but Dean objects to him on principle and pokes him in the ribs.

"Hey, buddy," he says. "I was just exercising my rights as a male of the species."

"Yeah, well, go and exercise them somewhere else," says the man.

Dean turns to Todd and says, "I was just exercising my rights as a male of the species. It's a free world, isn't it?"

Todd has been a witness to Dean's scrapping since high school. If Dean were in a seriously pugnacious frame of mind, Todd would take him in hand and get him out of there, but in Todd's view Dean's posturing is harmless. "Try to stay out of trouble" is his only remark.

To which Dean loudly replies, "She's a dog anyway. I can do better than that."

Todd laughs and says, "That's the spirit, buddy," and Dean snickers, pleased with himself.

Todd knows that Dean only gets like this when he's drinking. Some people can hold their liquor; Dean is not one of them. You wouldn't know it but Dean is sensitive, the kind of guy who cries easily and likes babies. When Dean finished high school he went in for the marines, but he wasn't red-blooded enough to see it through and left before he got a posting. That's when he went into sales. On the whole you'd have to say that Dean is easygoing. He's been known to lose his temper, but it takes a lot to provoke him. So it's really just a question of how the news is going to strike him, and Todd is finding that hard to predict. He can only hope that Natasha breaks it to him gently.

When it's nearing midnight and Todd is back in his car, he calls one of his cached numbers and after a brief conversation makes his way to the Four Seasons, just a few city blocks away. His date is one of several he keeps on tap, all with enough class to pass muster at a five-star hotel, all available at a moment's notice, especially when a man of his generosity is asking. It's on nights like this, when he hasn't seen Natasha and is too energized, too full of grace to go straight home, that he likes to take advantage of the luxury goods and services the city has to offer.

3
HER

Come Friday morning Jodi is still without plans for the weekend. Not her usual self, she hasn't been thinking ahead. During the week her habitual confidence gave way to doubt and hesitation and the guileless hope that Todd would change his mind and cancel his trip. But that's all over now. He packed his bag last night and took it with him to work this morning, planning to leave for the country directly from the office.

She takes her phone to the window and stands looking out at the view. The day is bright, with the blinding glare of a white sun glancing off white water. Needles of light penetrate her eyes and the sensitive skin of her face and neck. She's feeling raw and exposed, a bat faltering in daylight, but still she stands there, scrolling through her list of friends.

She calls Corinne first, then June, then Ellen, leaving each of them the same message: "What are you up to this weekend? Let me know if you're free for dinner. Tonight could work. Or tomorrow. Lunch would be good, too. Love to see you. Call me back." She turns away from the window, walks around the room, inspects the sideboard for dust, trailing a finger over the polished wood surface. Then she calls Shirley and leaves the message again. Shirley used to be a mental patient. Jodi met her during a practicum and liked that she was smart and zany, a poet who had won some prizes for her work.

Meticulous planning has its merits. Life at its best proceeds in a stately manner, with events scheduled and engagements in place weeks if not months ahead. Scrambling for a last-minute date is something she rarely has to do, and she finds it demeaning. It feels to her like begging. Why not stake out a spot on the street and do her soliciting there? She could make up cards and hand them out. *Abandoned woman seeking dinner date. Desperate so not fussy.* She doesn't have much hope that Corinne or June or Ellen or Shirley will be free to see her. Corinne and Ellen have kids, June travels a lot, and Shirley — well, Shirley doesn't always pick up her messages. But there's a limit to how many calls she's willing to make.

It isn't till later in the day — when no one has gotten back to her — that she decides to go ahead and try Alison, even though there's almost no chance that Alison will answer her phone or even respond to a message before next week. In fact, Jodi is so sure that calling Alison is a lost cause that when she hears Alison's voice on the phone she thinks for a second that she has a wrong number.

"You just caught me," Alison says. "I should be at work but it's one of those days. You won't believe the string of disasters, so I'll spare you the details. When I called J.B. to say I'd be late you'd have thought the sky had fallen in. It's silly because we don't get busy till after five. Men are such children. I guess throwing their weight around makes them feel important. It's a good thing women have the real power, right? Anyway, I'm doing double shifts this weekend, but Monday is free. How about dinner?"

Dinner on Monday does not solve Jodi's immediate problem, but she is happy to write it in her daybook. Alison is another one of her oddball friends, an outsider like Shirley, not someone she knows from university or her professional circle. She met

Alison in a cooking class, the one where she learned to clean squid and butterfly shrimp. Alison doesn't cook but went through a phase when she thought she should make an effort. Jodi doesn't exactly know what Alison's job entails but has to assume that — even though Alison is a server and not one of the girls — private dealings with customers come into it. Alison may get good tips for waiting tables, but she's got to be doing more than that, judging by her taste in restaurants and the wine she likes to order — vintage bottles that even Jodi finds pricey.

The next day, Saturday, she is client-free. After a wakeful night she fell asleep at dawn and stayed in bed till midmorning. Now she's dawdling over breakfast and the paper. It makes no sense that she feels at such loose ends. It's normal for Todd to be gone during the day, even on Saturday, when he generally spends the morning at his building site and then goes for a haircut and takes his car to the carwash. Whereas Sunday is another matter, a day to share a leisurely brunch and take the dog on a long walk by the water, something she looks forward to all week. But it isn't going to happen tomorrow.

Wishing that one of her friends would call her back, she turns the TV on and skims through the channels till she comes to a *Seinfeld* rerun. She's seen this episode before but has forgotten nearly all of it. Lately, it's been that way with movies, too. A year or two passes and it's almost like she has amnesia. It makes her think that if she had her life to live again — the exact same life with events unfolding in the exact same sequence — most of it would take her by surprise. As the episode comes to an end and she's seeing the final scene as if for the first time, she is hit by a landslide of loss and regret.

She takes refuge in a bath, a ritual that involves lowering herself into scalding water up to her neck. The clouds of steam, the cocooning heat, the sense of weightless yet heavy immersion (the body suspended, the water pressing in) are powerful tonics that can overthrow maladies of all kinds, but even though she soaks until the skin on her finger pads is puckered and white she emerges feeling peevish, abandoned, and tired. She falls asleep on the couch and wakes up an hour later, shivering in her damp bathrobe.

Disoriented, a lost dream stirring in her mind, she gets dressed, snaps a leash on the dog, and walks to the lake, joining the Saturday throng on the waterfront trail. The water is iridescent in the midday sun, and people are out in force, drawn by the escalating warmth, running, cycling, and rollerblading, or just strolling, most of them in couples or family groups, their arms and legs tanned, their voices ringing in the clear air. Freud ambles along at her side, wagging his tail at the children who ask for permission to pet him. She takes him across the grass to the strip of sandy shore, throws a stick, and watches him swim after it. The dog, at least, has an appetite for the day. He's an adaptable creature, easily distracted and easily gratified. He knows that Todd was not at home last night, but as he navigates the lake, nose up and ears trailing, Todd is the furthest thing from his mind.

When she's home again she swallows an Advil and checks her messages. Ellen has called her back, suggesting lunch one day next week. She changes into sweatpants, draws the drapes in the bedroom, and burrows into the unmade bed, taking up her novel, a story of three generations of women whose hardships include brutal husbands, ungrateful children, and the social and cultural deprivations of a small rural community. The story of their dreadful lives distracts her for a while, but when she's read to the end and closed the book, the return to reality is harsh. The sky in her window is a flat gray, the room is sunk in shadow, and the temperature has dropped. It's clear that none of her friends will call her back now; their dinner plans will be firmly in place, their evenings already in motion. She discards her rumpled clothes and puts on jeans and a flannel shirt, capitulating to her night at home.

In the fridge she finds half an apple pie and eats it out of the pie plate, first the apples, scooping them out with a spoon, and then the crust, picking it up with her fingers. Todd is not going to call her either. There will be no checking in to say that he misses her, no asking after her welfare. She somehow knows this, and with the knowledge comes a feeling of something unstoppable, like birds flying off before a storm. Twenty years ago their love erupted in a blaze of passion and shot like a rocket into orbit. That its momentum has lately been slowing is a shabby fact that she hasn't been able to face. Often it seems to her that the years from then to now have folded in on themselves, collapsed together like accordion pleats, bringing distant memories near.

On their second date they went to see *The Crying Game* and afterward stood outside the theater talking about the movie, shuffling their feet, bantering and laughing. A second date is territory unto itself, an energy field with laws and conditions all its own. By the third date certain things are understood, whereas a first date is an undisguised raw experiment. But the second date, the date in between, is a minefield of groping and fumbling, a trial of high hopes and rampant skepticism. A second date is a mutual frank admission of interest with no getting past the fact that it could blow up in your face at any moment, that everything about the two of you is tentative, merely conjectural. A second date is a sea of ambiguity in which you must swim or sink.

It was not warm that night; spring was not well advanced. Still, it was a time of year when people were optimistic about the weather and failed to bundle up the way they should. Jodi and Todd were no exception — she in a cardigan, he in a sweatshirt — but even so they started to walk, having a cursory notion of getting something to eat but no actual destination, and soon fell into a profound moving inertia, a hypnosis of ambulation they were helpless to break. They walked south on Michigan, wandered into the park, wandered out of the park, and circled back through the Loop. They did not hold hands or even link arms but applied themselves in earnest to the immediate task, the task of the second date, with an ongoing series of personal revelations and frank admissions.

"As a kid I used to be fat," he said as they crossed the Michigan Avenue Bridge.

"But not really fat," she said, unable to picture it.

"My nickname at school was Tubbo."

"Wow. How long did that last?" Not long, surely.

"Oh, till I was twelve or thirteen. That's when I started stealing cars."

"You stole cars?"

"Maybe I shouldn't have mentioned it."

"But you didn't really *steal* them."

"How do you mean?"

"You put them back when you were done."

"Hardly."

"But you didn't, you know, strip them and sell the parts or anything like that."

"No, no. Nothing like that. I'd just play the stereo and drive around. Pick up a friend, pick up girls. Pretend for a while that

I was some rich bastard who had it all."

"Did you ever get caught?"

"Never did. Lucky I guess."

She hadn't seen him that way at all. There was something about him, something — well, *lordly* was the word that came to mind — that defied this unexpected picture of his youth. Her view of him underwent an adjustment.

"When I was growing up," she said, "my parents went through cycles of not speaking to each other. One time it lasted almost a year."

"How is that even possible?"

"They would talk. They just wouldn't talk to each other. And if there was nobody around, if it was just us kids, then sooner or later it would be, like, Jodi, could you please tell your father that he needs a haircut. And he'd be right there in the room of course."

"So would you tell him?"

"Stupidly, most of the time, yes, I would repeat the message. I guess I was too young to figure out that I could stay out of it."

"They must have really hated each other."

"Sometimes it seemed like they did. But other times everything was fine."

"My folks were at least consistent," he said. "He bullied and she cowered. Always the same."

"I wouldn't have thought that." She was shocked and searched in her bag for her lip balm while her picture of him changed again. "Did he bully you too?" she asked.

"Not really. Mostly he just ignored me."

"What did he do, your father?"

"Worked in the parks, but it was seasonal. In winter he was mostly home. Hung out in the basement, had his chair down there and his stash. You'd hear him muttering, and you knew that by dinnertime he'd be dead drunk, and you'd be creeping around praying that he'd fall asleep and stay where he was."

"That sounds tough," she said, still adjusting.

"It was a long time ago. He's dead now. They both are." He stopped to tie a shoelace, bending over stiffly in the cold.

"In my family I think the hardest part was the pretense," she said. "I mean, a lot of the time things were great, but even when they weren't, he would go to work, she would get dinner, we'd all sit down to the family meal, they'd talk to us kids about what we did at school, and every night they'd get into bed together. Nothing was ever said. We'd all just pretend that it wasn't happening."

"What was their problem exactly?"

"Oh, you know, the usual. He wasn't good at monogamy."

"Monogamy wasn't designed for men. Or men weren't designed for monogamy. However you want to put it. Both things are true."

"You think so?"

"I know so."

"Did your parents have the same problem?"

"My old man had one love and that was whiskey."

"So why do you say that about monogamy?"

"All men cheat sooner or later, one way or another. My father cheated with the bottle."

Remembering this exchange in retrospect, she thinks that it ought to have caught her attention, made her stop and think. But the alarm bells that should have been sounding in her head were oddly silent.

As they headed north on LaSalle, past the Board of Trade, past banks and shops and the city hall, there was an overwhelming sense of walking through a tunnel, the single-point perspective created by the office towers that rose like cliffs on either side of them, the sliver of sky at the end with its magnetic forward pull. He talked about his father's dying, how his mother had devoted herself to his care. Up from his basement lair he wasted away on the sofa, and because he was dying anyway she let him have his bottle.

"He was yellow and he stank of alcohol and urine," said Todd. "His hands shook and he couldn't control his bladder. The day they carried him out of the house I had to put the sofa out in the trash."

"Your mother must have been a saint," she said.

"She should have left him years before."

"Why didn't she?"

"Some kind of perverse loyalty? Who knows? You can't get inside of somebody else's marriage."

"I get that. However things look to other people, the marriage bond can be indestructible."

"I suppose your father was a doctor or a professor or somebody important," he said.

"Not exactly. He's retired now, but he was a pharmacist. We had a drugstore at the corner of Park and Main. I used to work there after school. The whole family did. Well, me and my brothers. Not my mother."

"Why not?"

"I guess she had enough to do around the house. I don't know. Maybe it had to do with her disappointments in life. My mother trained as a singer, but she never got beyond the church choir. Her dream was to be in a Broadway musical. She knew all the songs and used to sing them around the house. My mother is a little zany. A little fanciful, let's say."

"Aren't girls supposed to take after their mothers?"

"That's what they say. But I think I'm more like my father."

"So which of your parents is the bad driver?"

She later developed a theory about why they'd stayed out in the cold for so long, but she can't remember it anymore, just that it had something to do with endurance and bonding. She does know that by the time they found a place to eat and were warming their hands on their coffee cups while they waited for their food, there was a feeling of unbending, a sense that barriers had broken down. And that come midnight they were back in the Bucktown mansion lighting candles and shaking out the sleeping bag.

4
HIM

He drops Natasha at her door and drives on toward home. The day is sultry with a hot sun and no breeze, a provisional return to summer. The Porsche is littered with garbage — crumpled napkins, discarded wrappers, empty cardboard cups, the evidence of the return trip — and too little sleep has left him bleary, but the smell of her clings to his clothes and skin, an intoxicating fug of her secretions laced with her perfume, lotion, and hair gel. Parts of him are still swollen, and he's already dreading the hours that have to pass before he sees her again. Spending continuous time with her has altered his brain chemistry, and the synapses are firing painfully in her absence.

Warily, he projects into the trial ahead, the evening at home with Jodi. First will come the dinner of measured conversation and moderate drink, to be followed by the bedtime ritual of turning out lights and sliding under covers fully clothed in freshly laundered pajamas. When was it that his home life became a penance? He can't recall the turning point, the moment when he lost his taste for the kind of comfort that Jodi so ably provides.

But when he reaches home his mood changes. He's greeted with such boisterous abandon and wanton affection that he bursts out laughing. How could he forget the dog? The rooms are cool and filled with the dulcet scent of roses, which bloom profusely from scattered vases. In the kitchen he finds an open bottle of white wine, cold to the touch, and beside it a plate of crackers topped with smoked oysters. The effect of these enticements comes as a revelation.

Jodi is not immediately visible, but the balcony door is standing open. He strips down and steps into the shower, turning the taps on full so the water pummels his skin, creating a pleasant sensation of numbness and washing away the cloying scents of the weekend. When he's toweled off and dressed in clean khakis and a fresh shirt, he snacks on the oysters and pours himself a glass of wine.

On the balcony, Jodi is lying half naked in the lounge chair, her bikini bottom a marvel of crimson spandex that clings like a second skin to her jutting hips and rounded mons. Her legs are in an elongated V that pulls his gaze to her crotch and up the center divide of her rib cage. Her breasts, small to begin with, are splayed and flattened by her prone position, the nipples inert in the heat of the day, presented for show like lucky silver dollars. She rarely sunbathes, he knows, because she doesn't tan. Her skin is tinted with a rosy flush that will chafe her later on, but she isn't in any danger now because the sun has moved on and left the balcony in shade.

"I thought I heard you come in," she says, lifting her sunglasses to squint at him.

She has an economy about her — physical, emotional — that has always drawn him in. Her self-possession rarely deserts her; she's a woman who rises to the top of any situation. And even after all the years he feels that he knows her hardly at all, that he can't really grasp what lies beneath the surface. As a force in his life Jodi is polished, a virtuoso who works on him artfully, whereas Natasha plugs directly into his primitive brain. If Jodi is up, Natasha is down. If Jodi is a gentle lift, Natasha is a ten-story fall.

The country innkeeper, when he and Natasha showed up to claim their room, did nothing to mask his disapproval. He asked them to repeat their names, looked grimly at his register, and said, shaking his head, "You're booked into the *honeymoon* suite," as though urging them to change their minds. "The one with the king-size bed and the Jacuzzi," Natasha affirmed. Based on the churlish stares that followed them through the weekend, you would have thought that Todd was having it off with his own daughter. When he and Natasha emerged from their suite at noon on Saturday and walked into the dining room for lunch, he might as well have been naked with lips rubbed raw and a giant erection. The way people were carrying on, Natasha could have been a girl of twelve.

That first day, on arriving back at the inn, hot and thirsty after a walk in the woods, they wandered into the lounge, an airy room with bamboo blinds and rustic maple furnishings, where the paunchy bartender, having taken their order, gave Todd a wink as he put Natasha's Manhattan down in front of her, a wink that meant, in bumptious macho parlance: "Get her drunk enough and even an old guy like you can get lucky" or "I made this extra strong because you're going to need all the help you can get" or

"Maybe I can have a go when you're done with her, whaddaya say?"

He could almost feel that Natasha was to blame, the way she let it all hang out — breasts rising from their moorings, navel ring winking, hair tumbling — and the way she liked to posture by deepening her lumbar curve till it bowed out her torso, as if she were Nadia Comaneci working the balance beam.

Twirling from side to side on her bar stool, she looped her fingers through his belt and nuzzled him like a newborn calf. "If we're getting married in June, and you promised me that, then we need to start planning the wedding," she said. "And we need to look for a place to live." Tugging on his belt, her lips approaching his ear, she added that spending the night together — the whole of the night in the king-size bed in their honeymoon suite — had changed things, that now there could be no going back. They had crossed a threshold, she said, and the old routine of sneaking around and hiding their love would no longer do.

Had he promised to marry her in June? Not that he could remember. As a way of putting her off, he said that he would have to talk to his lawyer before they could make any plans.

■ ■ ■ ■

Jodi gets up from her lounge chair and moves past him into the apartment. He catches the scent of her warm flesh layered with suntan oil and watches her walk away toward the bathroom. Her body is small and slight, in striking contrast to Natasha's with its broad back and deep curves. She returns wearing a short silk wrapper tied at the waist. When she sits down the robe falls open, revealing her thighs and the swell of her breasts.

"How was your weekend?" she asks.

"It's good to be home," he says evasively. "What did you do while I was gone?"

"Nothing much. Did you catch any fish?"

When she mentions fish her eyes crinkle up with merriment. If she knows or guesses the truth, she's at least not going to punish him with it.

"I wish I could tell you that I've stocked the freezer with pickerel," he says. "But I'll take you out to dinner if you like."

They go to Spiaggia and work their way through three delicious courses, washing them down with a robust amarone. He's wearing a dinner jacket and she's in an off-the-shoulder cocktail dress and a double strand of pearls. That night they make love for the first time in a month.

The next day opens with a series of misadventures. To begin with he gets to work at his usual early hour only to find that one of his keys — the one that opens the street door — is missing from his key ring. Standing on the sidewalk with his mobile phone he curses when he fails to connect with the janitor. He doesn't know how this could have happened; keys don't detach on their own from a steel ring. He nonetheless walks the three blocks back to his Porsche to search the seats and floor and then calls Jodi, waking her up, to ask if she'll have a look around at home. After that he waits in front of his building thinking that sooner or later someone will come along and let him in, but it's still early, and before long he gives up and goes for breakfast.

Starting time for the janitor is supposedly eight o'clock. At five to eight Todd is back at the building with a takeout coffee, but it's another twelve minutes before the janitor shows up. The twelve-minute wait finishes off what was left of his patience, and the entire responsibility for his wasted hour and a half comes down on the janitor's head. A quiet, mostly reliable man who's held his position for some years, the janitor quits on the spot and leaves without producing any keys. More minutes pass, another nineteen to be exact, before a tenant arrives and lets Todd in. By the time he's broken into the janitor's room to get at an extra set of keys, he has a message from Stephanie saying that one of her kids is sick and she won't be in to work. He spends the rest of the morning dealing with things that Stephanie would normally be doing, and when Natasha calls at lunchtime to ask him if he's spoken to his lawyer, he tells her that the world doesn't operate according to her whims.

Natasha's readiness to take offense, her proclivity to cry, to pout, to withdraw — this is all new to him, and he finds it wearing. Jodi doesn't behave this way. What is Natasha's problem? He'd like to take it up with her but prudently holds his tongue, and although the day is slipping away he talks her into meeting him for lunch.

When he shows up at Francesca's in Little Italy — a regular spot of theirs because it's close to the university — Natasha is seated by the pillar, reading a menu. As he settles into the chair across from her she fails to lift her eyes or otherwise take any notice of him, sticking with her menu as if she doesn't already know it by heart. Why can't she act her age and talk to him, call him a name or two, get it out of her system? On the other hand, meeting him here was no doubt a big concession for her to make, after the way he spoke to her. Ever so gently he takes the menu out of her hands and sets it aside.

"Let's not fight," he says. "I'm sorry."

Based on the look she gives him — unsmiling, apprehensive — he understands that she intends to break up with him. But it was such a little spat. There must be something else going on. Of course there is. The something else he's always feared. It's finally happened, and how could it not, given the throngs of likely young men who rub shoulders with her every day at school. He never believed that she would stay with him forever, in spite of what she says. The talk of marriage, that was just a sideshow, something to try on for size. She's like that, Natasha. She likes to speculate and presume, just to see what will happen. And why not? She has her whole life ahead of her and needs to figure out what she's going to be doing and who she's going to be doing it with. Whereas he is more than half done. Forty-six. Over the hill. A few more years and he'll be popping vitamin V. He can't compete with a rival half his age. He has to face the facts and let her go.

"I can't let you go," he says. "I love you."

Her eyes widen. She gives a little laugh. "Don't be silly," she says.

"Aren't you breaking up with me?"

"No. As much as you deserve it."

Their server appears and Natasha orders a meatball sandwich, so Todd gets that too, even though he has no appetite. Then he breaks his lunchtime rule and orders a beer. She isn't leaving him and he should be feeling relieved, but something isn't right.

"What is it?" he asks.

Ignoring the question she starts to talk about school: her nine o'clock class, what the professor was wearing, what he said about the Fauvists. At least she's decided to speak to him, but when the food arrives she digs in and falls silent again. He talks about his morning, the string of mishaps starting with the lost key. He's trying to entertain her, get her laughing, but there's something on her mind. He drinks down his beer and orders another. She doesn't come out with it till after she's eaten her meal, every scrap of it, and has a cup of tea in front of her. When she tells him it's like a kick in the head.

"How could this happen?" he yells. "I thought you were on the pill."

She shushes him. She's turned pale and seems confused. "I thought you wanted children," she says.

"Of course I want children," he shouts.

Of course he wants children, though *children* may not be the word for what he wants. Natasha wants *children,* meaning helpless little beggars who need her constant attention and bring her a sense of kinship and belonging. What he wants is not that. What he wants is descendants, heirs, or just one heir, preferably a son, someone who shares his DNA, a variant of himself to replace him when he's gone. As a younger man he never gave this any serious thought and would have kept on like that had he not awakened one morning with a lust for progeny that shot through him like a virus, and then, when he met Natasha, mutated into a rampant longing that never left him. It made him feel that his life, as it stood, was a wasteland. It gave his pursuit of her an urgency that was unrelenting. That she could love him meant that it was not too late.

"Of course I want children," he repeats. "Just not like this."

"Not like what?"

"Like this. With you springing it on me at lunch."

"When should I have sprung it on you?"

"We've never even discussed this."

"Yes we have. You want children."

"That's beside the point."

He's shouting again, and he can see from her face that he's lost her. She stands up, takes her knapsack from the back of her chair, and leaves the restaurant. He gets out his wallet, slides some bills under a plate, and hurries after her, fearing that she might have run off and disappeared, but there she is, standing idly by.

"I have to get to class," she says.

He drapes an arm across her shoulders and keeps it there as they walk up Loomis Street toward Harrison.

"I can have an abortion," she says.

"You would do that?"

"If that's what you want."

It's a ray of light, and with the hope it brings his panic subsides a little. He stops walking and swings her around to face him. "How far along are you?" he asks. "I mean, is it doable?"

She gives him a look of such intense hatred that he physically recoils.

"You're the one who brought it up," he says.

As the bickering continues he forgets to press his point about how this could have

95

happened. It doesn't occur to him that she might have done it on purpose. He is not by nature suspicious or vindictive, and without knowing it he moves past blaming her and starts on the process of puzzling things out, much as he would a plumbing leak or a bad debt. Now he's saying things like: "Don't worry . . . we'll get it straight . . . it's going to be okay." But this kind of talk falls short.

"You're still talking about it like it's a problem," she says.

"Okay, fine. But I'm not twenty-one. I have a history and that complicates things. I'm not, at the moment, a free man."

"Whose fault is that? You were supposed to tell her about us ages ago."

He wonders if this could be true. He doesn't recall any discussion with Natasha in which he agreed to talk to Jodi. He only knows that Natasha has been pressuring him to talk to Jodi.

"I don't think I was supposed to tell her," he says. "But I'll have to tell her now."

The reality of this is dawning on him. If Natasha won't consider an abortion, people will have to know. Maybe not immediately but eventually. Jodi will have to know. And Dean.

"I don't think you should tell your father,"

he says. "Not right away."

Natasha has started walking again. She's several steps ahead of him. "I've already told my father," she says, tossing the words over her shoulder.

He lengthens his stride and catches up with her. "You told Dean? When did you tell him?"

"After I spoke to *you*."

"I can't believe you would do that."

She shrugs, and he understands that she did it to spite him, because he was short with her on the phone when she asked if he had called his lawyer.

"What did you say exactly? You didn't tell him about me — about us."

"What do you think? I'm going to tell him and not say who it's with?"

"You didn't need to tell him at all."

She shrugs again, her pique and pride and truculence all packed into the single insolent gesture. As she walks on at a steady deliberate pace he has to make an effort to keep up with her. He feels like a cockroach scuttling along at her side.

"Slow down," he says. "Talk to me."

"What's to say?"

"Lots. There's lots to say. How far along are you? When did you find out?"

"I don't know how far along I am. I found

out this morning."

"You found out this morning? I thought you had a class this morning."

"I did it first thing, when I woke up. That's when you're supposed to do it."

Todd, who has never heard of a home pregnancy test, says, "You did *what* when you woke up?"

"There's this plastic stick that you pee on. You get it at the drugstore. If it's positive, a pink line comes up."

"A plastic stick?"

"That's not all. My period is late."

"But you need to see a doctor to know for sure."

"You so want it not to be true."

They're on Harrison Street now, heading east. The sidewalk is crowded with students moving in both directions. They're getting jostled in the congestion.

"When you told your father, how did he take it?" he asks.

"How do you think?"

"He wasn't happy."

"No."

"What did he say?"

"He said that he was going to wring your neck."

"That's all?"

"It's not enough?"

"He must have said more than that."

"Oh yeah, I almost forgot. He said that he was going to talk to Jodi."

He waits for her to disappear into Henry Hall and then turns back toward his car, already regretting the hash he's made of things. Clearly this is a sensitive situation, one that's going to follow him, and he should have been more tactful. Not that it would have made any real difference. Women have babies or not according to their whims — and what some guy wants, even the guy responsible, is completely beside the point. There's no recourse for the men of this world. Men are a race of suckers who don't realize that having sex is the biggest risk they'll ever take. His whole world changes as of now, and there isn't a damn thing he can do about it. He ought to have a voice here, but things don't work like that. In spite of what anyone says it's women who make the rules. In this case it's Natasha who makes the rules. And now she's upset with him, and he still has Dean and Jodi to face. Regardless of his feelings about fathering a child or an heir or whatever you want to call it, this right now is too complicated, too fraught, and moving too fast. It's like he's in a car that's careening along in the wrong lane, heading into oncoming traffic. It makes no difference that he doesn't know how he got here. It's going to be him who's held accountable.

As he passes in front of the UIC Pavilion he has his phone in hand and is speed-dialing Dean's mobile. He ought to take some time to get his thoughts in order, figure out what he's going to say, but time is passing and he needs to get to Dean before Dean gets to Jodi, if it's not already too late. He thinks he has a chance because Dean has only known for a few hours. The main thing is that he's willing to be humble, willing to give Dean plenty of space and take a certain amount of flak. Dean can be a little wild and a little unruly, and Dean can be stubborn, but he's not a blockhead. He may not like what's happening, but given time he's going to adapt because if Dean is anything he's loyal, and Todd is Dean's oldest friend.

But Todd is mistaken if he thinks that Dean has had enough time to come down to earth and have a rational conversation. Before Todd can form a single word Dean lets him have it.

"I thought you were my friend, you slimy son of a bitch. What the fuck are you doing with my daughter?"

Todd wants to say that he's sorry, that he

didn't mean for this to happen, that he never wanted to hurt Dean or put their friendship at risk, that Dean has every right to be upset. He wants very much to say these things and be forgiven, but most of all, right at this moment, he wants to ask Dean if he will please not speak to Jodi, if he'll give Todd a chance to talk to her first. Dean, however, is not in a listening mood.

"I'll rip your head off, you stinking turd," says his friend. "I'll have you arrested for sexual assault." And with that he breaks the connection.

Todd is riled now. The son of a bitch has got him going. He needs to simmer down, and it helps that he's striding along. Walking is a known remedy for getting a grip on yourself. Go for a walk, they say. Get outside and shake it off. It's one of those days when the sun is breaking through low-lying clouds and the odd spatter of rain hits the pavement with a hiss. Scattered showers. They moisten his head and shoulders and raise the smell of the pristine lawns that dominate the grounds of the university. He needs to focus on the future. Not the distant future — although that, too, is at stake — but the hours just ahead. Where will he be eating dinner? Jodi was planning to cook. And where is he going to be sleeping?

Something has to be done, but what?

His thoughts are a jumble of discordant notes, painfully sounding in his overwrought brain, beating on his temporal lobes. But something else is going on as well. Even in his alarmed, disgruntled, and apprehensive state, he's aware of a certain ambivalence. His thoughts are leaning mostly one way but not entirely, not conclusively. Faintly chiming in the fray is the hint of something wholesome, amusing, even comical, a punchy little ditty arising from the orchestral skirmish, having to do with Natasha and all that he feels for her.

He's known her for her entire life — from the day she was born, in fact — and in some antiquated part of himself he still regards her as a hapless child whose mother has died, a loud-mouthed brat in a school uniform, a pimply adolescent with braces, all of these rolled into one. If he had known then that she would be the one to bear him a child, he would have laughed out loud. It would have been a real knee-slapper.

He remembers the moment when he first saw her in her fully adult form, in the new and still surprising rendition that he has come to know and love. He was sitting at the bar in the Drake, waiting for Dean, and happened to look around when she walked

102

in, a beautiful stranger who caught his eye and glided toward him in all her succulent splendor, all her scandalous swank, hips swaying, breasts bobbing, earrings swinging — he didn't stand a chance. When she planted a kiss on his lips, a garden of hopes and dreams blossomed in his fertile mind.

"Natasha," she announced. "I'm meeting Dad here. He needs to give me money."

He hadn't seen her in years. She ordered a Manhattan, and by the time Dean showed up, twenty minutes late, they had passed the point of no return.

He remembers these things and smiles to himself as he walks along. But once he's back at his desk the trouble he's in catches up with him and he starts to pace. With Stephanie off he has the run of the place and his pacing takes him out of his office, into hers, and through reception, a full circuit. His hands are clammy and his mouth tastes like a rusty nail. He's resisting making the call to Jodi, has no idea what he's going to say, how he's going to broach the subject of his unofficial life, how he's going to talk about what neither of them has ever openly acknowledged. In his own mind nothing has actually changed. What is happening with Natasha has nothing to do with Jodi — and vice versa. But the prospect of his two worlds colliding, two worlds that belong categorically in separate orbits, is impossible to imagine, impossible to bear, a vision of the end of life as he knows it.

He waits through the program of rings until the recorded message comes on, his own voice telling him there's no one at home to take his call. He ought to feel relieved. He gets the flat tin out of his drawer, scrabbles in the leavings for a roach, lights up, and takes it to the window. A few tokes is all he needs, just enough to clear his head. That bastard Dean will have called her by now. Though it's possible they failed to connect. Right now that's the best he can hope for.

He locks up and walks to his car. It seems to him that the afternoon rush hour starts earlier now than it once did. It used to be that people worked from nine to five, but now there are all these alternate schedules, and nobody puts in an eight-hour day anymore. Sitting in traffic makes him impatient, aggressive, hostile. He uses his horn, changes lanes, crowds the car in front of him. His thoughts vie for space in a mental arena that's crammed too full.

Jodi's parking spot, the one next to his, is vacant. Riding up the elevator he can't remember when he was last at home on a weekday afternoon. For all he knows Jodi might have had a lover for years, could be carrying on this very minute in his own bed. The teenager two doors down comes to mind, the tall boy with the ball cap. Jodi says he's good at math and plays the violin. How does she know so much about him?

When he opens the door the dog comes barreling out and rockets up and down the hallway. His next-door neighbor, en route to the elevator, stops to say hello and laugh with him at the dog's antics. A woman in her sixties, she is nicely made, with legs that still look good in sheer stockings and high heels. When she moves on he takes the dog inside and advances into the living room. There's proof of Jodi's absence in the motionless air and the half-closed blinds, but he nonetheless checks each room in turn. Finding nothing but a neatly made bed, fresh towels symmetrically arranged, cushions standing upright, and magazines aligned, he looks around for the portable handset, spies it on her desk, picks it up, and scrolls through the caller list. Dean's name appears three times, logged in at half-hour intervals, starting at noon. There is no new message. If Dean left a message Jodi has already listened to it and possibly called him back. Perspiring now, he feels at a loss.

If only Dean were not such a hothead. Dean should learn to pace himself, wait till he cools down and not pick up the phone to destroy someone's life just because he's a little bent out of shape.

He retraces his steps to the parking garage and drives uptown to the Drake. It's still early but the great thing about a hotel bar is that it's never empty, so you never have to drink alone. In any given hotel at any time of the day or night there are going to be customers because people come to hotels from all over the world and they're all ticking away on their own private clocks. He orders a double shot and throws it back before starting on his pint. As the drink flows through him the knot of panic he's been carrying around since lunch begins to dissolve. His muscles relax; the clamp on his nerves loosens its grip. A chink opens up in his defenses, and into it rushes the very concept that he's so far been unable or unwilling to ingest. Fatherhood. The feeling of it swills around inside him and gradually — as he drains his pint and starts on another — takes on a simple, rudimentary reality, like so much vapor condensing into palpable drops.

Looking around the room he sees men of assorted shapes and sizes, men who have no

106

doubt fathered children because that's what men do. He feels love for them, each of them individually and all of them as a group. This is his tribe now, his fraternity, and these men must henceforth accept him as a fellow procreator, a sanctioned member of the assembly of breeders, a contender of proven virility, a dynasty builder. In spite of the way it's happened he can't deny that this is what he wanted — what he's wanted ever since he met her and what he's always wanted, really, even if he didn't know it because he was too busy proving himself in other ways. This. The great carnal enterprise. The primordial swamp of genesis and propagation. Certifiable verifiable paternity. The ultimate fulfillment. And this, now, is something to be shared with her. He needs to tell her all that he's thinking and feeling, applaud her fertility, take credit for his own, engage in a dialogue of mutual veneration. He takes out his phone, doesn't understand why she won't pick up, how she can still be mad. Their quarrel was trivial and meaningless. If she would just pick up he could ask and receive her forgiveness and they could move on into their future, their new way of being in the world.

He returns to his pint and his musings, trying her at intervals, finally remembering that it's Jodi he meant to call. There's a reason why he needs to speak to Jodi. He's going to tell her the news before Dean can beat him to it. But he needs to preserve his mood of celebration, and in keeping with this, instead of making the call, he buys a round for the house, which is filling up as five o'clock approaches. People around the room lift a glass to him, saluting his generosity. He spreads the word that he's going to be a father, and congratulations are offered. When a group at a nearby table raises a cheer on his behalf, he says with earnest candor, "I'm just hoping that my wife doesn't know." Leaving the well-wishers to puzzle this out for themselves.

5
HER

The dismal thoughts that plagued her over the weekend have largely gone from her mind. Whatever he did and whoever he did it with — that's over now, and she's never been one to live in the past. If she were inclined to dwell on things gone wrong she would have left him or strangled him years ago. Besides, she's had her little revenge with the key, and to that extent at least, she feels satisfied.

With breakfast over she skims through her file on Sad Sack, who is about to appear for his Monday morning session. When she's buzzed him up and he's put his bony frame in its baggy suit in her client chair, she eyes him as if he were a wild boar that she somehow has to capture and tame, and he looks back at her morosely. It is Sad Sack's great conviction that he got a raw deal in life. He believes with all his heart that fortune has set itself against him and that nothing he can do will make a difference. This is Sad Sack's litany, the essential overriding bias that defines him and underwrites his joyless passage through life. He isn't an overly complex man, but given his obstinacy it's difficult to make any sort of impression on him.

Most of Jodi's clients would benefit by taking themselves less seriously, and her style of therapy involves a certain amount of coaxing and cajoling, which is not exactly by the book, but the way she deals with her clients' problems is similar to the way she deals with her own. Sad Sack in particular responds to a little good-natured goading, and after she's listened to him complain for a while she says: "I'm going to charge you extra for the carping. I know the only reason you're here is because your family can't take it anymore. Why don't you tell me one good thing that happened over the past week, just one thing. I bet you can if you try."

The challenge, as slight as it is, stops him in his tracks. He looks at her blankly, jaw dropping, and then without warning he reflexively grins, showing her a set of beautiful white, even teeth. It transforms him completely.

"Seriously now," she says, seizing the moment. "Think back over your week. Just one positive experience."

He is not quite ready for this exercise and shares with her instead the problems he's been having with his car. But Jodi is pleased nonetheless. It's the first time she's ever seen him smile.

After Sad Sack she sees a new client for the first time, a woman who is so self-effacing that minutes into the session Jodi has her mentally indexed as Jane Doe. Her presenting problem is that she can't stand up to her husband, a jealous man who rabidly monitors everything she does. The session is spent gathering information — going through the questionnaire about background and childhood that gets the ball rolling. The trouble is that Jane doesn't remember much of her early years. Her memory is pretty much a blank up to the age of eight.

Afterward, Jodi feels hyped and shakes it off at the gym. Lunch is a cheese and arugula sandwich and a glass of water. When she's showered and dressed she returns to her desk to put her client files away and check her messages. Alison has called to confirm dinner, and there's a message from Dean Kovacs, who says that he urgently needs to speak to her. She can't imagine why. She knows Dean well enough — during the year or two after his wife died he often came to dinner with his daughter, and she still sees him from time to time at this or that gathering — but Todd is normally the intermediary. Dean and Jodi have not developed a friendship independent of Todd. She calls him back and leaves a message in turn.

The headliner on her afternoon agenda is a seminar on eating disorders sponsored by her professional association. Although she does not treat eating disorders, she likes to stay informed and enjoys mingling with colleagues. She's left herself time for errands en route, and as she's getting ready to leave she gathers up the checks she's collected from clients and assembles items of clothing that need to go to the laundry.

Her first stop is the bank. In spite of what Todd likes to say about her practice being a hobby, she probably earns as much as the teller who takes her deposit and more than the barista at the Starbucks next door, who makes her a takeout latte. Enough, anyway, for basic household needs and a few extras. At the laundry she waits for Amy to talk to a man about the bloodstains on his shirt. The man is prim looking, with tasseled shoes and longish, manicured fingernails. He seems agitated, even embarrassed about the state of his shirt, but Amy is a pro and betrays not a glimmer of interest.

Jodi steps forward in turn, places her garments on the counter, and waits while Amy goes through them — shaking them out, looking for missing buttons and other flaws, checking pockets, and sorting them into piles. When she comes to the worn pair of khakis belonging to Todd, she takes an object from a pocket and passes it to Jodi, who glances at it and drops it into her purse.

She is parked illegally and hurries back to her car. Her next stop is the framer on the near west side where she picks up the Rajput painting that she took in last week. She's running late now but has a string of green lights and makes it to her seminar at the library center with several minutes to spare. The lecture room is humming, with some people sitting down but most of the crowd standing around in pairs and groups. Scanning the faces she sees quite a few familiar ones, but before she can make any rounds a presenter takes the microphone and asks that everyone be seated.

The first speaker is a woman in herringbone tweed and sensible shoes. She's short and makes a joke about her height as she peers over the lectern and adjusts the microphone downward. Appreciative titters ripple through the audience. The ice broken, she restates her credentials, which have already been detailed by the presenter who introduced her. She is a doctor of social psychology and senior program director for an eating disorder clinic on the West Coast. Jodi has heard that the anorexics at eating disorder clinics are force-fed, which sometimes turns them into bulimics, and that many of them run away. The senior program director says nothing about that. She talks up the clinic's staff, evaluation process, therapy plan, and nutrition classes. Eating disorders, she says, are difficult to treat, and patients require specialized care that they can only get in an institutional setting. Learn to recognize the symptoms, she advises, adding that the assistance of a trained therapist can be helpful as part of an aftercare program. She refers her audience to a stack of brochures on the information table.

The second and final speaker is the author of a book titled *You and Your Child's Eating Disorder.* He's a medical doctor, early forties, with a haggard face and a kindly manner. He began his investigation of this subject, he explains, while coping with the anorexia that each of his three daughters developed in turn as they moved into adolescence. He talks about standards of beauty and the American obsession with food and diet. He talks about self-image and self-hatred. He talks about how he felt when his daughters returned time and again from treatment centers only to relapse into their self-destructive habits. Not that he himself has any answers. He wrote his book to offer moral support to other parents in like situations, to tell them that it's not their fault and that not all afflictions can be cured, whether physical or psychological. As a doctor this is something he can say with conviction. We sometimes have to live with unpleasant realities.

The discussion period turns on the apparent contradiction arising from the two presentations. The doctor reiterates that treatment centers have failed him. The senior program director takes refuge in figures: her clinic's success rate — high — and its recidivism rate — low. The doctor's daughters, she says, may belong to the small percentage of cases that resist treatment. The doctor questions the program director's figures, inquiring about follow-up studies and methods of collecting data. The two become increasingly embattled, and the assembled audience of therapists and counselors is spellbound to the end.

Jodi sticks around for coffee, which she drinks on her feet, standing in a circle with her colleagues as they cheerfully dissect the squabble that just took place. Her mind briefly wanders and she thinks of her visit to the laundry and what she has in her purse. She takes it out and shows it to the woman standing next to her, who happens to be a psychiatrist.

"Sleeping pills, right?"

The psychiatrist takes the container and looks at the label.

"Right," she says. "Eszopiclone." And absently hands it back, still engaged in the general conversation.

As Jodi makes her way out of the building she tries to puzzle out what Todd would be doing with a bottle of sleeping pills prescribed for Natasha Kovacs. She hasn't seen Natasha in years, and as far as she knows neither has Todd. He did have dinner with Dean last week, though she can't think what that could have to do with it. Unless Natasha happened to join them. But he would have mentioned it.

On the drive home she calls up a mental picture of the teenage Natasha — Natasha as she last saw her — a big girl with a forward manner. A little on the manic side, which could account for the sleeping pills.

That and the fact that she's now in university. As Jodi well remembers, university can be stressful. It's important to study and get good grades, but there are compelling distractions. You stay up late with friends, drink too much coffee and alcohol, take the odd upper, and eventually get so strung out that you no longer sleep. Not until she's parking her car does she remember Dean — that he called her, that she called him back, that it's his turn again. When she gets in she checks her phone, but there are no messages.

She unwraps her picture and props it on the mantel. The gilt frame brings out touches of gold that she hadn't noticed in the feathers of the peacocks. The woman in her finery is lovely but today seems wistful, even forlorn. She gives off a sense of being cloistered and secluded, even trapped, in her beautiful garden. Maybe the frame is too ornate, too bold for the delicate little painting with its vulnerable central subject.

Jodi knows that you can come to your senses in a blinding flash because she's seen it happen with clients, but that's not how it happens to her. In her case it's been coming on incrementally for some time. You could almost say it started with the onset of Todd's depression — that's when things took a turn for the worse — and then again with his depression lifting the way it did, as if he had suddenly found a reason to live. That was in the spring or early summer, and she was happy to have him back even though he seemed distracted a lot of the time. But now events are accelerating, taking on a sickening forward thrust, and she knows why Dean is calling.

She changes out of her day clothes into a simple black dress. Standing in front of her wardrobe mirror she's vaguely surprised to see herself looking perfectly well. Her complexion is pale, but she's always had a natural pallor. People remark on it, tell her that she ought to see a doctor. Once in a while she resorts to a powdered blush to give her cheeks some color, but the contrast with her milky skin can make her look vulgar, so most of the time she leaves well enough alone.

The phone rings as she's transferring her wallet and keys to a clutch bag. She picks it up and checks the call display. She can't talk to Dean right now. It's time to leave for the restaurant. She's already running late, and Alison will be waiting. She'll speak to Dean later, she decides, but she nonetheless carries the phone to the foyer and leaves it on the console table while she puts on her coat, and on the sixth ring, irrationally, she picks it up and presses the talk button.

"Dean," she says. "You've been trying to reach me."

Alison is a chunky blonde with apple cheeks and bobbly blue eyes. Being close to Jodi's age — a little past her prime — is good reason in Alison's opinion to wear her heels a little higher and her necklines a little lower. Twice divorced, she has settled into a functional independence and regards her short-lived marriages as little more than minor disruptions in her life, temporary and unavoidable, like bad weather not her fault, unexpected squalls in otherwise placid waters.

The Garnet Club is Alison's home base and social sphere. She often spends her day off sitting at the bar sipping a cola. The staff and regulars are like extended family, and she is den mother to the girls, who squabble over everything — schedules, costumes, music, territory. Alison's boss, the club manager, can see that she is the glue that binds things together, and so she is allowed certain freedoms. This is what Jodi has gathered from Alison's talk.

Tonight they're having dinner at Cité on the top of Lake Point Tower, where they like

119

to watch the sun setting over the city. Spotting Alison across the room, already seated with a glass of wine, Jodi smiles with pleasure. Alison, as always, strikes her as larger than life, a vivid presence with a generous measure of vitality. In the cooking class where they met, Alison emerged as a natural leader, helping people with their knife technique even though she never did take to cooking. For her part, Alison found it impressive that Jodi was paid money to give advice, something that she herself has always done for free.

"Is that the Duckhorn?" Jodi asks, taking a seat.

"How can you tell?"

"You always have the Duckhorn." She waves the server over and orders a glass of the same.

"So how are you keeping, sweetie?" Alison asks but doesn't require an answer. The question is merely a prelude to her newscast. "You'll be glad to hear that Crystal broke up with her boyfriend," she says. "Took her long enough. And Ray's wife finally died, poor thing. It's hard on Ray, but at least now he can move on."

Jodi knows that Crystal is a stripper who suffers from low self-esteem. She's heard a lot about Crystal's hard-earned money and the way her boyfriend spends it. Ray is one of the regulars, an elderly man who is treated by the girls like a favorite pet.

"I'm just so relieved for them both," Alison says. "It takes a weight off. It really does."

Jodi's wine arrives and she raises her glass. "Here's to better times ahead for Crystal and Ray."

Alison touches her glass to Jodi's and forges on, eager to share a treasury of detail about Ray's wife's final illness and Crystal's boyfriend's reaction to getting the boot. Jodi understands that Ray and Crystal are like brother and sister to Alison — what happens to them is part of Alison's own life story. Alison has a heart like open country, and although she chides herself for getting caught up in other people's lives, other people's lives are what she is all about.

The restaurant is more subdued than usual, all the action taking place in the blazing sky beyond the windows where the sun is busy with its feverish descent. The closer it gets to the horizon the more dramatic are its effects. Alison rambles on, pausing only when the server comes to take their order. Her voice is soothing and distracting, a steady, dependable patter, like rain on a roof. Not until their wine has been replenished and their food is on the table does she stop to take her bearings and consider a change of subject.

"You're quiet tonight," she says.

It's true that Jodi would normally be interrupting her with questions and comments. She nods and says, "I must be tired."

She isn't aware of lying or trying to conceal anything. Rather, she has the sense that dealing with Todd all these years has indeed tired her out. In fact, she would gladly share with Alison everything she learned from Dean, but the news is thrashing around inside her like a trapped bird, giving her a kind of psychic vertigo. "I don't understand it," she says, referring, however obtusely, to the stupefying revelation — the pregnancy, the wedding, the magnitude of the betrayal, the scope of the intrigue — but even as she speaks, the words and even the thoughts behind them seem to dissipate and lose all meaning. If someone has to talk it had better be Alison.

"How are things with Renny?" she asks, knowing that once Alison gets started on her first husband it's like she's on a train that she can't get off. Loser that he is, Renny has worked his way under Alison's skin, and her lament is one that she often repeats: "I'm crazy about that man. I'd marry him again if he'd ever grow up."

Renny comes from a small town in Quebec, where he was raised by a French father and an English mother. His full name is Sylvestre Armand René Dulong. He's done jail time for drug trafficking. Alison met him at a Montreal nightclub where she waited tables one summer. He used to come in with his biker friends, and they'd sit near the stage so they could slide hundred-dollar bills into the girls' G-strings. Renny would tip Alison the same, even though she was just a server.

Alison's courtship with Renny, a high point in her life, featured heaps of cocaine, sex from dusk to dawn, and joy rides up and down the mountain on his Harley. The marriage itself lasted under a month. He didn't tell her he was seeing someone else — just stopped coming home and let her figure it out for herself. But he still drives from Montreal to surprise her, and he still likes to give her a whirl.

"He's always trying to get money off me," Alison is saying. "He knows I'm at work most nights so he calls at four or five in the morning when I'm trying to sleep. Of course, he would never ask for it up front. That's not Renny. It's like he's giving me this fantastic opportunity to invest in some deal he's got going. I put in ten Gs and get back fifty. If he's dealing on that level then why is he broke?"

Jodi is doing her best to stay alert and follow along. She feels like she's perched on a treetop in a high wind.

"What I need," Alison says, "is a nice, quiet, steady guy with a good income. Guys come into the club, they're hitting on me all the time. Married guys. What do they take me for?"

Alison sips her wine and frowns at her manicure. The server takes their empty plates and leaves them with dessert menus.

"The quiet, steady guy may be a myth," says Jodi. "Biologically, men are predators."

"Tell me about it," says Alison.

"Women like to believe that their men are nicer than they actually are," Jodi adds. "They make excuses for them. They don't see the whole picture, just bits at a time, so it never seems to them as bad as it really is."

Jodi looks at her dessert menu, which the server has placed squarely in front of her. The words are floating — little boats set adrift in white space. "It's hard to choose," she says.

"You like the crème caramel," says Alison.

"Okay," says Jodi.

"But we don't have to stay for dessert. If you're feeling too tired."

"We always have dessert."

"But we don't have to. How are you feeling?"

"Actually, I'm a little dizzy," says Jodi. *Dizzy* is not the word for what she's feeling, but it's a convenient shorthand for a volley of symptoms that she can't itemize or describe.

Alison's concern is immediate and genuine. She gets the server's attention, gives him her credit card, asks him to rush it, takes Jodi's arm, and insists on driving her home.

"Don't be silly," says Jodi. "It's a ten-minute walk."

Alison ignores this. As they leave the restaurant she keeps a protective arm around her friend, and when the valet brings her car she buckles her in as if she were a child. When she gets Jodi home she makes her lie on the sofa and brings her a cup of tea.

"Where's Todd?" she asks.

Jodi shakes her head. "It's still early."

"Maybe I should call him."

"God no."

"Why not?"

"I'd rather you didn't."

125

"So," says Alison. She sits in an armchair and rests back. "What's he done?"

Jodi doesn't immediately answer. Alison waits. The moments that pass are taut, marked by a distant sound of water rushing through pipes and the ticking of the Keininger mantel clock. Jodi resists divulging her news because right now it's nothing but words in her head, a story she was told that she could still try to forget.

"Have I ever mentioned someone named Natasha Kovacs?" she says finally.

"I don't think so," says Alison. "Not that I can remember."

"Todd has gotten her pregnant," says Jodi.

"Oh dear," says Alison.

Having made a start, Jodi finds that going on is less of an effort. "Natasha can't be more than twenty or twenty-one. She's Dean Kovacs's daughter. Dean is an old school friend of Todd's."

"That's disgusting," says Alison. "How could he do that to you?"

"He's planning to marry her. That's what Dean says."

"He doesn't have to *marry* her. How ridiculous. She can have an abortion."

Jodi finds herself rising to Alison's show of outrage. "He *wants* to marry her. According to Dean he's *dying* to marry her."

126

"Well, maybe Dean doesn't know what he's talking about. Or maybe the marriage is Dean's idea. Maybe Dean is the old-fashioned type who thinks that you marry the girl if you get her pregnant."

"I don't think Dean wants Todd to marry her. I think that's the last thing he wants."

"Okay, well, let's not go off half-cocked. Better get the story straight first."

Jodi shrugs. Dean has no reason to deceive her. The way he tells it is probably as close to the truth as it's going to get.

After Alison has left she gets up from the sofa, smooths her hair and dress, and goes into the bedroom. The clothes she wore to the seminar are draped across the made bed: beige trousers, white shirt, flesh-toned bra and thong, sheer panty hose. Her Fendi leather handbag is on a chair, and under the chair her Jimmy Choo leopard pumps are lying askew. Surveying her beautiful clothes gives her a measure of comfort. It isn't that she's insecure about her looks, but it could be that the bloom is not as fresh as it once was, that a younger woman might enjoy advantages that she herself can no longer claim. At one time she could throw on a pair of Levi's and a T-shirt, and she can still do that, no question, but there's reassurance in dressing well.

She picks up the shirt and undergarments and drops the items one by one into a hamper. The trousers she arranges on a hanger in her wardrobe. The shoes go into their original box, which she places back on the shelf with her other shoe boxes. She partially emptied the handbag before she went to dinner, but it still contains a number of items. She opens it, turns it upside down, and dumps its contents onto the bed: ball-point pen, tiny notebook, assorted receipts, loose change — and the sleeping pills. The pill bottle, one of those clear plastic vials with an oversize twist-off cap, makes the sound of a baby's rattle as it rolls into a slight depression in the duvet. She picks it up and reads the print on the label: *Kovacs, Natasha. Take 1 (one) tablet at bedtime as required.*

She's feeling better now. "Almost back to normal" are the words she used to reassure Alison, and they were very nearly true. She's at least regained a sense of being held down by gravity, and the objects around her are keeping their shape. Methodically, finding it soothing, she goes through her nighttime routine: turning down the bed, plumping the pillows, tidying away this and that stray object. She changes out of her dress, removes her makeup, and brushes her hair. By the time she hears Todd's key in the lock, she's sitting on the sofa in her robe and slippers reading a travel magazine. She waits while he scrabbles around in the foyer disposing of his jacket and keys and change. She hears him clear his throat and mutter a word or two under his breath. She even hears his shoes as he approaches, dragging on the pile of the carpet.

"You're still up," he says.

He comes around the sofa to stand in front of her and kisses the top of her head. She closes her magazine, puts it aside, and gets to her feet. There's something about his posture. He's caught wind of Dean's call and thinks that she may have stayed up to confront him. He places a hand on her shoulder, searching her face.

"Alison was here," she says. "We ate at Cité and she drove me home. How was your day? What did you get for dinner?"

"I had a burger at the Drake," he says.

He smells of alcohol and fried food. His nose is shiny and his voice is pitched high. She picks up the magazine she was reading and adds it to the stack on the coffee table. When she turns back he's still standing there looking at her.

"What?" she says.

"Nothing. It's good to see you."

"You should get the dog walked. I'll wait up for you."

When he gets back she's in the kitchen using a wooden spoon to stir a pot of Ovaltine. Now he becomes talkative. He wants to tell her about various things that happened at the bar over the course of the evening — a couple making out, really going at it, and a gang of priests getting soused. There was some kind of religious convention at the hotel. He talks about the mishap of the morning — the missing key — and laughs about his bad temper. "Poor guy," he says, referring to the janitor. "But he was gone so fast. You'd almost think he was waiting for an excuse."

She puts four slices of bread in the toaster and pushes down the lever. As he talks on, she responds mechanically with nods and murmurs. He doesn't seem to notice that she isn't really listening. When the toast is ready she butters it, spreads it with strawberry jam, and cuts it into triangles. These she arranges on a plate, which she places on the bar top. He pops one of the triangles into his mouth and takes a turn around the room. He comes back, picks up the plate, and continues to pace.

"You didn't talk to Dean today," he says.

"By any chance."

"Dean," she says. "Why would I talk to Dean?"

"No reason."

"I can make more toast," she says.

"Dean is a bastard," he says. "I hope you know that."

He's getting dangerously close to confessing. She's relieved when he moves to the fireplace and turns his attention to the newly framed picture on the mantel.

"This is quite the picture," he says. "The detail in these things is phenomenal."

"How do you like the frame?"

"The frame. I didn't even notice it." He laughs. "Good job. I like it."

When he comes back with his empty plate, his mug of Ovaltine is waiting for him. It's not too hot and he gulps down half of it in one go.

"I love you, you know," he says combatively.

She's standing at the sink washing the pot and the wooden spoon. "That's nice," she replies, looking at him over her shoulder. "How's the Ovaltine?"

"Good." He puts the mug to his lips and recklessly drains it.

"Give me that." She holds out her hand.

He comes around the bar top and gives

her the mug. As she rinses it under the tap, he presses against her from behind, circling her waist with his arms. "You're too good to me," he says.

When she wakes up on the sofa it takes her a while to remember why she's here, and then there's a moment of escalating panic. Last night, after getting Todd undressed and sitting him down on the edge of the bed, after giving him a push and watching him collapse backward like so much dead meat, his jaw slack and his eyes already closing, after lifting his legs off the floor and trying without success to roll him into his proper place, she covered him with the duvet and left him there, lying across the mattress on a diagonal.

Eleven pills. That's how many were in the vial, round blue tablets like buttons on a baby's smock. She spilled them into her hand and counted them out as she dropped them one by one into her mortar. A woman who grinds up sleeping pills in her kitchen mortar and stirs the resulting chalky powder into her husband's bedtime drink could potentially attract a lot of negative attention, could even make a name for herself, but that's not how she was thinking about it at the time. It was more a matter of the just and appropriate thing to do. The pills were in his pocket; he was careless enough to leave them there; it was only right that he should be the one to ingest them. If he ingested the pills they would disappear, and in the process the score between them would be settled.

Unfortunately she failed to notice the dose, and it's now too late to check because the information is gone — the label scraped off and flushed away, the vial itself down the chute with the rest of yesterday's trash. Not that knowing would be any help because she has no idea what dose would be likely to kill him or how much he'd had to drink or what the exponential effect of the alcohol would be. Looking back now she sees that she couldn't have been in her right mind, taking a risk like that without even stopping to think.

She's aware of her fondness for ledger keeping, a term that marriage counselors use to castigate their clients for keeping a running tally of who did what to whom, which is not in the spirit of generosity that supposedly nurtures a healthy relationship. The way she sees it, generosity is admirable but not always practical. Without some discreet retaliation to balance things out, a little surreptitious tit for tat to keep the grievances at bay, most relationships — hers included — would surely combust in a blaze of resentment.

The thing is, eleven sleeping pills did not then and do not now strike her as very many. The alcohol could tip him over the edge, but he's a big man who can take a lot of abuse. The most likely outcome, the intended outcome — and let's not forget she has a pharmacist for a father — is that sooner or later he's going to wake up.

Avoiding the bedroom and its en suite bath she makes use of the powder room off the foyer. Still in her bare feet and night-gown she busies herself opening drapes and blinds, folding her blanket, and pounding the sofa cushions till they've decompressed and resumed their natural shape. When she's given the dog his breakfast she sits down at her desk to check her daybook and her e-mail. Bergman has canceled, leaving only Mary Mary, her first client of the day. It's a bit of good luck as she can't have any fuss while clients are here, and if he's going to get up and stagger around, chances are he won't do it before eleven, by which time Mary Mary will be gone.

When it's no longer possible to avoid the bedroom, she enters like a wary animal, all nose and ears in the lurking gloom. The stagnant air has a sour note that fondles the back of her throat, forcing into her mind the appalling thought that he might have survived the pills and alcohol but choked to death on his vomit. She's heard of that happening. If he's breathing, he's doing it soundlessly. Pausing at the foot of the bed she studies the swell in the covers, the menacing alpine ridge. As far as she can tell, its shape has not altered since she last looked at it some eight hours ago.

She dresses quickly and in the bathroom brushes her teeth, ties back her hair, and applies her daytime makeup — mascara and a light gloss of pressed powder. Her face in the mirror is incongruous, youthful and pretty to the point of reproach. Passing again through the bedroom she watches and waits for an intimation or portent of the kind of day it's going to be, but receives no sign.

The closet in the foyer yields up a leash for the dog, and there she also finds her Nikes and a windbreaker. She and Freud take the elevator down to the lobby, where she waves to the doorman and greets a neighbor who is coming in as she is going out. It's good to be under the open sky and breathing the fresh, unsullied air. Only now, as it's leaving her, does she notice the constraint she's been under, creeping around like a felon in her own home. At least there's been no recurrence of last night's sickness or vertigo or whatever it was. That was a new one on her and something she really didn't care for.

She follows her usual morning route, walking the shoreline to the pier and then cutting back through Gateway Park. The sky is gray and the lake a dull bottle green, but the bracing air and her pumping legs give her some new life. When she's back inside with her takeout latte, she cautiously opens the bedroom door and without crossing the threshold peers intently into the gloom. As far as she can tell, nothing has changed.

Mary Mary is a twelve-year-old girl whose parents send her to Jodi because she's wayward and rebellious. She loves her therapy sessions, which get her out of school and make her feel special, but makes a point of being pushy and intrusive. The child has boundary issues. If there's trouble with Todd, Mary Mary is sure to put her nose in it. Jodi counts herself lucky when Todd stays put and the girl comes and goes without any hitches.

Standing on the balcony to cool her head,

she takes stock of her situation. While she was in with Mary Mary, Todd's phone was sounding from its place on his dresser behind the closed door of the bedroom, where she left it last night when she was emptying his pockets as she helped him get undressed. Todd keeps his phone in vibrating mode, and throbbing on the wood surface it sounded like there were workmen in there with electric hammer drills. Loud enough to wake him, she would have thought, especially given that Todd is so keenly attuned to his phone. His phone going off, to him, is like a crying baby to its mother, calling for immediate, tender attention. And he isn't the type to ignore it, roll over, and go back to sleep. Todd is someone who springs out of bed the second he opens his eyes.

She watches a pair of gulls swooping and diving out on the lake. Far from hesitating or prevaricating, when they spot what they want below the water's surface they attack at high speed, headlong and brash. Their raucous calls — a gullish version of chuckling and gloating — don't seem to warn off their prey, who are swallowed whole before they know what hit them.

She's tempted now to push on with her day as if there were nothing out of the ordinary going on. Turning a blind eye is something she knows how to do. She's adept at leaving well enough alone, waiting to see what happens. It's time for her workout, and after that she would normally have lunch. She's been looking forward to the small fillet she has thawing in the fridge. But when Todd wakes up he's going to be asking questions. "Why did you let me sleep so late? Didn't you think that something might be wrong?" And in the event that he doesn't wake up the questions will come from elsewhere. The paramedics. The police. She should make up her mind what she's going to say if she's put on the spot — what her story will be, how she can account for her behavior, the fact that she did nothing, nothing at all, when her loved one failed to get out of bed in the morning. She can just hear some enterprising policeman saying to her: Mrs. Gilbert, your husband was dead for six hours — or eight hours or twelve hours — before you called 911. And on it would go from there. Didn't you think you should at least look in on him? Didn't you realize? Didn't it occur to you? Didn't it just happen to enter your mind? That your husband might be sick. That he might be in distress. That he might be unconscious. That he might be *dead,* Mrs. Gilbert.

Unconscious, she thinks. He could be unconscious. And on the heels of that thought comes another more ominous one — the thought that he could be in a coma, a possibility that has somehow eluded her up to this moment. Like a winking intruder the term *brain damage* slides into her mental landscape and with it a vision of Todd as a human vegetable, failing to either live or die, belonging to no one, not even himself, but calling the shots nonetheless as people scurry about to feed him, bathe him, massage him, sit him up, and lie him down as days and nights become months and years and his loyalties, along with his assets, remain in escrow. And even so there will be questions. She's starting to feel that she is seen and judged, her every move logged to be used against her. It's no comfort that Freud has been nosing the closed bedroom door off and on all morning. Mrs. Gilbert, even your dog knew that something was wrong.

6
HIM

He sits on the toilet, elbows on knees, face in hands, urinating in a fetid stream. It's all he can do to stay upright. He thinks about coffee, the smell and taste of it, and that propels him from the toilet to the shower, where he turns the taps to cold. The icy pellets are pure unmitigated pain but a poor match for the jackhammer going off in his head. He lifts his face to the spray, takes some in his mouth, gargles, and spits it out. He hawks up some phlegm and spits that out too.

When he's finished toweling off he stands at the sink to lather his face. His fingers are numb and clumsy with the razor. He has an idea that he's overslept, and this is confirmed when he returns to the bedroom to dress. Jodi is already up. It must be later than he thought. Still, it's not until he's fully clothed and pulling on his wristwatch that he checks the time.

He finds her in the kitchen, beating eggs with a whisk. "My watch is running slow," he says, hovering. "Battery must be dead."

"Coffee's ready," she says. She fills a mug, stirs in cream and sugar, and hands it to him.

"What time is it?" he asks. "My watch says half past one."

"It's half past one in the afternoon," she says.

"You're joking," he says.

"That's what time it is," she says.

"It can't be," he says. "I'm meeting Cliff at ten."

She shrugs. "You'll just have to call him and tell him that you overslept." She pours the eggs into a sizzling pan and moves them around with a fork.

"But that's crazy," he says. "Why didn't you wake me up?"

"You needed to sleep it off."

"Jesus," he says. He drinks some coffee, presses a hand to his temple. "I must have really tied one on. I can't remember getting into bed."

Hit by a wave of fatigue, he takes his coffee to the table. She has it set with a place mat, a knife and fork, and a napkin.

"I had to help you get undressed," she says. "You couldn't even get your shoes off."

141

She turns the eggs onto a plate and adds bacon and potatoes from a pan that's been keeping warm on the stovetop. She carries the plate to the table and sets it down in front of him. He picks up his fork.

"Thanks," he says. "I'm starving."

As he eats, his tongue gets in the way, a foreign body in his mouth. He shovels in the food nonetheless, feeding his weakness and fatigue. He'd like to collapse — go back to bed, curl up on the floor — and compensates by sitting up straight and planting his feet.

"I didn't think I drank all that much," he says. "No more than usual, anyway."

He tries to remember what happened at the bar — what time he got there, how long he stayed, how many rounds he ordered — but the math eludes him. What he does remember is his celebratory mood. And in the spirit of celebration, it's possible that he overindulged.

"I mean, okay, it might have been a little more than usual," he says.

"You probably needed the extra sleep."

"Tell that to Cliff. And Stephanie."

She brings the coffeepot to the table and refills his mug.

"Jesus, Jodi. I don't understand why you didn't wake me up."

142

"Are you planning to be home for dinner?" she asks.

"The way I'm feeling," he says.

"I'll make you a nice cassoulet. Pork is full of iron."

His phone starts up as he's lingering at the table, and he follows the sound to the bedroom. Natasha's number on the call display gives him a little boost. One thing he does remember is that last night she wasn't speaking to him.

"Where are you?" she asks. "I've been trying to reach you all morning."

"Sleeping off a hangover."

"You're still at home?"

"Almost out the door."

"What did she say?"

He struggles to grasp her meaning. His mind feels stuck, a burned-out engine sunk in a pool of sludge.

"Maybe you can't talk right now," she prods.

He glances at the open door. Hears the tap running in the kitchen. "Only for a minute."

"So? What did she say?"

"What did who say?"

She gives a noisy little sigh. "How upset is she? Is she going to be decent about it?"

The pregnancy, he thinks. Did he promise

to tell Jodi?

"I got home late," he says. "I haven't had a chance to talk to her."

He's resting a forearm on his dresser. Its white surface is mottled and cracked, an antique effect that cost him more than he would have paid for the real thing. "You know I love you," he says.

"For God's sake, Todd. What happened after she spoke to my father?"

"Jodi didn't speak to your father."

"Yes she did. Yesterday. He told her everything."

"That's impossible."

"How is it impossible? It happened. What's going on there? Are you okay?"

He sits down heavily on the bed. He's starting to wonder if he's caught some sort of bug. "I'm fine," he says. "There's nothing to worry about. I'll have to call you back."

He breaks the connection and it dawns on him that this is typical of his and Jodi's life together: the stubborn pretense, the chasms of silence, the blind forging ahead. He must have known this, but the weirdness of it, the aberrance, has somehow never struck him. Other couples are loud, vocal, off and on again, working things out, but with Jodi and him it's all dissimulation. Put up a front, go through the motions, don't say a word. Act as if all is well and all *will* be well. Jodi's great gift is her silence, and he has always loved this about her, that she knows how to mind her own business, keep her own counsel, but silence is also her weapon. The woman who refuses to object, who doesn't yell and scream — there's strength in that, and power. The way she overrides senti- ment, won't enter into blaming or bicker- ing, never gives him an opening, doesn't al- low him to turn it back on her. She knows that her refusal leaves him alone with his choices. And yet he can see that she suffers with it.

He understands suffering; he was raised Catholic. What he understands is that life has suffering in it, can't not have suffering in it, because in life there is everything. Life is a mosaic of everything, and there are no clean edges either. In the mosaic of life things overlap because nothing is all one way. Take, for instance, his father. He came to despise his father, and that's a given, but there were times with his father he can think of even now with something like pleasure. An afternoon at the airport watching the planes come and go. He must have been seven or eight at the time. He loved seeing the rotund bodies of the jumbo jets lumber

across the tarmac and then lift off with ef-
fortless grace, the sunlight glancing off their
wingtips. For years afterward he wanted to
be a pilot, and his father encouraged him,
told him he could be whatever he wanted to
be. There was something like love between
them then, love mixed with other things of
course, getting back to the principle that
nothing in life is just one way. The old man
had goodness in him, even laughter and fun,
but the darkness at the center was growing,
always growing, and when your father is at
bottom a drunk and a bully, there comes a
sense of biding your time, waiting for the
day when you'll be big enough and strong
enough to intervene, and you look forward
to that day as one of ultimate liberation,
which it does turn out to be, but that's not
all, and here again is the lesson that life is a
mixed bag.

The day came when Todd was sixteen. By
then he was growing tall and husky, had
gained strength and confidence working
construction over the summer, heaving
sacks of cement and buckets of tar. It was a
Saturday in fall, cold and rainy, a day of
hanging around the house doing homework
and watching TV. The old man had been
restless, testy as a land mine and surfacing
at intervals from the basement to nag and

carp at his wife. Anyone could see there was a storm brewing. It was just a matter of when it would erupt. But there was always this underlying optimism, a stubborn disbelief that things could go very badly wrong, something his mother felt, too, he knew, because she said to him as she peeled potatoes, "He'll settle down when he's had his dinner." But then, when they were sitting with their plates in their laps watching something on TV (an episode of *Bewitched* is what he remembers), and meek as she was his mother reached out with her napkin to dab at a spot of gravy on her husband's chin, they were suddenly, all three of them, on their feet with their dinner overturned and the old man holding her hair in his fist, and in Todd's ears there was a rushing sound, and with black spots decimating his vision, he swung his fist, throwing a punch, as wild and clumsy a punch as ever there was, and one that landed he knew not where, and his father without ceremony folded up like a collapsible chair and fell to the floor and lay there bleeding from his nose, and in the days that followed, the boy, now a man, was overcome with grief, despising how it all lay bare between them, how there was no more father and no more son but just two adult men in hateful and impoverished proximity.

Now, at home in the afternoon on a weekday, when he ought to be at work, sitting on the bed holding his phone, confused by what Natasha has told him, his eyes roam idly around the room taking in the height and breadth of it, the ample proportions, tall windows, receding ice blue of the walls. There's no sound anywhere in the apartment and no sound from the outside. When you're this high up you don't even hear the birds. It couldn't be more peaceful, and yet he feels his weight dragging him down and his spirit besieged as if by devils or wild dogs.

As he understands suffering he also understands devotion, and he's made his offerings with an open heart, his offerings to his beloved, to Jodi. He's provided her with comforts, yes, but not just that. He's been attentive, devoted, massaging her feet sometimes for hours when they're home together watching a movie, and spending his weekends in the kitchen helping with her jellies and jams, endlessly stirring the pot, the watery mixture that seems like it will never thicken. She loves it when he puts on an apron and turns domestic. She feels close to him then. It's the kind of intimacy she craves, a companionship that makes her happy. And he's taken it on willingly, even religiously, with a devout spirit, and he'd do more for her if she asked, but Jodi rarely asks for anything. If she asked more of him maybe things would be better. His mother was like that too — didn't ask — but that was for the best because his father would not have responded well. As far as cheating goes the old man was in a different league. Cheating with the bottle is not a mere distraction, not an evening's entertainment, but an out-and-out commitment, a contract, a pledge, and it led him to turn away from his wife utterly and with finality. Todd's mother was a forsaken woman, her loneliness a mist that enveloped him throughout his childhood.

He stands up and braces himself on the doorjamb. This is no ordinary hangover. Maybe food poisoning, the burger he ate at the bar. But if so wouldn't he be throwing up or at least sitting on the can? Instead, he feels like crying, giving up, giving in. Conscious of holding himself together, putting one foot in front of the other, he finds Jodi on the sofa, legs curled underneath her, not reading a magazine or a cookbook, not talking on the phone, not doing anything. He sits beside her, lets his head drop to her shoulder.

"I'm spoiling your afternoon," he says.

"Not really." She seems distracted, a little remote. "I'll do some grocery shopping and then get started on dinner. Maybe a chicken soup would be the thing."

"You must have other plans."

"Nothing important. Taking care of you is what matters right now."

"I feel like getting back into bed."

"Why don't you? Sleep it off. Get a fresh start tomorrow."

"Chicken soup sounds good. Are you going to make it with dumplings?"

"Whatever you like."

"What would I do without you. I'm sorry I'm not a better husband."

"Don't be silly," she says. "You're under the weather, that's all. I'll make up the bed for you. Why don't you lie down here until it's ready."

7
HER

When her kitchen devilry, her little bit of domestic mischief, instead of going down in history retains its status as a private and incidental matter just between the two of them, she counts herself vindicated. The speed of his recovery — within twenty-four hours he was right as rain — was a meaningful confirmation of her good instincts. She didn't think that eleven pills would kill him, and they didn't.

With disaster averted she is back in her comfort zone, able to laugh at her fears. Dean's version of things is almost certainly unreliable; that's what she's decided. She's come to the conclusion that Dean is not to be trusted. For the moment at least, he isn't himself but a man whose basic assumptions about reality have been forced into abrupt revision. His oldest friend turns out to be a predator; his daughter is not the sensible girl he took her for. It's a given that he's temporarily out of his mind. Besides which Dean has always been too quick off the mark. Prone to theatrics. A bit of a prima donna. She, Jodi, is the one who knows Todd best, and one thing she knows for sure is that home is important to him. Not just for Todd but for most men, home is the counterpoint that gives an affair its glamour. An affair by definition is secret, temporary, uncommitted, not leading to the complications of a longer-term arrangement — and thus its appeal. Todd has no intention of marrying this girl.

As a child Natasha was unremarkable, and after her mother died she ran wild. Jodi remembers her with black lipstick and spiky hair, a potbelly and chewed fingernails. It's hard to imagine that she's grown up to be in any way attractive. What Todd is drawn to is her youth, a girl half his age taking an interest in him. Men are like that; they crave the reassurance. Certainly Natasha Kovacs is not a *force*. Not anyone to be *reckoned* with. Todd is in it for the short term. That's his pattern, and everyone knows that the best predictor of future behavior is past behavior.

It's a good thing that she, at least, is stable, mature, and loyal, capable of holding a marriage together. The world is full of damaged people and without the sane ones to take up the slack no couple would be safe. She does it willingly, gladly, pleased to be the fully functional member of the union, the one with the clean bill of mental health, the one who enjoyed a happy childhood and emerged without a psychological deficit. She's clear about this, the fact that she is capable and sane. During her school years she went through a course of psychotherapy. Her badge of self-knowledge has been hard-won.

The psychotherapy came about through one of her profs at the Adler School, who thought she would benefit from finding out firsthand what it felt like to sit in the client's chair. Delving into her own psyche, he said, would show her how to help others do the same. She knew that he didn't make this recommendation to all his students and wondered why he had singled her out but never got around to asking. What she did know was that some schools make a personal course of psychotherapy a basic requirement for graduation. Jungian students, for example, are subjected to rigorous personal analysis throughout their training.

After university, when she was making up her mind to do additional studies and before settling on the Adler School, she looked into the Jung Institute as one of her options. She liked Jung's idea of individuation, the process of realizing oneself apart from one's racial and cultural heritage, in Jungian terms a way of attaining wholeness. People must arrive at their own understanding of life and its meaning, aside from what their elders may have taught them. But on the whole she found the Jungian approach to be arcane, having a locked-box kind of appeal that arose from Jung's attraction to mysticism and symbolism. A Jungian once told her that to live meaningfully would mean to experience herself as a participant in a symbolic drama — a suspension of disbelief that she could never quite attain. Adler appealed to her more with his pragmatic views on social interest and goal constructs.

The therapist she chose, Gerard Hartmann, was an Adlerian and like herself a counseling psychologist, but Gerard was older and had more credentials and more experience. She was in her twenties then, and he was in his forties. On Tuesday mornings she arrived at the vintage high-rise on Washington Street near the park in time for her ten o'clock appointment and sat with him in a room that was heated and air-conditioned indiscriminately, which got her into the habit of bringing a couple of sweaters, whatever the temperature outside, that she could put on or peel off as needed. The other important thing she brought to her sessions was her understanding of the underlying premise of psychotherapy, a premise that broadly cuts across the schools of thought, namely: Whoever you are and wherever you come from, you grew into your present shape and form in the garden of your early childhood. In other words, your orientation to life and the world around you — your psychogenic framework — was already in place before you were old enough to leave the house without parental supervision. Your biases and preferences, where you are stuck and where you excel, how you circumscribe your happiness and where you feel your pain, all of this precedes you into adulthood, because when you were very young, in your naive, impressionable, developing self, you assessed your experiences and accordingly made decisions having to do with your place in the world, and these decisions took root and grew into further decisions that hardened into attitudes, habits of mind, a style of expression — the you of you with whom you have come to identify deeply and resolutely. Having understood this theoretically through her schooling, she was prepared to encounter it practically in her therapy. Her ease and composure in facing this prospect sprang from her belief that in her case it would be painless, given her good beginnings and healthy outlook.

She took an immediate liking to Gerard, who had a large measure of the kind of manliness that emanates from sheer size and bulk — big head, big feet, broad chest and shoulders, impressive height. He was hairy to boot, with a lush, dark mane and sprouting wrists, and he smelled of cigarettes and car upholstery, smells that she associated with men and masculinity — her father, her uncles. Gerard also had a bit of a squint. The way he looked he could have been a cowboy, but he fought that image by always wearing a suit and tie and never removing his jacket, apparently oblivious to the fluctuations in the temperature of his consulting room.

Sitting across from him on the first day, taking in the pen and notebook that he kept on the arm of his chair but rarely used and his habit of giving her all the time in the world to answer any question, she thought he looked tired, even worn-out, had been through too many difficult wrangles with clients. But his habitual rueful expression said that he regretted their pain, and hers, too, and that he was caring, sympathetic, and safe.

"Tell me the very first thing you remember" was the way he began, and she recounted the memory that came into her mind.

"I was in the hospital having my tonsils out, but that part my mother told me later. The part I remember is standing up in my crib and looking around the room at the other babies in cribs and feeling distraught when one of them started to cry."

He waited, so she said, "I couldn't understand why that baby was crying. And I wanted to find out."

Still he waited, and finally she said, "I guess I had an early calling to psychotherapy."

That made him laugh. She was glad he had a sense of humor.

He asked for more childhood memories, and she came up with another half dozen, and then he asked for still more. She was of course familiar with the Adlerian approach to early recollections and knew that Gerard wouldn't care if her accounts were accurate or even true. To an Adlerian, your memories are simply your stories; their value lies in the way they reflect your attitudes. Fertile ground for the therapist, but she had never applied this filter to herself. Not being the sentimental type, she did not keep memorabilia, not even a photograph album, and she rarely thought about the past. What surprised her now was the groundswell of feeling that each recollection brought with it. The remains of days gone by were not the antiquities she thought they would be, not fossils, but fresh, still alive and jumping.

She remembered a party dress with a tartan pattern and velvet trim, her mother using a curling iron to set her hair in ringlets, the time her tongue stuck to an icy railing, spraining her wrist falling out of a tree, baking cookies with Granny Brett, her father reading her stories, her older brother pushing her on the swing, playing house and hopscotch and clapping games with the other kids, giving her friend a bracelet that she would have preferred to keep for herself and when her friend lost the bracelet regretting her generosity. From school she remembered a pretty girl named Darlene who she wanted to emulate and a girl named Penny who gave a wrong answer to the question: How many in a trio? Penny said two. With each event came the appraisal, what she had decided at the time: She liked being a girl, was not going to benefit by being a show-off or a daredevil, men were nice to her, playing with others was fun, it was okay to be selfish when it mattered, she could copy the things she liked about Darlene (her excellent posture, for example), she was smarter than Penny, and she had the potential to make something of herself.

The disclosures continued over the next few sessions. She told Gerard about her entry into psychology, that she'd seen it as a calling — but may have been misled. From the age of seven or eight she'd been known in her family as the house shrink, the one who could pacify her younger brother, Ryan, who was prone to nightmares, tantrums, and self-biting. "Get Jodi," they said when he was bleeding or thrashing around in his bed.

She doted on Ryan. She'd hold him close and rock him to sleep or distract him with jokes and games. The upshot was that her parents praised her and she took the praise to heart. But comforting your little brother bears no resemblance to working with clients on their blind spots and grappling with their anger, jealousy, loneliness, and greed.

"We do our best," said Gerard.

"What if your best isn't good enough?"

"If your clients know that you care about them, that's half the battle. Emotional support in itself can do wonders. After that you rely on your training and your wits."

"What about aptitude? That has to count for something."

"It's like any other job. You work at it. You get better with practice."

Gerard grew in her esteem, became an anchor that kept her stable in uncharted waters and also, in a way, her muse. A nod, a word, a gesture from Gerard could be a marker and a prompt. His dependable squint and mellow vowels were coconspirators in the enterprise of drawing her out. Even the room itself, the neutral colors, the uniform light, and the quietude, with only an occasional burst of voices from the hallway or a distant bump or thump as of a door closing, but muffled, as if under water, could turn the crank of her memory, take her back to the jurisdiction of her earliest years, bringing them once again to life.

In spite of all this she did not have high expectations, did not foresee much of anything coming from her work with Gerard. Her inclination was to take it for what it essentially was: part of her education, another leg of her training. Because, after all, it wasn't as if she had come here with problems. Indeed, her life at the time was going exceptionally well. The client who had shattered her confidence by committing suicide, young Sebastian, was slowly but surely receding into a measured distance where the picture included factors other than her own negligence, and meanwhile she and Todd were in their blissful third year of being a couple, still in the brash, lingering phase of going everywhere together, going out just to be seen in all their concupiscent glory. She had never been more in love and had never entered so fully into the pleasures of the flesh, not even in her first year of university when she went through a phase of what she could only describe, even then, as wholesale promiscuity.

Inevitably, she and Gerard got onto the subject of her parents' marriage, especially their silences, which apparently struck him as fertile ground for discussion, judging from the way he kept coming back to it. But it was old terrain for her and held no surprises.

Gerard: How was it for you when they weren't speaking to each other?
Jodi: I guess it could make things tense for us kids.
Gerard: Did it make you tense?

Jodi: Sometimes it made me laugh. When there were dinner guests and my parents were fawning over them — you know, focus on the guests so you don't have to talk to your spouse — I'd look over at Ryan and he'd be crossing his eyes and clutching his throat and I'd start to laugh and then he'd start to laugh and we'd be sitting there shaking with laughter and trying not to spit out our food. That happened a few times, actually. That kind of thing.

Gerard: Laughter is a great release.

Jodi: I don't know that it was such a big deal, them not speaking. I mean it was for them, obviously. But I didn't see that till I was older.

Gerard: What did you see?

Jodi: What he put her through. What she had to put up with. It was a small town and everybody knew what was going on. I think it was the humiliation that got to her more than anything. The idea that people pitied her. She felt demoralized.

Gerard: So your father was unfaithful and your mother felt demoralized. What was the effect on you?

Jodi: Funny, I just remembered this. I followed him to her house once.

Gerard: Tell me.

Jodi: She was a customer. She'd come into the pharmacy. And I'd always notice what she was wearing and how she acted and what she bought. Cough drops, usually. And Valium. He was always filling her prescription for Valium. She'd get dressed up — lipstick, skirt, heels — it was all so obvious. She was very unashamed, and I found that shocking in a way.

Gerard: Go on.

Jodi: She came in one Saturday when I was there helping out, and as soon as she left with her purchases he took off his lab coat and asked me to mind the store, but I closed up and followed him instead. I guess until then there was room for doubt. But it was very graphic, very final, seeing him climb her porch steps and ring her bell, and seeing her open the door and let him in.

Gerard: Did you say anything to your mother?

Jodi: What would be the point?

Gerard: Did you talk to *him* about it?

Jodi: No. I think that even then I understood. This woman, she was a widow. It was one of those Vietnam stories —

163

husband comes home in a wheelchair and a few months later dies of an overdose. My father started something that he may have regretted, but he couldn't just abandon her.

Gerard: And your mother didn't leave him.

Jodi: It would have meant breaking up the family.

Gerard: In her position, what would you have done?

Jodi: If I had three kids? I guess I would have done the same. Stuck it out. But you learn from their mistakes, right? I won't put myself in that position.

Gerard: How do you mean?

Jodi: I won't get married. I won't have a family.

Gerard: You say that very emphatically.

Jodi: It's how I feel.

Gerard: In a way it puts you in the position of paying for their mistakes.

Jodi: I want to be in control of my life. I want to be happy.

Gerard: Happiness is not something we can prescribe.

Jodi: If I ended up like my mother I would only have myself to blame.

But her parents' troubles were adult

troubles and hadn't much affected her life as a child. It would have been hard to improve on her thriving middle-class family with its solid core values of hard work, earning power, community spirit, and education. Or on her stable, balanced childhood filled with summer holidays, piano lessons, swimming practice, church on Sundays, and sit-down family dinners. Growing up, she was loved, praised, disciplined, and encouraged. She did well at school, made and kept friends, went on dates with boys, and entirely missed going through any sort of awkward phase. An only girl in a family of three children, she was cushioned between an older and a younger brother, and in her talks with Gerard it came to light that this, too, had worked to her advantage. She was spoiled but no more nor less spoiled than the baby of the family, her younger brother, Ryan. And her older brother, Darrell, was enough years older to be a mentor and not a rival.

At times, during her work with Gerard, her undeniable advantages could make her feel awkward, even apologetic. The way he looked at her (quizzically, hopefully), his habit of waiting for her to say more, to add something to the mix — this could cause her to falter and question herself. There

165

were moments when she felt like a fake —
or like he must think she was a fake. It
became a concern that he suspected her of
dissembling, hiding some deeper truth
about herself, failing to disclose a darker,
bleaker side of her story, resisting him,
resisting therapy. But he never actually said
such things, and so she had to conclude that
it was all in her mind, a smattering of
paranoia, a slight discomfort with the psy-
chotherapeutic process.

8
HIM

Over the next little while Todd is taken in hand by Natasha, who insists that he accompany her all over town on various errands and excursions. Every day he breaks from work at odd hours. They visit the obstetrician, look at rental apartments, and buy things for the baby — toys, a carriage, a matching crib and dresser — which Todd has to store in the damp basement of his office building for lack of anywhere else to put them. All the more reason, says Natasha, to hurry up and find a place for them to live.

In the third week of September he signs a lease on a two-bedroom apartment in River North. Natasha likes it because it's newly renovated, with a teak and granite kitchen and a Jacuzzi. She also likes that they can move in on the first of October, which is just around the corner.

After the lease signing, which takes place

midmorning on a weekday, Natasha declares that celebratory sex is mandatory, so they check in to their usual room at the Crowne Plaza and Todd does his best to perform in spite of the news he received from Cliff earlier in the day about the leaky basement at the Jefferson Park apartment house. They knew that moisture was getting in, but Cliff is saying that it's worse than they thought, that yesterday's downpour was a wake-up call. As soon as he can get away he drives to the site to see for himself the seepage along the west wall (where he plans to put the laundry room) that is only going to get worse. This will mean a major dent in his profit margin and does not leave him in a good mood, coming on top of today's lease signing. Paying for two residences in the same city is a fool's game, but what choice does he have? Given that Natasha has his balls in a vise and things with Jodi have still not come to a head. Although Natasha insists that Jodi knows the truth, he's not entirely sure that he believes her. He's thought about having a talk with Jodi, but when he runs that conversation through his mind it comes to a dead end, considering that he himself has not made any final decisions about his future, that leaving Jodi is by no means a fixed item on his agenda.

Natasha can nag and Natasha can pressure, but he will come to his own conclusion in his own time.

Another thing that's taxing his patience is Natasha's jealousy of Jodi. Natasha wants him to leave Jodi and move to a hotel. It isn't right, she says, that he goes home to Jodi every night when she, Natasha, is incubating his baby. Worse, she's developed a ghoulish curiosity about his and Jodi's life together. She wants to know what they talk about, what they eat for dinner, what they wear to bed. He tells her that he and Jodi are friends, that they haven't made love in years. He even told her once that Jodi wished them well. But nothing seems to appease her. If only she would get a grip and settle down. He's been with Jodi for a long time. Natasha is young; she doesn't understand the pull of the years. She's impatient and lacks perspective, has a hot head, tends to be stubborn and willful like her father.

She's also a born mother, a nurturing type who wants a big family, and he likes that, can just about imagine himself as a patriarch, the benevolent head of a brood of boys and girls in staggered sizes. He sees them lined up as if for a family photo, clean and pressed, quiet and well behaved. Above all else, kids need to mind their manners; you

169

can't have them running wild and taking over. When his boys are old enough he'll teach them the trades, show them the city, explain to them how the neighborhoods have grown up through the years, how property values have changed, how to spot a deal when they see one, his accumulated knowledge passed on and not gone to waste. It's a different life from the one he's been leading, and in many ways it appeals to him, but so far it's just an idea, a projection, a possibility. Natasha needs to be patient and take things as they come because nothing is fixed. Nothing is decided. He won't move forward till a clear path opens up in front of him. He isn't going to heedlessly walk away from the home he's made with Jodi and everything they've shared for so many years. Jodi is his touchstone, his world, his promised land. When she came into his life — when she showed up a sight for sore eyes in a downpour at a congested intersection, when she helped him consecrate the Bucktown mansion, when she decided to believe in him and came another day to help him paint and balanced on the ladder with supreme grace, back then on any given day he wanted only to inhabit her — her flawless skin, her supple form, her open heart. And then, as things progressed, as their togetherness deepened, something in him shifted, the ground solidified beneath his feet and he lost the sense that he couldn't take a right step, that any step he took would land wrong.

In his boyhood home there was never any sense of equilibrium; it was always a matter of uncertain alliances: his mother protecting him from his father, his father setting him against his mother, his own confusion and shifting sense of loyalty. He spent a lot of time with the Kovacses, eating dinner with Dean and his family and sometimes sleeping over, finding it strange and impressive that Mr. Kovacs was always present at the table, that he'd compliment his wife on the meal, that he was rarely seen with a drink in his hand. Mrs. Kovacs would invite Todd to join them for Thanksgiving, and one year she asked him to come along on their summer vacation, to keep Dean company she said. She was nice that way, making it seem as if he was doing them a favor instead of the other way around.

When he met Jodi's parents they reminded him of Mr. and Mrs. Kovacs. They had the same easy air of cordial good nature, and their home had the same feeling of dependable middle-class comfort, and sitting down with them to a pot roast and a glass of apple juice, he felt a keen sense of déjà vu. He was impressed by the ease between Jodi and her mother as they got the meal on the table and by the camaraderie between Jodi and her father, who teased her about her rapid advancement through the education system, calling her Frau Doktor Jodi, which made her becomingly blush. He felt himself to be an interloper from an underclass, the boyfriend who had opted out of an education and entered into the perilous, possibly doomed life of a struggling would-be entrepreneur. He was broke, untried, and unproven, and it went without saying that he would not pass muster with Jodi's parents.

But Mr. Brett — a stocky man with black-framed glasses, a man who didn't smile even when he joked and who, according to Jodi, had been a firm disciplinarian with his children — turned out to be gracious and attentive, and Mrs. Brett was also very nice, a handsome woman with an air of refinement who welcomed Todd with a great show of warmth.

When everyone was seated with their napkins in their laps, Jodi said, "Todd is restoring a grand old mansion in Bucktown. The previous owner turned it into a rooming house and left it in a mess. Todd is doing the city a great service, if only they knew it."

"Is that so, Todd?" said Mrs. Brett.

"Sounds like a challenging project," said Mr. Brett.

"He's doing all the work himself," Jodi added. "He knows all the trades and he's really good at them."

"What kind of timeline are you on?" asked Mr. Brett.

"Well, sir, I guess I'm just going as fast as I can," said Todd.

"He's brilliant at the business end of it too," said Jodi.

He hadn't exactly lied to her but he'd never told her the truth either — that the Bucktown mansion was as good as quicksand, that the swamp of debt was about to suck him under, that he would end up working construction, a job he'd done summers during high school and then again for several years afterward — and at this critical moment, the moment when he was meant to swagger a little in front of Jodi's parents, his confidence deserted him entirely.

"It takes guts to do something like that," said Mr. Brett. "But now's the time for it, while you're still young and have the energy."

"You bought the drugstore when you were young," Jodi said to her father.

"Your mother and I were about the age you two are now," said Mr. Brett.

"The worst thing is to let your dreams slip away without fighting for them," said Mrs. Brett.

"Mom wanted to be a singer," said Jodi. "She has a beautiful singing voice."

"Used to have," said Mrs. Brett.

"Running your own business is the way to go," said Mr. Brett. "Doesn't matter what you do, as long as you're your own boss."

"Some people care more about security," said Todd, doubtful of all this approval.

"That will come in time," said Mr. Brett.

"You have to start somewhere," said Mrs. Brett.

"What sort of a house is it?" asked Mr. Brett.

Todd obligingly answered that it was built in 1880 but that — unlike many Chicago mansions of the period — it was more Gothic Revival than Victorian, was a bit of a monstrosity, in fact. "It looks like your typical haunted house," he said. "And it's gone to ruin. Even the grounds are a mess, all rubble and weeds. I'll need to rent a tiller to turn the soil."

"You'll want to put in your grass seed

anytime now," said Mr. Brett. "Give it a chance to root before the cold weather comes. Or your sod, if that's what you're planning, but seed does better in the long run, and it's cheaper."

"Take his word for it," said Jodi. "He knows about grass."

"I noticed the lawn when we came in," said Todd.

"The lawn is his pride and joy," said Mrs. Brett.

"Don't let grass intimidate you," said Mr. Brett. "Growing grass is simple chemistry."

Later, when Jodi and Todd were out walking, Todd said, "I love your parents. They're so nice."

It was late summer, a time of year for lush, fading blooms and dusk descending with slow, archaic majesty. The evening light lingered in the western sky as they rambled through the quiet streets, past Jodi's old high school and the United Methodist church she had attended with her family and the houses of friends who, like her, had grown up and moved away. Jodi by then was solidly in his life, but there was still a flavor of mystery about her, a glamour with origins he couldn't quite divine. What he did know was that he'd never met a girl he wanted so much to impress. He longed to live up to her faith in him, to be the man she needed and deserved. Walking beside her in the radiant dusk, in the otherworldly trafficless quiet of the small rural community, lapped by scented breezes, the air itself a lulling bath, he felt that his life could finally begin, that she was the god he would worship and the talisman that would make things come out right.

By the time they returned from their walk, the sky had darkened and the streetlights were on. The plan was to stay the night and drive back the next day after lunch. He knew that the visit would be a chaste one because Jodi had forewarned him that her parents were the old-fashioned sort, and true to form Mrs. Brett made a point of showing him into the room that had once belonged to Ryan, the younger boy, whereas Jodi, he understood, would be spending the night in her own room down the hall. He found this endearing, even commendable, the impulse of the parents to cocoon their daughter as best they could, at least for the time she was under their roof. Like most parents they no doubt saw their grown child as a youngster still, and on some level he must strike them as a menacing stranger who had somehow found his way into the family compound. Still, he was content to

176

take their hospitality at face value and not concern himself with whatever might be crawling around under the tribal bedrock. He knew, for instance, that there was some sort of trouble between Jodi and her brothers — that she didn't speak to the older one and that she worried about the younger one, who had turned out to be a black sheep of sorts — but the brothers didn't figure in the general conversation, and nor was there any sign of strife between the parents.

A few months later, in the glory days of autumn when the treetops burned with color and the side-angled light cast the city in a golden glow — he always feels in fall that there should be trumpet blasts or bugle calls — after he'd sold the Bucktown mansion and consolidated his future, in his own mind at least, he and Jodi found a small apartment in the Loop and merged their belongings and their lives.

He wanted to marry her, intended to marry her, and thought about ways he could propose that might overturn her resistance. Being together was perfect, she said, and why mess with it, but it seemed to him that she might be persuaded, flattered himself that he could slip past her guard. Commitment appealed to him, a fortress of togetherness, a pledge to guarantee their future. If you couldn't secure your stronghold at the outset, how could you expect it to survive when the storms blew through? He wanted them to vouchsafe their love, give it over to something greater than the two of them.

In the end he decided that the best tactic was to simply spring it on her, hoping that she might just concede in a spirit of spontaneity, and he tried this many times, but she never would take him seriously. He'd say, "Let's get married," and she'd say, "Can we stop at the supermarket first?" He was a little stung by it, but there was something to admire in her resolve. Anyway, boys don't grow up dreaming of their wedding day. Having her promise — hearing her say the words, take the vow — would have meant something to him, but her love and devotion were never in doubt. She belonged to him; they belonged to each other. And they were happy. She took care of him in surprising ways, making an art of their household arrangements, easing the burden of day-to-day life, and it was new to him, this domestic gratification — that she was there for him when he got home, how pretty she looked, how delicious the dinner, that his clothes were clean and pressed when he needed them, that she wanted to do this for him.

He found it so tender, so exquisite that he feared it couldn't last, but the two of them together had a surprising innate stability. With Jodi it was never about the sex — or not mainly about the sex. Or let's say it was about much more than the sex. Jodi had emphatic core values, knew what she wanted. With Jodi you could relax. There was no hidden agenda, nothing jumping out at you. And yet there was more to her than just this. There were depths that he couldn't fathom, fires that didn't warm him, places beyond his reach. There was substance to her. She was everything a man could want and so much more.

9
HER

"Mrs. Gilbert?"

"Yes."

"This is Natasha Kovacs speaking."

There's a pause while Jodi considers cutting her off. She is not going to benefit from having this conversation.

"Please don't hang up, Mrs. Gilbert."

What can she possibly want? Jodi wonders.

"I'm not the person you think I am," says Natasha. "Please believe me, I feel terrible about what's happened. Todd and I both do. I guess in a way I'm calling to say that I'm sorry. That we're both sorry."

How is it that her life has arrived at this implausible culminating moment when she's done her best for so many years to make things work, to be helpful and accommodating, a good wife and companion, often in adverse and trying circumstances? Todd is not an easy man to live with, and yet she's made a success of it, held things together, created and maintained a peaceful, agreeable life for the two of them.

"I wanted to tell you that I appreciate everything you did for us, for me and my father, after Mom died," says Natasha. "Please don't think I've forgotten. The birthday presents. The time you took me shopping for school clothes. You went the distance, Mrs. Gilbert. You were the only one who stepped in to fill the void, and it made a difference. I always think of you fondly and I never wanted to —"

She can't allow this prattle to continue. What can the girl be thinking?

"Natasha," she says. "You do realize that this is going to end badly for you. And you can stop thinking of me as a mentor. I no longer wish you well, and there's nothing we need to discuss."

In spite of this Natasha persists.

"I can understand how you would feel that way," she says. "Maybe you hate me, and I wouldn't blame you if you did. But you've got to give me credit for trying. It wasn't easy for me to call you, Mrs. Gilbert. I didn't know if you'd even speak to me, in spite of what Todd says. He tells me that you're happy for us, but maybe that's just wishful thinking on his part. You've been with him a long time. I know you're going

181

to miss him. At least until you get used to it. He did tell you, didn't he, that we've leased an apartment in River North?"

She stops, waits for a reaction. Met with silence she forges on.

"I'm sorry if that comes as a shock, Mrs. Gilbert. We need to make a home for the baby. It's a beautiful apartment. Maybe you'll come and see us once we've settled in. We'd love for you to visit. In a way you'll be a kind of auntie."

Jodi has been pacing, marking out a warped figure eight. Clockwise around the sofa and chairs that face the fireplace, past the wall of windows, counterclockwise around the dining table, and back again. Now she comes to a standstill. Todd is the one at fault here. It's Todd who has exposed her to this. Shame on him for picking on this child, so naive and spiteful, so desperately insecure. Todd can be insensitive, but how can he string the girl along so heartlessly, his best friend's daughter, too. The poor thing has no idea who Todd really is or how he operates.

"Natasha," she says. "I understand that you are in over your head and don't quite know what to do about it. What are you — twenty, twenty-one? Your father tells me you're still in school. He says you're bright, too, but I have to tell you that I'm not getting that impression, based on the choices you're making. Based on where you seem to be headed in your life.

"Anyway the point is that none of this is really my problem, and I don't like you or care about you enough to try to help you, and I'm busy and have to go now, and I strongly discourage you from calling me again."

There are times, and this is one of them, when she thinks that not marrying Todd might have been a mistake. Sometimes it's hard to remember why she objected to marriage so emphatically. A reaction more than a decision. Aversion, distaste, something on a visceral level. He wanted to marry her and even proposed. He proposed more than once, she recalls, but the time she remembers best, the time it was special, happened on a day in August, a day of brilliant sunshine and sweltering heat.

They were standing waist-deep in the lake, watching a sailboat moving off into the distance. They'd been watching it for a long time, caught up in its slowly diminishing size, and now it was little more than a speck, tiny and formless, buoyed up by the swell of the horizon.

"You'd never know it was a sailboat," he

said. "It could be anything."

"It's so small," she said. "It could be a grain of salt."

"A grain of salt. That's about the size of it."

"Balanced on the edge of the world."

"See how it's almost vibrating?"

"Shimmering. As if it were humming."

"Getting ready to dematerialize."

"Vanish into eternity."

"It's going to be spectacular."

"Like seeing the impossible."

"Like seeing into the cosmic works."

Clinging to each other, giddy with anticipation and eyestrain, they were doing their best not to blink for fear of missing the beat in time when the laws of physics would collapse and the impossible would happen — a sailboat disappearing right before their eyes. Still wet from their swim, young, in love, sheltered by the overarching sky, they absorbed this experience as *something,* an exaltation, a moment of breaking through and coming together, a celebration. And when miraculously it happened, the sailboat disappeared, and there was no gap — not an instant — between when he saw it and when she saw it, when they shouted out in unison, a spontaneous cheer, that's when he said it. "Let's get married." An exuberant thought for an exuberant moment. A moment that she would like now to recapture and reconsider.

10
HIM

On the morning of October first Todd wakes early. He lies on his back holding his penis, grasping at the trailing wisps of an erotic dream. When the dream is finally, irrevocably lost he turns on his side and shimmies across the expanse of bed that separates him from Jodi. She has her back to him, knees drawn up. Wrapping an arm around her waist he molds himself to her curled spine. She makes a sound low in her throat, but her rhythmic breathing is not disrupted. Filled with the scent of her, a blend of clean hair and warm skin, he closes his eyes and sinks into a drowsy torpor. It isn't till he wakes for a second time that the trouble he's in overtakes him, bursting on his thoughts like a thunderclap.

Moving Day.

He sees the words in block letters on a blinking marquee, as a wispy banner in a blue sky, drawn with a stick in wet sand. At

186

no point did he actually come to a decision, and even now he can't say that his mind is made up. But he feels a forward momentum, an urge to make a break for it, get out of his comfort zone, shake himself up. It's something like pulling up roots and moving to a foreign country, the feeling that people must have who do that, an appetite for the exotic, an impulse to create themselves anew. He knows that his restlessness is partly biological but favors a story of renewal. He knows, too, that what he's about to do will make him a walking cliché, but his instinct for self-forgiveness is strong.

Natasha has insisted that he take the day off work. He's agreed to show up at her place around ten, to coincide with the arrival of the movers. Her junky furniture and kitchenware will at least give them something to start with. One thing Todd is not going to do is fight with Jodi over household goods. Whatever happens he will not turn this into a petty squabble. The breakup is going to cost him, that much he knows, but the fear he has about his financial future is still indeterminate, a specter without shape or form. He's avoided giving it substance in the same way that he's avoided a lot of things. Calling his lawyer, for instance. Telling Jodi that he's leaving.

It's going to be awkward now; he gets that. With something like this it's a bad idea to wait until the last possible moment. When it comes to any sort of change or disruption, women are very involved with timing. But who knows, maybe Jodi will be understanding. She is good-natured, not possessive or territorial, and she has a way of taking things in stride.

He gets out of bed and dresses without waking her. It's hard to grasp that this is happening, that tonight he won't be coming home, that he'll never again sleep next to her in this familiar room, that their life together, which he always envisioned as something like rolling hills, was really a train on a track, moving toward a final destination. He tries and fails to picture the rental apartment in River North. He was in it for fifteen minutes at most, and for ten of those minutes he was getting things settled with the landlord.

When Jodi makes her appearance he's sitting at the table thumbing through the morning paper and working on his third cup of coffee.

"You're still here," she says.

An explanation is required, but although he's been dawdling for close to an hour, he's given no thought to what he ought to say.

"Are you going out with the dog?" he asks.

"Yes, why?" She's holding a leash in one hand and keys in the other.

"I'll come with you."

She frowns. "What's going on?"

"Nothing. Just. I need to talk to you."

"Tell me."

"Wait till we get outside."

In the elevator they stand three abreast facing front: him, Jodi, the dog. Someone should be waiting with a camera in the lobby, ready to snap them when the doors open. This moment in time is worth capturing, the family group just before it breaks apart, tectonic plates once aligned shifting into disjunction. Everything different. No going back. It could be worst of all for the dog, who won't understand what's happened and will sleep with one eye open, expecting him home at every moment. As they head toward the water tears are streaming down his face. Jodi doesn't comment. Maybe she hasn't noticed. She's said nothing since they stepped outside, when she remarked that it was a bright day and put on her sunglasses. She must know what's coming, especially if she spoke to Dean, as Natasha claims. Her silence strikes him as

189

dense and purposeful, a barricade.

They cross the bike path to the grass verge by the lake and let the dog off leash. The waterfront is busy for a weekday morning. People are taking in the early autumn sun, storing it up for the winter ahead. She stands facing inland, framed by the luminous backdrop of sky and water. He sees himself in the lens of her sunglasses, shoulders slumped, runnels glistening on his cheeks. Her eyes are hidden but he senses that her mood has changed, that she somehow knows and understands.

"I'm sorry," he says.

He draws her to him and sobs into the top of her head. She makes no move to resist and slackens in his arms. They share a moment of wracking grief, pressed warmly against each other, breast to breast, heartbeat to heartbeat, together as one in the morning light. Only when they break apart and she changes position, making a quarter turn and taking off her sunglasses, does he see his mistake. She is dry-eyed and scowling, brows drawn together, eyes full of suspicion.

"What is it?" she asks. "What did you want to tell me?"

He's sorry now that he got himself into this. It would have been better to leave her a note, something brief and inconclusive to ease her into the new arrangement. Why have a confrontation when no confrontation would be kinder to them both? The face-to-face encounter is too harsh, the finality it's bound to create. There's no need to build a wall out of talk. Words are like tools, easily turned into weapons, creating closure where none is needed. Life is not words. People by nature are awash in ambivalence, swept along by winds that are fickle and skittish.

"I thought you knew," he says. "I thought you talked to Dean."

Her expression doesn't change. The look she's giving him is narrow and flinty. He feels as if he's shrinking, withering from within.

"Don't," he says. "Don't make it hard for me. It's not like I planned this. It's just the roll of the dice. We don't decide everything that happens to us. You *know* that." He feels like a jerk. She hasn't said a word but she has him on the run. He turns away from her and looks across the grass to where two men are tossing a Frisbee back and forth.

"What exactly are you saying?" she asks.

"Listen. I'm sorry. I won't be coming home tonight."

"What do you mean you won't be coming home? Where will you be?"

"I'm moving out," he says. "You really didn't know?"

"You're moving out? Where are you going?"

"You remember Natasha Kovacs." He makes it a statement rather than a question. "It isn't that I don't love you."

The noisy public quarrel that ensues surprises them both. For years they've kept their differences at bay. The worst of it is that the argument centers on irrelevancies. As he knew she would, Jodi fixates on his timing.

"Good of you to tell me," she says. "I'm so happy that you didn't wait any longer. I wouldn't want to be the last to congratulate you."

He hates it when she's sarcastic. "You're right," he says. "I screwed up. I'm guilty. I made a mess of it."

"Oh well, it's your loss," she says. "I could have thrown you a party. Bought you a gold watch."

"I'm sorry I didn't tell you sooner."

"And why is that? Why didn't you tell me sooner?"

"Because I didn't know myself what I was going to do."

"You knew I'd kick you out is why you didn't tell me."

"That's not true."

"I *would* have kicked you out."

"Yes, but that's not what I was thinking."

"What *were* you thinking, Todd? Just tell me that. What was going through your mind? Why would you wait until the second you're walking out the door to share the news with me?"

"I told you. I didn't know what I wanted. It's complicated. The situation is complicated."

"You signed a lease on an apartment over a week ago. You signed a lease! How complicated is that?"

"So you did know. You knew all along."

"I didn't believe it. I didn't think you would go through with it."

Both of them are shouting, flinging the words across the space of years. Part of him wants to relent, tell her that it's all a big mistake, that he doesn't know what he was thinking. He understands that this is in her mind too — it's what she would like and maybe half expects — for the whole ugly mess to end up a tempest in a teapot, conclude with a show of forgiveness and later on an evening on the town, champagne cocktails, a walk along the river in moonlight. It's a pleasant vision, and he could almost go there.

Without warning she lets out a howl and charges him with fists clenched. He's twice her size and catches her wrists with little effort. She swings a knee but he has her at arm's length and holds her off. In the end she tires herself out, and he lets her go. Her hair is disheveled, her face is contorted, and she's panting. People are staring. He looks around for Freud and spots him in some nearby shrubbery, digging a hole the way dogs do — rump in the air, tail waving, paws flying.

"Okay," she says. "Go and get your things. You have ten minutes. I don't want to see you when I get home."

11
HER

As the northern hemisphere hurtles away from the sun, the lengthening nights and disappearing days strike her as a punishment designed for her selectively. Harsh winds whip up rain and fog, whistle through trees, and slam into windowpanes. Leaves that were green just last week have turned the color of piss and dung and are piling up on the pavement. For Jodi, the reckless speed of these meteorological changes stands in mocking contrast to the thudding march of time, every day a weight that she drags behind her.

Mornings, when she opens her eyes, cheek on the pillow, breath moving in gentle waves, the first thing she sees is the over-stuffed chair in the corner, its wide seat and squat arms, its slipcover of silky polished cotton with a light and dark design of vines. She traces the leafy pattern with a child's eye, her mind suspended in a pleasant meditation, till the moment comes when she faces the fact that getting out of bed to start her day is the violent and pointless thing she has to do.

Curiously, it's not so much his physical absence that causes her pain. It was often the case that he didn't come home till after she'd fallen asleep, and he was normally gone before she woke up in the morning. What bothers her most is the blow to her routine. She misses the hours spent poring over cookbooks, composing a menu, shopping for ingredients, putting a twist on his favorite foods. And then there's the weight of the chores that always fell to him — walking the dog after dinner, taking her car to be serviced. Even putting the trash in the chute feels like a sad and onerous thing that she should not be forced to do. The daily paper poses another problem. Having quit her practice of carefully refolding it and leaving it for him on the coffee table, she finds that its absence can take her by surprise. At times she stands in his wardrobe, rearranging his jackets. One day she took all the T-shirts out of his drawers, shook them out, refolded them, and put them back again.

Her shattered routine leaves her at loose ends, but worse still, much of what she used to enjoy no longer brings her any pleasure at all. Stepping outside in the morning and taking the measure of the day. Fondling the dog's velvety ears. Slipping into a four-hundred-thread-count Italian shirt and doing up the small pearly buttons. She has no taste for any of it, and now, when she waves to the doorman as she passes through the lobby, she can only imagine his pity and curiosity. Without a doubt she is the subject of gossip and speculation throughout the building. Her neighbors, she notes, are different in their treatment of her, even if it's just their intonation when they say hello or the way their eyes linger on her face.

It's no help that Dean has been leaving tirades on her voice mail, piling *his* distress on top of *hers*. She knows that, like her, Dean has been sideswiped — dealt the kind of lateral blow that you never see coming — and maybe it eases his pain to rant and rave, but Dean's pain is not her problem. Of course, given her profession, people do this to her all the time, as if they think she's programmed to deal with their complaints.

The best hours of the day are those she spends with clients. She loves the challenge of the consulting room, the complexities her clients bring to her — the life puzzles, the guard coming down, the learning to trust, the tides of resistance. Some are more locked in than others, but by and large people who bother to seek her out are motivated to change, steeped in enough emotional pain to make the effort. Her clients bring out the best in her. She likes herself more when she's with them, especially now, with her world shaken and her optimism failing. With clients she can be patient, compassionate, receptive, and they reward her with their progress, the fitful forward movement, the cracks that open to the light. The other day Jane Doe said about her husband: "When he tells me what to do it makes me feel safe. I like the shelter of subservience." Astonishing. An absolute first for Jane in owning her predicament, a plain acknowledgment that, concerning her marriage, she is less a victim and more a participant, a bold step on the path to self-realization. It also provided a clue as to why Jane has stuck it out, not that Jodi finds it puzzling that she has. There are lots of reasons why a woman stays with a man, even when she's given up on changing him and can predict with certainty the shape that the rest of her life with him is going to take. Her mother had a reason. Every woman has a reason.

There was a time when she used to say

about Todd: "He's a weakness of mine. I have a weakness for him." She said this to herself and to her friends in the way of a justification. Bending yourself out of shape for a man is not a popular thing to do these days, certainly not the emancipated way of going about a relationship. Sacrificing your values on the altar of love no longer holds up as an ideology. Tolerance, beyond a point, is not widely preached, even though, inevitably, when two people rub shoulders on a daily basis, when they inhale each other's way of being as a life premise, there is going to be a sacrifice of sorts. You will not be the same person coming out of a relationship as you were going into it. Not that she understood this then, in the beginning. When she confronted him, when he apologized, when they shed tears, when they reaffirmed their love, when they did this time after time, she didn't sense the renunciation that was going on within her, because after all he was Todd, and he was precious to her. Even his sedition could be precious, his way of remaining true to himself. He wasn't cruel about it, never unkind. You could never say about Todd that he was mean-spirited or spiteful. Quite the opposite was true. If you crossed Todd he'd give you another chance, and if you crossed him a hundred times he'd give you a hundred chances. But Todd was bound and determined to live his life, and all she could do in the end was accept this, even knowing that what she had become was a version of her mother. In spite of making different choices, in spite of living in different times, in spite of being forewarned by her education in psychology, which taught her that the buck passes from one generation to the next, the predicament she landed in was the very one she had set out to avoid.

She does better on days when there's something to look forward to: her flower-arranging class or dinner out. It's hard to be peevish in a room full of fresh-cut blooms or surrounded by well-dressed strangers in the festive social space of a restaurant. She makes an effort to pace her dinner dates, methodically rotating through her friends to avoid calling on any one of them too often. When she talks about her situation she does it with an air of detachment, sometimes laughing and toasting the power of youth. Her friends, she finds, are relieved that she's taking it so well.

It's only with Alison that her guard comes down. Jodi and Alison have been getting together often, more so than usual — for an early lunch before Alison's shift or dinner on her day off. Alison is the only one of her friends who demurs when she makes light of her situation. She's also the only friend who picks up on the fact that Jodi has been waiting for Todd to come home.

"Honey, I know you're hurting, but you can't be naive about this. The man reviewed his options and made up his mind to leave. What you need is a divorce lawyer. We have to keep a roof over your head, make sure you get your fair share of what's coming to you. After spending twenty years wiping the man's ass."

"I don't think that Todd would want to deprive me."

"A man in his predicament? I wouldn't count on it. Anyway, much better to play it safe."

It's a comfort that Alison is looking out for her, but she is not receptive to Alison's advice. What's knocking around in her head is that people act on impulse, make mistakes, and regret them later. Maybe he needs to know that he's forgiven. Maybe he's waiting for a sign. And really, when you think about it, no actual harm has been done. Even the baby is not a major complication, doesn't need to be. He won't be spending a lot of time with it while it's an infant. Infants need their mothers. And

201

when it's older — well, it might be nice having a youngster around to liven things up.

12
HIM

Refusing to look back he throws himself headlong into his new life, beginning by shopping for clothes to replace the wardrobe he left behind. Natasha tags along and he allows her to influence his purchases, with the upshot that his look becomes more stylish and up-to-date. His belt has a larger buckle; his shoes taper to a point. He learns to wear a T-shirt with a blazer and jeans. The new clothes have designer labels and they fit him better. He likes the reinvention of himself and gets into the swing of it, letting his hair grow out and cultivating a roguish stubble. All in all it makes a younger, sexier man of him. He looks like someone who is still in the game. And then there's the payoff that trumps all others: When he and Natasha are out together people no longer mistake him for her father.

Evenings are spent getting dinner, going for walks, going shopping, making love. If

Natasha has schoolwork Todd takes over things like dishes and laundry. If Todd goes to the bar Natasha goes with him, although — given that she's pregnant and therefore not drinking — she usually drags him away before he can really get started. For this he takes some ribbing from the boys, Cliff in particular, who refers to Natasha as the she-boss. On weekends they pack a lunch and drive out of the city or eat pizza and watch movies or babysit for people in the building. Natasha says they need to make friends with their neighbors.

One Saturday they pass the afternoon getting matching tattoos — armbands of intertwining foliage, his and hers. The needles bring tears to his eyes — he wasn't ready for the pain — but he likes the idea of a rite of passage, an initiation of sorts, something to symbolize the start of their life together. The tattoos were Natasha's idea. Tattoos, she says, are permanent and nonnegotiable — unlike wedding bands. Not that she wants to forgo a wedding. On the contrary, she has moved the date up to mid-December, which is ideal, she says, because not only will it be Christmas break but she will barely be showing and will still fit into the dress of her dreams.

His workdays are spent in a state of

heightened energy and purpose. The buyer he's been courting for the Jefferson Park apartment house has come through with a signature, so now it's just a matter of finishing the work. This includes digging out the west foundation, waterproofing the exterior wall, and replacing the concrete walk that will be damaged in the process. The whack of cash he was counting on for the new office building will be a smaller whack than he foresaw, but right now he's riding a wave of optimism and feeling that he has Natasha to thank for all of life's blessings. He won't soon forget the ordeal of his depression. Before Natasha, life was hardly worth living. Now, his renewed spirits are rippling outward, creating promise for the future. He stands firmly by the choices he's made and the path he's taken. His advice to everybody would be: Don't allow anything or anyone to stop you from living your life.

Eventually, he knows, he'll have to settle things with Jodi, something he is not looking forward to. He's seen enough of his friends through breakups to anticipate the shock to his income and assets. What he needs to do is call his lawyer. It's not as if putting it off is doing him any good. Even now Jodi is out there spending his money. Her credit card statements come to his office and are paid by Stephanie — along with the condo fees and other household costs.

In spite of these concerns it's only Natasha's nagging that eventually prompts him to action. Natasha is adamant that he close things out with Jodi. She has pried out of him every detail of his and Jodi's financial arrangements and is livid that he allows things to go along as if nothing has changed, as if he and Jodi were still together.

Todd's lawyer, who sees him through the ins and outs of property deals, is also a practitioner of family law. A man in his sixties, Harry LeGroot has been through three divorces and knows what it means to make mistakes and pay for them. He married his first wife when he was a student in law school, and although he hasn't set eyes on her in thirty years he is still required to send her a monthly check. The second and third wives, in addition to bleeding him of money, are living in palatial homes that he foolishly bought and paid for while he was married to them. Harry himself lives in a rental unit and prays daily for their deaths. Dear Lord: Please take Shoshana; please take Becky; please take Kate. But Shoshana, Becky, and Kate are in no hurry to leave this world.

Todd meets Harry for lunch at Blackie's in Printers Row, where they order steak sandwiches and draft beer. Harry has silver hair that he combs straight back, playing up the prominent features and high forehead. He's wearing a light gray worsted suit and a charcoal dress shirt with no tie. Harry and Todd go back more than two decades, almost to the start of Todd's career in property development. Their relationship thrives on business, but they like to conduct it in restaurants and bars, where they can feel good and open up to each other on a personal level. For Todd, Harry is a father figure as well as an expert navigator in the arcane sphere of city bylaws and urban politics. And Harry, whose failed marriages have used up his own tolerance for risk, admires the audacity and stamina that power Todd's success.

When they're settled in with their food and drink, Todd delivers his news. "You're not going to like this," he says. "I've left Jodi."

Harry bites into his sandwich, chews, swallows, runs his tongue over his upper and lower teeth, drinks from his pint glass, and belches politely with a hand over his mouth. When he speaks, his voice is a deeply purring baritone.

"Here you are with a gorgeous home, a beautiful wife who loves you, and all the recreation on the side that a man could possibly want. Not to mention a life mercifully free of the kind of financial drain imposed by bloodsucking ex-wives who hate your guts. And now you want to throw it all away and join the ranks of pussy-addled middle-aged men like me whose brains are in their pants. I'm disappointed in you, Todd. I thought you had more sense." He shakes his head sadly. His watery blue eyes wander around the restaurant. "How old is she?" he asks.

"How old is Jodi?"

"How old is the home wrecker. And please don't tell me you're planning to marry her."

"Stop it, Harry," says Todd. "You haven't even met her."

"I don't need to meet her. Whoever she is, she's not worth it. And if she's younger than you, she'll make your life hell."

"There's a reason you're such a cynical bastard," says Todd. "I pity you, Harry, I really do, because in spite of all your marriages you've never found the real thing. Natasha and me, it's something you'll never understand. It's like I was dead and now I'm alive. Yes, she's younger than me, but that means we can have a family. I'm going to be a father, Harry. Congratulate me. At least you have your children. Imagine what you'd be without your children."

"Fatherhood is wildly overrated," says Harry. "Don't you watch TV? The courts award custody to the mother, your ex-wife, who makes a vocation of turning your kids against you, and you get to see the people who despise you growing fat and lazy on your profits while you work your sorry ass off and never get ahead."

"You're breaking my heart," says Todd.

"You think you're immune?" says Harry. "Whatever else happens, Jodi gets half."

"Okay," says Todd. "That's what I need to know. Jodi gets half of what, exactly?"

"Half of your net worth, doofus. Half of your investments. Half of every property you own. You two have been together since you were practically children. Since before you bought your first house. That means she has an interest in every last cent, right down to the change in your piggy bank."

Todd sits with his lower lip dangling, trying to take it in. It can't be right, what Harry is saying. He's thinking back, doing his best to remember what actually happened.

"I'd already bought my first house when I met her," he says. "I remember that because I took her there to show her, and it was gutted. So no, when I bought the house I didn't

209

even know her. And we didn't move in together till after I'd sold it."

"Living together is one thing," says Harry. "When did you get married?"

"We didn't," says Todd. "I mean, there wasn't an actual ceremony."

"You're not married?"

"It's a common-law marriage."

"You're joking," says Harry.

"Is that bad?" asks Todd.

"Poor Jodi. I could almost feel sorry for her."

"She didn't want to get married. She didn't see the point."

Harry is wild-eyed and grinning like a monkey. Todd thinks he's being mocked. "What does it mean?" he asks.

"It means we should have another drink," says Harry. "We need to celebrate."

13
HER

On a Tuesday, after her workout and before lunch, she calls him on his cell phone. He picks up and warbles the notes of her name.

"Surprise!" she says. "Where are you?"

"I'm in my car. How have you been?" He sounds flustered, wary, no doubt assuming that she's called to berate him.

"I'm fine," she says. "I've been thinking about you. In a good way."

"Really," he says. "I wasn't expecting that."

"Well, you know," she says. "It is what it is. We can only go forward."

"I'm glad you feel that way," he says. "I've been thinking about you, too."

"That's nice," she says. "Do you miss me?" She hadn't meant to ask him that.

"Of course I miss you. I miss you every day."

She takes a breath and lets it out. "I'm here," she says.

211

"Yeah. Well. I didn't think . . ."

"I know. We parted on not such great terms."

"Even the sound of your voice," he says. "It's nice."

They are both acting a little coy, choosing their words with care. Her plan was to test the waters first and if he seemed receptive to follow through with her invitation.

"Listen," she says. "Why don't you come for dinner?"

He doesn't immediately reply. She waits, listening to the sounds coming through the receiver: traffic, a radio announcer. When she pictures him at the wheel he's in the same cargo pants and sweatshirt he was wearing the morning he left. She thinks daily about the fact that he went away with only the clothes he had on. He must have done some shopping, but she can only conjure him up the way he looked then.

"I'd love to," he says finally. "When do you want me?"

"I was thinking tomorrow."

"Tomorrow," he repeats, sounding doubtful.

What can be going through his mind? Does he have to account for every evening out? Is he even allowed an evening out?

"Tomorrow it is," he says.

"Can you come at seven?"

"Seven," he agrees. "Can't wait to see you."

The conversation proves to be transformational. As she puts the phone down she's already living in an altered world, a world created by the resurgence of their love as it once was, a younger love, untarnished and all of a piece, not prone to dismemberment — pulling the other apart and considering the bits, this one good, that one bad. In those days even her eccentricities were dear to him: her addiction to spending, her aversion to clutter bordering on obsession, her habit of saving wine corks and cheese rinds, her love of panty hose, which she still wears even with jeans, her undemonstrative nature. He used to scribble affectionate notes and leave them in unexpected places before he left for work. He'd play with her hair, join her in the shower. And likewise, back then there was nothing about him that she didn't adore. The way he drank his coffee, blowing on it with lips pushed out comically, long after it had cooled. The way he showered, soaping himself from head to foot till he all but disappeared in the lather. The way he carved butter into slabs and set about paving his toast. She even loved the way he drove, cutting people off and laughing when they gave him the finger. She loved him like that for a long time, even after she knew him well. The renewal of her love she attributes to their separation. The shock of losing him has affected her deeply, reactivated her pulse, flushed out disused chambers of her heart.

She spends the rest of that day and all of the next in a thrall of counting down the hours. The time unfolds in visits to the supermarket, cheese shop, fishmonger, florist. In chopping herbs, making marinades, cleaning squid, trimming vegetables. She takes the dog to the groomer and goes for a manicure, pedicure, bikini wax, facial, and massage. Impatient during sessions with clients, she cuts their time a little short. She goes to bed late and gets up early. There are bouts of trying on outfits. She has a lot riding on this, she knows. A drink in a bar or dinner in a restaurant would do just as well. But she's been overcome by a persuasive euphoria, and all she can see is the stars in her eyes and all she can hear is the music in her head.

Lapses of this kind are part of her history, marked by a buildup of excitement around some upcoming social event. When she was a girl, she and her mother indulged in them together. A sense of occasion, a flirtation with promise and possibility, that's what makes for the high times in life. But even on ordinary days, even in the face of disappointment, a positive outlook is her mainstay. She's good at rebounding from setbacks, resisting the undertow, riding the waves. Staying afloat is what she does well — something that Todd has always remarked on. He likes her buoyancy; it's kept him from falling permanently into a black hole and from getting too addicted to alcohol, getting addicted the way his father was. Though during his depression she wasn't able to help him.

She tried to get him into therapy, but he wouldn't have it. "That's your world," he said. "Leave me out of it." Maybe she should have tried harder. He would have benefited from the practical approach of an Adlerian like Gerard Hartmann. As far as difficult childhoods go, Todd's could set an example. Any child with an alcoholic father and a victimized mother is going to be damaged, and Todd has done well for himself considering, but the real story is told in his lying and equivocation, his inability to talk about his feelings, his aversion to authority, and his compulsive risk-taking, which has worked out for him in business but along with his never-ending affairs reflects the deep-seated feelings of inferiority that drive him to continually prove himself. According to Adler, having a good measure of self-esteem leaves us free to be task oriented rather than worth oriented in all that we undertake, whereas feelings of inferiority keep us focused on ourselves. That's Todd in a nutshell.

Jodi first encountered Adler in university, but it was through her studies at the Adler School and her work with Gerard that she gained a solid working knowledge of Adlerian principles. Along with Jung, Adler was a colleague of Freud's in Vienna in the early twentieth century, but Adler and Jung, each in turn, broke away from Freud and formed their own schools of thought. That Adler's school is pragmatic and socially attuned is nowhere quite so evident as in his three main life tasks, which he identified as hallmarks of mental health: (1) the experience and expression of love, (2) the development of friendships and social ties, and (3) engagement in meaningful work. In these terms Jodi could only be counted as utterly sane — and as her therapy with Gerard progressed this fact became somewhat glaring. Whichever way they turned, whatever line of inquiry they pursued, they ran smack-dab into her inspired relationship with Todd, her excellent social skills, and her professional dedication. She'd done her time in the client's chair; did she really need to continue on with her weekly sessions? The question was often in her mind, and it came to a head when she suggested to Gerard that they call it quits. But Gerard was inclined to stick with it, and so they did. He asked questions, listened, and took notes. Jodi reported her dreams and talked about her family of origin: her parents, her older brother, Darrell, and her younger brother, Ryan.

She was three years older than Ryan but had no memory of his entry into the family, no mental picture of how he looked the first time she saw him. Ryan had been in her life as far back as she could remember, and her interest in him had always been proprietary. When they were little he was more or less on a par with her favorite stuffed animal — hers to coddle, indulge, dress up, teach, scold, and generally boss around. Back then he was compliant, sweet, good-natured, and he easily surrendered to her well-meaning despotism. It wasn't until he was older, no longer a toddler but a boy, that the outbursts started, the nightmares and self-inflicted wounds that had everyone so worried, but all of that passed in the end, as did his many other phases: obnoxious prankster, contrary know-it-all, paranoid loner.

She had loved him through it all and loved him still, even though she was far from reconciled with the way he had ended up: with the fact that after opting out of university he had spent his twenties traveling in India and Southeast Asia and had ever since been living half the year in Kuala Lumpur teaching English and half the year in Baja California Sur, where he surfed and waited tables; with the fact that he was a certified, card-carrying black sheep who would one day be too old to continue doing what he was doing and what would become of him then? — without money, far from home, and too proud to ask for help.

She had no way of getting in touch with him because he didn't have a phone or wouldn't give her the number — she wasn't sure which — and so she had to wait for him to call, and thankfully he did call every now and then, though it was rare for her to actually lay eyes on him. At that point, during her Gerard days, she hadn't seen him for a very long time, not since meeting him at the airport on one of his hasty stopovers. He called her at six in the morning, and she met him for a breakfast of refrigerated sandwiches bought from the airport kiosk and eaten off their laps. It was late November, but being en route from one tropical climate to another he was traveling light, with only a knapsack for luggage. Aside from his T-shirt, jeans, and sandals, he was wearing a string of blue glass beads and a black straw hat with a skull-and-crossbones motif on the crown and the brim turned up at the sides. He'd grown a little stocky and needed a shave but had the same blue-eyed elfin look that he'd always had and seemed fine, just too old to be stuck at this place in his life — still single, preoccupied with surfing, ignoring his talent and potential. As a boy he was good at gymnastics and drawing, took an interest in insects and plants, talked about becoming an athlete, an illustrator, a biologist, and other things. During high school he was a camp counselor and wanted to be a teacher — not a teacher working on the fly but a teacher who would see his students through and make a difference.

She had recurring dreams about Ryan in which he was lost or on the run and she was frantic to get to him but couldn't manage to book a flight or board an airplane. She still thought about him every day, or rather, he was ceaselessly present within her, a constant companion distinguished by his worrisome absence. Her instinct was to help and protect him, but he made that impossible. She knew that if she ventured to comment on his lifestyle he would think twice about ever calling her again. Their parents had made this mistake and subsequently had to get their news of him from her. Besides, it wasn't as if he gave her any openings. He liked to keep his distance, Ryan, avoiding talk of anything significant, never letting her in, clowning around and making light of things. All she could do was laugh at the stories he told of his misadventures and resist the urge to offer him money, unwilling to hurt his pride.

By contrast, her older brother, Darrell, had followed in their father's footsteps, taking his PharmD in Minneapolis and then returning home to marry his high-school sweetheart. Their parents held out hope that Darrell would stick around to run the family drugstore, but in the end he chose to move on and was now the director of pharmacy at a large teaching hospital in Canada.

Darrell was six years older than Jodi and a boy, but from the start he was a bright light in her life — a kind, obliging, fun-loving mentor who had time for her and could make her laugh. It was Darrell who took her trick-or-treating on Halloween, Darrell who taught her to tie her shoelaces by the bunny-ears method. She even remembered a dolls' tea party at which Darrell served up the mud pies and lisped the voice of Barbie's little sister, Skipper. When she was older he helped her with homework and played cards with her, even though by then he was in high school and she was still a kid. Darrell was one of those rare, good-natured, obliging boys who got along with everyone — the ultimate easygoing, earnest, diplomatic young man who was destined to do well in life because everyone was eager to help him on his way.

Gerard took an interest in her family life and plied her with questions.

Gerard: Which of your brothers did you play with?

Jodi: I played with Ryan. Darrell would play with me, but that was him coming down to my level.

Gerard: Who did you fight with?

Jodi: Ryan and I would sometimes fight.

Gerard: You've told me that Ryan went through phases — compliant and good-natured as a toddler, then later obnoxious, contrary, paranoid. (Here he was referring to his notes.) What would you say about him overall? If you had to use one word to describe him.

Jodi: Sensitive. Ryan was the sensitive one. We used to tease him about it.

Gerard: And what kind of a kid were you?

Jodi: I had a reputation for being bossy.

Gerard: Who did you boss?

Jodi: Everyone, but only Ryan would do what I said. Until he got older, that is.

Gerard: When you were growing up what was your father like?

Jodi: He expected a lot from us. But he was stricter with the boys than he was with me.

Gerard: So you were let off easy because you were a girl. What was your mother like?

Jodi: A little on the dreamy side. She did a good job of cooking the meals and keeping house, and she did her community service, but she pretty much lived in a world of her own.

Gerard: What kind of community service did she do?

Jodi: Organized food drives. Volunteered at the soup kitchen. My father coached Little League.

Gerard: So community service was a family value.

Jodi: They were big on community service. Also getting an education.

Gerard: Who had the most community spirit among you kids?

Jodi: Darrell. He used to read to seniors every Saturday. He did it for years.

Gerard: And who had the least community spirit?

Jodi: That would have to be Ryan. I can't remember Ryan ever getting involved in that kind of thing.

Gerard: What about you?

Jodi: I helped with bake sales at the church. But I didn't have Darrell's zeal.

Gerard: Who got the best grades in school?

Jodi: Darrell.

Gerard: Who got the worst grades?

Jodi: Ryan.

Gerard: Who was the favorite?

Jodi: Darrell. Everybody loved Darrell.

Gerard: And the least favorite?

Jodi: Ryan. The way he was, it was almost like he didn't belong to us. Sometimes they would call him their little foundling. My parents did. They called him that when he was acting up.

Gerard: Who conformed and who was the rebel?

Jodi: Darrell and I conformed. Ryan was the rebel.

Gerard: So Darrell carved out his place as the favorite, and Ryan distinguished himself as a rebel. Where did that leave you?

Jodi: I was the girl. I was not expected to compete with the boys.

Gerard: But you held a more favorable position in the family than Ryan did. And you fought with him and bossed him around.

Jodi: I think that in my own mind I was taking care of him. But maybe he didn't see it like that.

Gerard: How do you think he saw it?

Jodi: I guess he needed to get out from under me. Because we were very close as kids, but we're not close anymore.

Gerard: How does that make you feel — that you're not close anymore?

Jodi: It's hurtful, I guess. The distance he's put between us. And I worry about him. But maybe it's my own fault. I suppose I was more competitive than I give myself credit for.

14
Hɪᴍ

He leaves the office and navigates the old familiar route. As he takes the ramp to Upper Randolph Drive and sees the condo in the distance, he waits for an onslaught of nostalgia, but it doesn't come, maybe displaced by the scrap heap of everything else he is feeling. At the top of the heap is apprehension. He has no sense of what to expect. She was friendly enough on the phone, but these are unusual times. Whatever happens he should try to get his hands on a few of his things while he's there — some sweaters and his winter coat at the very least. He'll have to leave them in his trunk or Natasha will know where he's been. She might figure it out in any case. Natasha has the nose of a jackal. Tonight he's supposedly dining with Harry, going over contracts, but she may find a way to check on that. This will be their first evening entirely apart since moving in together.

Easing the Porsche into parking spot number 32, he grapples for a moment with a lordly sense of possession. Absurd as it is he can't quite suppress his territorial instincts. These two hundred square feet of pavement are his — he owns them — and he also owns spot number 33, where Jodi's Audi sits — and for that matter the Audi is his property too.

He travels up the elevator and with pride of ownership still goading him uses his key to enter the apartment. The complex smells of her cooking welcome him before he's through the door, eliciting the nostalgia he's been waiting for. Freud is there to greet him, prancing and spinning at his feet. The dog looks well — eyes bright, coat shiny and lush. He moves through to the living room, seeing it with fresh eyes, as if he's been away for a very long time. The place has an opulent feel that he must have become inured to when he lived here, or maybe he's already been corrupted by the squalor of his current domicile, where Natasha's habit of cluttering every available surface with the litter of her daily life is the reigning principle of her housekeeping.

He looks for Jodi in the kitchen and doesn't find her, but when he turns around she's there in front of him, smaller than he remembers and different in other ways too — more fragile and with a longer neck, whiter skin, and features somehow re-arranged. How can she have changed this much just because he wasn't looking?

She's wearing her everyday beige trousers and white shirt. Maybe to her this is a noth-ing occasion, not the momentous coming together or breaking apart that he's been alternately envisioning. Her eyes show the glimmer of a question as they touch on his cashmere jacket and longer hair. He meant to kiss her but turns toward the kitchen instead.

"Should I make the drinks?" he asks.

The old routine moves them past the awkward beginning, but as he takes down the glasses and gets the Stolichnaya out of the freezer, and as she chops parsley and places tiny crustaceans on a platter, it becomes chillingly clear that nothing is remotely as it was. They could be strangers, so courteous and stilted is their conversa-tion, so carefully do they gauge their move-ments and monitor the space between them. When they've clinked glasses and taken their first warming sips of alcohol, he sits on a stool and watches as she cuts a lemon lengthwise into quarters. She smiles as she offers him an appetizer, but all he can see is the distance in her eyes. As he chews and swallows, and as she moves around the kitchen in her prim white shirt buttoned to the clavicle, he tries to remember what she looks like naked.

Their conversation during dinner fixes on their work, while other subject matter is avoided: his new living arrangements, her lonely nights, his impending fatherhood, anything to do with the future. The elephants in the room are alive and well. He doggedly talks about plumbing and mildew. She offers updates on her clients. When he hears that Miss Piggy is pregnant and doesn't know if her husband or her lover is responsible, he has to laugh. He's never felt kindly toward Miss Piggy or for that matter anyone who carries on a long-term extramarital affair, in effect, a form of polygamy. A passing fling is one thing, sex with a prostitute is one thing, but dividing your loyalties as a way of life is a faithless path to take and one that can only end badly.

Jodi, for one, always understood this about him; Jodi could see the bigger picture. As long as he and Jodi were together he belonged to her, and she knew that. A lot of women — probably most women — would make a fuss about the little diversions, get all wound up over the trivial dalliance here and the minor detour there. It's possible that he took Jodi's tolerance and forbearance too much for granted, didn't credit her enough for putting up with him. An easy mistake to make. Jodi has a knack for acceptance. She isn't easily threatened or thrown off balance. She moves along in a measured way and with a sense of scale, doesn't get alarmed or take things to extremes.

As they work their way through the salad, the squid, and the salmon en croute, he begins to feel as if he never left. Here they are in their usual places at the table, eating their dinner off the everyday plates. Not only is she wearing her ordinary clothes, but she hasn't bothered with the crystal, the silver, or even a tablecloth. The food is good, but Jodi has always known how to cook. The table is set with candles and cloth napkins, but this, too, is normal.

And then he gets it. She's intentionally giving the occasion a commonplace twist. This is not something that can happen only once, not a special event but a staple, something to be repeated. She wants them to go on as usual, behave as if nothing has changed. Making him dinner is part of ordinary life, and routine pleasures have always been her mainstay, the crux of her happiness, the theme of her existence. A bottle of wine, a homemade meal, the delights of the domicile, predictable diversions, dependable comforts. He sees exactly where she's coming from. It's almost like a game.

He's been guilty of underestimating her. She has an admirable practical intelligence. There's a lovely clarity about her. It crosses his mind that men are going to notice her, that maybe they already have. It could be that in the time he's been gone other men have eaten their dinner off these very plates. And it could be that these other men have loved her, slept in his bed with her, made use of the toiletries he left behind. These are not pleasant thoughts and he struggles to quell his spiraling imagination, the part of him that wants to get up from the table and rage around the room, assert his dominance, his ownership.

"What have you been doing with yourself?" he abruptly asks.

"Oh, you know," she says. "The usual things."

"Uh-huh." He rearranges himself in his chair. "Who have you been seeing?"

"Is this the third degree?" she asks mildly.

"Not at all," he says.

"Ellen, June, Alison."

He drums his fingers. "Have you been seeing anyone, you know, romantically?"

Her eyes open wide. He can tell that she's surprised not only by the question but by the very idea.

"Okay, okay," he says. "But you're attractive. It's going to happen. Men are going to pursue you. If they haven't already started."

She has the food on her plate triangulated: salmon — peas — squash, the dividing trenches forming a loosely drawn peace sign.

"Which men?" she asks. "I don't *know* any men."

"Well, ha ha, the world is full of men," he says.

"Not in my profession. Psychology is full of women."

"Adler and Freud and Jung are men," he says, naming the stars in her professional constellation.

"Times have changed. It's all women now."

He ought to shut up, he knows, but can't get the image out of his head now that he's conjured it up — a nameless, faceless male standing naked in his bathroom, still wet from the shower, schlong dangling, helping himself to the towels, the toothpaste, the shaving foam he left behind.

"You've been friendly with the Carson kid

from down the hall," he says.

"Joel Carson? He's only fifteen."

"I've seen the way he looks at you."

"He's a nice boy. Very sweet and in-nocent."

"Teenage boys are not innocent."

"Well, maybe not. But I'm old enough to be his mother."

"You may be old enough to be his mother, but you're not his mother. And I bet he can tell the difference."

"Todd, you're being ridiculous."

"When I was his age I was in love with my history teacher. Her name was Miss Larabee and she was pretty and refined but also tough-minded and a hard marker, and she really turned me on. Come to think of it she was a lot like you. I thought about her all the time. I'd imagine calling her up, taking her out on a date. I even offered to fix her car once. But it wasn't her car I was interested in."

"Well, if that's what's going through Joel's head he gives no sign of it. The one time he was in here he stood by the door with his hand on the knob as if he couldn't wait to escape."

"When was he in here?"

"He came in once to borrow a magazine. There was an article on the violinist, what's-his-name, the one who did the solos for *Angels and Demons*. Joel plays the violin beautifully." She gets up to fetch another bottle of wine, brings it to the table and opens it, refills their empty glasses. "Not that it's any of your business," she says. "Under the circumstances."

"When did you hear him play?" asks Todd.

"I heard him play at his school concert."

"You went to his school concert? Man, you are really tight with this kid."

"Yeah, right. Joel Carson and I. Well, now that you've guessed, I might as well admit it. We've been having a torrid affair for quite some time now. It started on his fifteenth birthday. Or was it his fourteenth? Or maybe it was his twelfth. Funny, I can't remember. Maybe he was only nine or ten when we fell in love."

"Okay, I get it," he says. "But you're attractive, beautiful, you know that, and anyone with eyes in his head is going to notice you — even a pimply kid who plays the violin."

"Joel is not pimply."

"Whatever," says Todd, losing interest in the Carson boy. "The point is that you're a knockout and you're fantastic and I've loved you from the first moment I saw you, and yes you were soaking wet and you'd just

233

smashed up my car, but you were magnificent. And you still are."

He sees her eyes welling up, reaches across the table for her hand, suddenly understands that he's been wandering rootless, that he woke up one day in someone else's life and couldn't find his way home. Sitting here now, clasping her hand in his, he feels that time is passing at a distance, like a train on a faraway track, that in this open-ended moment all the thoughts and feelings that he's pushed aside are gathering in force.

"I've missed you," he says. "I've missed coming home and I've missed getting into bed with you and I've missed waking up beside you — and all I can say is that I must have been out of my mind to think I could give you up."

She grips his hand and the tears start to flow, his and hers, watering their shrunken hearts and wilted love. They look into each other now, past the strangeness and the distance, and when at last they dry their eyes and she gets up and serves the chocolate mousse, they spoon it up like greedy children, lick out their bowls, and laugh at themselves.

After the table has been cleared and she's at the sink rinsing dishes, sleeves rolled to the elbows, hair coming loose in tendrils, he approaches her from behind, slides his arms around her waist, and rests his chin on the top of her head.

"I love you," he says.

She turns to face him, swiveling in the circle of his arms, hands clasped to her chest as if in prayer.

"I'm still getting used to the change in you," she says. "It's not just the hair and clothes. You look younger. Have you lost weight?"

His hands explore the delicate bones of her back and shoulders, relearn her subtle curves and childlike proportions. He's already grown accustomed to Natasha, her sturdy frame and padded hips, the exaggerated recess of her waist.

"It's an illusion," he says.

She murmurs into his chest, her breath warming his skin through the cotton of his shirt. "If I'd passed you in the street I wouldn't have known you. I would have walked right by without giving you a second glance."

"I would have stopped you and introduced myself."

As she smiles up at him and says, "I don't speak to strange men," he feels her letting go, collapsing against him as if she's turned to jelly.

"You need to get over that," he tells her.

With very little effort he scoops her up and holds her bodily in his arms as if she were unconscious or a corpse. Even her dead weight is doll-like and negligible. As he carries her across the threshold to the bedroom he remembers this about Jodi, the peculiar slackness that overtakes her when she's aroused.

15
HER

She's lingering over breakfast when a call comes in from the office of Harry LeGroot. The caller is Harry's assistant, an earnest girl named Daphne, whom Jodi has met once or twice in the past.

"Mr. LeGroot has asked me to contact you," says Daphne. "He would like to be in touch with your lawyer. If you would be so kind as to provide us with a name and phone number. Mr. LeGroot would like to get the process started."

Jodi hears the words but they whistle around her like random gusts of wind. If Todd has some legal business that he wants to run by her, he should speak to her about it himself.

"Mrs. Gilbert? Are you there?"

"I'm here," she says. "Tell me again. What is it you want me to do?"

"You really don't need to do anything, Mrs. Gilbert." Daphne's tone is friendly yet businesslike. "The main thing is that Mr. LeGroot would like to get the process started as soon as possible, so we will need your lawyer's name and telephone number."

Todd and his motives, intentions, and whereabouts have been on her mind since the night he came to dinner, the night they made a new beginning. The way it worked out she couldn't have wished for a more idyllic coming together, a more gratifying renewal of their bond. She was right to invite him, right to make the first move. She didn't like it when, afterward, he got up and left, but she could take it in stride knowing that nothing worthwhile happens overnight, that things coalesce in their own way and in their own time. It could be that they'll date for a while before he moves back home, that's what she's been thinking, and she can resign herself to that. But she doesn't understand why he hasn't called.

Still holding the phone she moves into the living room where the sun gleams off the furniture and picks out the colors in the carpet.

"Sorry, Daphne, I don't quite follow you," she says. "Why not tell Harry to call my husband and go over the matter with him. I'm sure that would be the best solution."

At this, Daphne exclaims as though she's

been struck. "Oh, Mrs. Gilbert! I'm so sorry. I thought you knew."

She's evidently made some sort of blunder, but instead of signing off to regroup and perhaps consult her employer, Daphne holds her ground, stumbling through an explanation that Jodi refuses to hear and offering advice that isn't welcome.

"If I were you, Mrs. Gilbert," she concludes, "I would hire myself a really good divorce lawyer."

Which prompts Jodi to hit the off button.

Having tidied away her breakfast things she pulls out the files on her two Friday clients and reads through her notes. First is Cinderella, a plain girl lacking in self-esteem. A night proofreader for one of the local dailies, her constant complaint is that life is passing her by. Jodi has been proactive in pointing out options, encouraging her to take small steps that could have exponential effects. She might, for example, take a course, join a gym, or do any number of things to improve her appearance, such as getting contact lenses or a good haircut. If you need to get out of a mental rut it's often easiest to change something on the outside and let the inner changes follow. When you make an effort on your own behalf, circumstance will quite often veer helpfully in your direction. Jodi believes this. She's seen it happen. It's ultimately what prompted her to take the initiative in inviting Todd to dinner.

Her second client, the prodigal son, is a young man with a trust fund whose parents routinely pay his debts. Because he's young and still finding his feet, because he hasn't yet discovered his potential or his limits, and because his parents chip away at his confidence, Jodi offers him unconditional support. He needs to find things out for himself. And if she took his parents' side he would simply shut down.

Not until late in the afternoon does she get the call from Todd that she's been more or less expecting since her conversation with Daphne. She feels uncertain about him now and doesn't know quite what to think. But insofar as she is still holding out hope — for some sort of promise for the future — she is quickly brought to her senses.

"You know my situation," he says. "I'm struggling to stay on top of things right now."

"I'm confused. You need to explain to me why I need a lawyer."

"Why does anyone need a lawyer? You need a lawyer to look after your interests.

Listen to me, Jodi. This doesn't need to be personal. It doesn't have to come between us. Let the lawyers sort it out so we can still be friends."

Her mental reckoning jams like a faulty calculator. She has failed to compute things correctly, and now she's at a loss. "Friends. Is that what we are? You'd better explain that because I don't get it."

"Jodi, Jodi, you need to relax. We love each other. We share a history. Things change, that's all. It's healthy for people to evolve and move on. That's something *you're* always telling *me.*"

"Fine. People evolve. So if that's the case then what were you doing here the other night? What was that about?"

"Would you rather we didn't see each other? How does that make sense? I miss you. I'd like to see you once in a while."

"You'd like to see me once in a while."

"Of course I would. Don't you feel the same?"

16
Him

Natasha is busy with plans for the wedding, which is coming up fast. Every night at dinner she monologues about flowers, menus, table settings, music, vows, favors, and cake until he wants to gag her. She's already taken him shopping for a suit, and that at least was rewarding. When he tried it on in the store he was dazzled by the elegant cut and the youthful silhouette it gave him. He didn't look at the price tag and waited outside while she paid for it with the credit card he'd given her. The wedding is costing him a fortune, and on top of everything else she's pushing for a honeymoon in Rio. This is not a good time for him to be throwing money around.

One thing that meets with his approval is the decision in favor of a church ceremony. She was back and forth on that for a while, and he made a point of nudging her in the right direction. Not that he's a religious man, but neither is he a nonbeliever. Ritual and tradition have their place, and marriage is one of those places, because marriage is above all an act of faith.

The guest list includes a great many aunts, uncles, and cousins on Natasha's side, whereas Todd's lineup amounts to a handful of buddies — Harry, Cliff, and some of the guys, and of course their wives. The cloud hanging over the proceedings is Dean, who remains steadfast in refusing to attend. He is still not speaking to Todd and has barely exchanged a word with Natasha. The last thing he said to her was that he'd rather die than see her married to the likes of Todd Gilbert. This had Natasha in tears. Dean needs to smarten up. If he had any sense he'd be happy for his daughter. She's going to be well-off, an affluent woman living a life of ease. Would he really prefer that she marry some young punk who can't provide for her? There's a lot he'd like to say to Dean, if only Dean would give him the chance.

He's beginning to wonder when life with Natasha is going to settle down, become more stable and orderly, more like what he had with Jodi. Natasha behaves in such unexpected ways. She certainly isn't glowing and contented, as pregnant women are supposed to be. On the contrary, she's turned into something of a viper, and he can't predict what will set her off or when she's going to strike. Still, he's doing his best to be understanding and accommodating. She's under a lot of stress with the fall term ending and the wedding coming up and the trouble with her father. Maybe the stress is what's causing her to gain weight, even though the baby is not yet showing. It could also be the cause of the rash she's developed on her forehead. At least she hasn't lost interest in sex, which is what he thought would happen based on what his buddies have told him. Some of them — guys who had *never* cheated — were forced to take refuge in massage parlors and the adults-only section of the classifieds. He counts himself lucky that Natasha wants him as much as ever, but it's funny how the tables have turned. Natasha is now standard fare, whereas sex with Jodi the night he went to dinner had the agreeable tang of adultery. He'd almost forgotten about Jodi's weird stillness, the way her eyes lose focus and drift sideways while he's driving into her. He used to find it irritating, but that night, for some reason, it was kind of a turn-on. Life can throw you some real curveballs.

He could miss Jodi if he let himself. It's

the daily patterns that make a marriage, the habits you fall into as a couple. These become a kind of background rhythm for your life. With Natasha, things have yet to settle into a beat that he can march to. But he can't afford to be sentimental. The law says that he owes Jodi nothing, that she is nothing more than an ex-girlfriend whose free ride is now over. She ought to thank him for his generosity during the years they were together. That's what Harry says. Harry wants to serve her with an eviction order, which will give them legal recourse if they need it. What he and Harry are hoping for is that Jodi will see reason and move out without a fuss, but if she decides to get stubborn about it, they'll have the eviction order to fall back on, meaning they can get the sheriff to forcibly remove her. He hopes it doesn't come to that, but it's entirely up to her.

With so much on his mind the last thing he needs is this health scare. Go to the dentist for a routine cleaning and come away thinking you're at death's door. Wherever dental hygienists go to school, they clearly don't learn any tact or diplomacy.

"It's a *lesion*," she said. "Looks like *thrush*." She prodded the spot with her gloved finger. "Have you been tested for

HIV recently?"

It came out of nowhere, so much so that he laughed out loud, but with her finger in his mouth it came out more like a protest.

"No need for alarm," she hastened to say. "Could be that it's absolutely nothing to worry about. This kind of thing can develop for any number of reasons. Quite often, though — and I'm obliged to tell you this — it's associated with a suppressed immune system. Best get it checked out and be on the safe side."

Thrush. The name of a bird. A harmless word that doesn't trouble him. It's *lesion* that's the kicker. The resonance of the word *lesion* with HIV and AIDS is clear in his mind because sometime during the past year he and Jodi watched a rerun of *Philadelphia,* in which the appearance of a single lesion on the forehead of Andrew Beckett, played by Tom Hanks, leads swiftly to his demise.

The virus has never before presented itself as something to personally concern him. When it first hit the news back in the early 1980s he was a sexually voracious adolescent having volumes of unprotected sex because copulating repeatedly in the back of a vehicle does not lend itself to precautionary measures, which in any case don't make for a fabulous experience. But his only concern at the time was the risk of pregnancy. HIV was not something you had to think about unless you were gay, or so the story went. And somehow he never moved past that kind of thinking.

A dental hygienist is not a doctor, but a dental hygienist does look inside a lot of mouths, and maybe learning to identify certain abnormal conditions, even those that have nothing to do with teeth, is part of the general training. When he got back to the office he locked himself in the washroom and turned his cheek inside out to see for himself the small patch of white fungus cleaving to the mucous membrane like a dab of spackling paste. And now he can't keep his tongue away from it. Still, in all likelihood this will turn out to be a false alarm. The women he sees who pose the most risk are professionals, who won't come near him unless he's wearing a condom. Condoms sometimes tear, it's true, but that's no reason to obsess. It's just a little fungus, after all, and he finds that he can put it out of his mind for hours at a stretch, especially during the day when he's busy, though sometimes when he wakes in the night all he can think about is death. His own death, of course, but also the death of those around him, the fact that one day in the not-too-distant future every person he knows, every single one, will be dead and gone, along with all the people he doesn't know, to be replaced by a crop of strangers who will take over the structures left behind: the buildings, the professions. His building and his profession. When he gets on this jag the only thing that comforts him is the thought of his unborn child.

17
HER

Dear Ms. Brett,
I am legal counsel to Todd Jeremy Gilbert, who — as you are no doubt aware — is the sole and rightful owner of the premises at 201 North Westshore Drive ("the Premises"), where you are presently residing.

My client directs me to inform you that your residency of the Premises is hereby terminated. He orders you to quit the Premises no later than 30 days from the date of this letter. By that date, you must vacate and surrender possession of the Premises free of all occupants and personal belongings.

Your compliance in this matter will prevent any further eviction action against you. Should you fail to comply, my client will not hesitate to exercise all available remedies under the law.

Very truly yours,
Harold C. LeGroot
LeGroot and Gibbons
Barristers and Solicitors

In years to come she will think of this letter as marking a radical shift in her disposition, as quietly killing off the girl she was and ushering in an updated, disenchanted version of herself. Looking back she will see the transformation as being practically instantaneous, akin to falling into a dream or waking up from one, but she'll be wrong about this. The truth is that the change happens gradually, over the days and weeks that follow. There are stages to it, the first being denial. This is involuntary, not hers to manipulate or control but merely reflexive, a spontaneous form of defense that cushions her from catastrophic loss. It happens in the way that birds, like encroaching thoughts, can circle but not alight, or as a message picked up by your microreceiver might be compromised by static, or the way you can be shot and continue to walk in the direction you were going.

It was the man with the ponytail who handed it to her. He approached her in the lobby when she came in with the dog. The doorman must have tipped him off. It was a rainy Saturday morning. She closed her umbrella and gave it a shake, waited for him to speak.

"Ms. Jodi Brett?"

"Yes."

She took the envelope he foisted on her, heard him say the words.

"Consider yourself served."

Riding up in the elevator she read it twice. Once inside she left it with the mail in the foyer and carried on to the kitchen, where she got the coffeemaker going. Now, waiting for the coffee to drip, she eats a shortbread cookie out of a package and gives one to the dog. Moving into her office she puts some files away and checks her voice mail. A woman has called about her overweight daughter. She returns the call, explains that she doesn't treat eating disorders, and rhymes off some referral numbers from a list that she keeps in her desk drawer. Forgetting her coffee she moves from room to room straightening furniture and picking lint off the carpets. She finds a cloth and some Lemon Pledge and sets about dusting and polishing. The moment arrives when her thoughts return to the letter, and she registers a response of sorts, a level of annoyance that prompts her to drop the cloth she is holding and pick up the phone.

"So," she says. "What's with the letter from Harry?"

"Jodi," he says. "I've been meaning to call you."

"You *should* have called me. How could you let this happen?"

"Harry sent you a letter?"

"Some guy handed it to me in the lobby."

"What does it say?"

"For crying out loud, Todd. It says I have to move."

"Jesus," he says. "That's a mistake. That wasn't supposed to happen."

"Of course it's a mistake. A very upsetting mistake."

"Jodi, listen. As far as I knew, Harry was going to wait till I talked to you."

"Talked to me about what?"

"I wish I didn't have to do this, I really do. But surely you can see that I have no choice. I can't *afford* to keep the condo. And it doesn't *look* right. Please try to understand."

"You can't be serious."

"But to spring it on you in a letter. That was not my intention."

"What is going on here, Todd? What kind of game are you playing?"

"Listen to me, Jodi. I want you to know

that I'm not going to haggle about the furniture. Whatever you want is yours. Take it all if you like. I want you to have it."

"Todd, what's got into you? You need to come to your senses. I'm not *moving*. And you don't *want* me to move. Think about it. Think about our life together."

"Jodi, try to be reasonable. Things have changed."

She hits the off button, puts the phone down, and walks away from it. What does he mean he has no choice? It's just like Todd to dramatize his circumstances, relinquish responsibility, pretend that it's not him running his life but a force beyond his control — a way he has of excusing his bad behavior. She knows of course that he wants to buy another office building; he's talked about it for years. It's going to be his next big project, possibly his last, the one that will set him up for life. This will be no four-story makeover with a warren of suites rented out to mini-startups and struggling entrepreneurs. He has something bigger and grander in mind — a building that's on the map — and he thinks he can make it happen by selling the condo out from under her. Their waterfront condo with its unobstructed view of the lake and its bamboo floors and spacious rooms, with its walk-in wardrobe in the master bedroom, and in the kitchen the terrazzo countertops and stainless-steel appliances and built-in effing coffeemaker. Pay no attention to the middle-aged Caucasian female and youngish golden retriever who happen to be living here. They will be gone in no time.

When Dean phones later in the day she's feeling just reckless enough to take the call.

"Dean," she says. "Sorry I haven't returned your calls. I'm sure you know how it is."

"I do know how it is," he says. "I know very well how it is."

"I get that this is tough on you, Dean. You've been on my mind."

"Well, and you've been on *my* mind. I keep on saying to myself that I'm not the only one who's been hit by this, that Jodi has been sucker punched, too. Well, you know what I mean. It can't be very pleasant for you either."

"No. It hasn't been pleasant."

"I know. I know. That's what I've been thinking, and I wanted to reach out, let you know that I feel for you, that you're not alone. You and I, we're in this together."

"That's kind of you, Dean. To think of me

when you have so much to deal with yourself."

"No, no," he says. "I really wanted us to connect. You're just the person I need to talk to. Well, you know. Try talking to my daughter. I'm just glad her mother isn't here to see her throw her life away."

"I'm sure her mother would be very upset by this," says Jodi.

"Natasha has always been a good girl, and the thing is, she doesn't have to do this. I don't think she understands that she can just walk away. What she really needs is someone who can talk sense to her. A woman, you know. She won't listen to me. Someone who knew her mother. Someone like you. I think you could really have an influence on her."

"You flatter me, Dean."

"Did you hear that she's moved the wedding date up? Second Saturday in December. Bloody hell. She wants me to give her away. Can you believe it? I'd rather see her boiled in oil."

"I know you don't mean that."

"Have you talked to Todd about it? Why do you think he keeps calling me? What do we have to say to each other? Thirty years of friendship and he throws it away. I'm telling you, he could cancel the whole thing tomorrow and it wouldn't make a speck of difference. It's too late. He's crossed a line. I'm sure you feel the same."

Dean is such a good talker he could have this conversation without her. An asset for a salesman, no doubt. Keep your mark distracted; leave no room for independent thought.

"Look, Jodi, why don't you let me buy you a drink. Or better still I'll take you to lunch. We need to stick together, share the burden, show each other support. What do you say I come pick you up tomorrow? We can go for Chinese."

He doesn't just want to commiserate; he has an agenda for her. Curious how he thinks that she, of all people, could have an impact on Natasha. It's actually kind of sweet. Not something she can hold against him. But lunch would be a mistake.

18
HIM

He's in his Porsche driving north on Michigan, heading for the Illinois Center. The gym has become a refuge of sorts, the only digression he's allowed on his way home from work, and he's taken to spending more hours getting fit, even when he's not in the mood for it, even when he badly needs a drink. Like now. The conversation with Jodi has unsettled him. He can't understand what her problem is. Does she think he's going to support her for the rest of his life, while he and his family do without? It's not as if he's trying to hard-line her. He offered her the entire contents of the apartment. Does she have any idea how much that's worth?

He thinks about calling her back but gets Harry on the line instead. "What did you think you were doing sending Jodi that letter?" he says. "I was going to talk to her first. We discussed that."

"Must have been Daphne," says Harry. "I'll have a word with her."

"That's right, blame your assistant," says Todd. "The point is that Jodi is now officially pissed off and digging in her heels. Damn it, Harry, don't you think I have enough problems?"

"I have news for you, Todd. She was going to be upset no matter how she found out."

"We'll never know now, will we, Harry?"

"Just keep your objective in mind, why don't you. The important thing is to get this done, and there isn't much time."

Harry is probably right in that it wouldn't have mattered how she found out, but the eviction notice seems unnecessarily cruel. And it makes him look bad. Ruthless. Cold-blooded. Still, it's done now, and maybe that's for the best because he really needs her out of there. Natasha asks him every day if Jodi is gone yet and what he's planning to do if she won't leave. An ugly scene is the last thing he wants. Jodi locking herself in, the sheriff breaking down the door, marching her out of the building. She would never forgive him.

It could be that she just needs time to adjust. If nothing else Jodi is practical. Give her a week or two and she'll find herself a cozy little rental where she can settle in and feel at home. It won't be anywhere central, given her income. She'll have to move to a suburb, someplace like Skokie or Evanston, at least until she revs up her practice and starts seeing clients full-time. It'll do her good to take her profession more seriously, take *herself* more seriously. Maybe she'll even get a real job, put her education to better use. She'd do well in the corporate world, and she'd make good money.

Wherever she lands he hopes she'll let him come and visit, maybe even make a thing of it. In odd moments, when he lets himself, he misses her terribly, misses her cooking and her common sense, the ease and comfort of their life together. Maybe it's the season that's making him nostalgic. Autumn can be glorious but menacing too — the long shadows, brisk winds, scurrying leaves, impending frost. He doesn't want to knock Natasha, but coming home isn't what it used to be, and the clutter is the least of it. Natasha seems to thrive on chaos: neighbors dropping off their kids, people showing up for dinner, the TV blaring even when she's studying. And it will only get worse when the baby is born.

He has the heat turned up in the Porsche, the airflow directed at the windshield to keep the glass from fogging up, the radio tuned to the news. The announcer's voice is buttery and rich, comforting in spite of the words being spoken, reports of the day's calamities. It's only just past five and night is falling fast. The short days would be hard to take if you lived in the country, but the city generates its own light, a bright mirage in all the colors of the rainbow. Seen from outer space it would look like a glowing dome, the force field of the great city where he lives. He's been driving these streets all his life and every stretch of pavement, every city block is known to him. In his younger years he used to fantasize that he owned it, that the city was his — the streets, the buildings, the power generators, the water purification system, even the sewers — the entire infrastructure. Even now, when he's on the street or when he walks into Blackie's or the Crowne Plaza, he has a sense of being in charge.

How he loves driving around in his car listening to music, scoping out the neighborhoods, watching the street life. In your car you're in your own private world and in the world at large, both at the same time. He likes snacking in his car, too, and usually has some licorice whips or salted peanuts in the glove compartment. This is not much different, he has to admit, than his father's love of holing up in the basement with his bottle and his transistor radio. You have your throne, your dignified perch (in the old man's case a dilapidated La-Z-Boy) that places you at the center of your world, and there you sit like a goddamn lord. Sometimes in his car he even starts to *feel* like his father, gets a taste of him. The way he used to nod to himself, for example, a barely perceptible nod pertaining to nothing in particular. Todd does that sometimes too — nods his head to the air currents or the ebb and flow of traffic.

19
HER

She's sitting in the office of Barbara Phelps, BA, LLB, the lawyer recommended by her friend Ellen. Barbara is petite and older, possibly in her midseventies, with hennaed hair, penciled-on eyebrows, and tiny wrists. Her power suit sags on her puny frame but she carries herself like a pillar. According to Ellen, Barbara took her law degree when that was still rare for a woman and has devoted her career to turning dependent, unhappy wives into liberated, freewheeling ex-wives — a sisterhood of prosperous divorcées.

Barbara's offices, on an upper floor of a Loop office tower, are furnished with inhospitable Bauhaus furniture and gigantic ab-ex canvases that testify, in dollars spent, to the woman-power on which her practice is built. She has seated Jodi in a Wassily chair and asked her some preliminary questions. Now, as she fans herself with Jodi's eviction letter, she patiently explains that Jodi was a fool not to marry Todd while she had the chance, because at this junction Jodi has as much right to her home as a colony of cats.

"Without a marriage license you have no interest in anything he owns. He has you at his mercy, my dear. No judge is going to rule against him. Common-law marriage does not exist in this state."

Jodi feels that Barbara has somehow failed to grasp her situation.

"I've been a wife to him for twenty years," she protests. "Everything we have we built up together. He can't *make* me move. If I refuse what can he do?"

Barbara shakes her head. "You have no legal right to be there. If you choose to ignore the law, you'll make things worse for yourself in the end. Most likely scenario, you'll be out on the street with little more than the clothes on your back. It will happen in front of the neighbors. I don't recommend it."

"I've made a home for him," says Jodi. "I've cooked, kept house, looked after him. He can't kick me out just because he finds me inconvenient."

"He can. And by the looks of it he will."

Jodi tries to absorb this. It makes no sense,

fails to accord with her notion of justice. But then she sees where Barbara is going. "Okay," she says. "I get it. It's *his* condo."

"Right," says Barbara. "It's *his* condo."

"But he'll have to support me," says Jodi.

"Why?" asks Barbara.

"Because he always has. It's our arrangement."

"On the contrary," says Barbara. "Under Illinois law you are not entitled to any kind of maintenance. But all things considered, your position is not a terrible one. You have his verbal permission to take away whatever items you want. If he's sincere about that, you avoid squabbling over household goods, and you avoid the pain of losing your possessions. So. You preserve your dignity *and* your belongings."

Thinking about it on the way home, Jodi doesn't see it like that. How is her dignity preserved by allowing him to turn her out, with or without her belongings? They're ganging up on her: Todd, Harry, and even this Barbara Phelps, who's supposed to be on her side. What they're doing may be legal, but it's far from humane.

On arriving home she takes off her coat and shoes and lies down on the sofa. Napping is not a habit with her but she feels like a rock sinking in muddy water. When her eyes open again the sky beyond the windows has lost its color and left the room in semidarkness. She gets up, changes out of her Valentino skirt suit, and gives the dog his dinner. Watching him eat, she can only wish that she had half his appetite. Doubtfully, she stands in front of the open fridge and scans its contents. In the end she takes the vodka out of the freezer, pours a small amount into a tumbler, and adds a splash of tonic. She doesn't normally drink alone, but this is a special occasion, calling for a celebration of sorts. She's always been a woman in charge of her life, someone who manages well, but today she's been toppled, and it turns out that all it took was a little shove, a gentle boot; her position was that precarious. Two decades of believing that her way of life was secure, and it turns out that she was hanging by a thread all along. Ever since moving in with Todd she's been as good as delusional — there's no other way to think about it. She built her life on a faulty premise, on wishful thinking. The person she thought she was has never existed.

She downs her drink and pours another, this time omitting the tonic. Thirty days. That's what she's been granted. Thirty days to extract herself from her own present tense, much as you'd extract a sliver from living flesh. This is what it's come down to. She's been reduced to the status of a foreign body in her own intimate surroundings.

She knows women who have gone through something like this, and none of them are in any way role models. These women, whose numbers include her friend Ellen, have not emerged with any degree of wisdom or grace, have not succeeded in reclaiming their lost years or reviving their goodwill. And yet most of them are better off than she will be. Most of them at least got to keep their homes.

The Adlerians would have a heyday with this, the muddle that she's made of things. They're big on routing out the error in the client's way of life, the screwy private logic and harebrained assumptions. All that privilege and opportunity and she drove it into a wall. She could do this because she took it for granted that life would treat her well, that there was no need to look ahead or take precautions. It was a form of hubris; she sees that now. If Gerard Hartmann had spotted this back when she was his client, he would have set her straight in no time. Indeed, it's highly likely that Gerard would have saved her from herself entirely if she had let him, if only she had stuck it out with him. He knew his stuff, Gerard, and had an instinct about her that drove him on — in spite of the fact that she appeared to have no problems and was not (in her own opinion, at least) in need of his services.

Which is not to say that her sessions with Gerard were a waste of time. Once they got into her relationship with Ryan, she could see it was a knot that needed to come undone. And picking it apart was not even all that painful. Gerard was good at what he did — skilled and knowledgeable, with exceptional insight. He was also the kindest and gentlest of inquisitors.

Gerard: About Ryan's outbursts. You mentioned nightmares and self-inflicted wounds. What was the problem exactly?

Jodi: He'd wake up screaming some nights. He'd be screaming and kicking and wouldn't settle down. Other times he'd bite himself till he drew blood. He'd go for his arm or the fleshy part of his palm.

Gerard: Was he taken to a doctor for this?

Jodi: They must have taken him to a doctor. You would think.

Gerard: Do you know if there was any

sort of diagnosis or treatment?

Jodi: He was never labeled as having a mental disorder if that's what you mean. It was just a phase. He did eventually grow out of it.

Gerard: When Ryan was acting out, how did your parents handle it?

Jodi: It was me who handled it. That was *my* job.

Gerard: How did that become *your* job?

Jodi: It became my job because my parents only made things worse. Dad would get all disciplinarian, and Mom would just, you know, stand around and helplessly wring her hands.

Gerard: Did your parents call on you to intervene, or was that your own idea?

Jodi: I think it was my own idea at first, and then after a while they just assumed I would handle it.

Gerard: How did that make you feel?

Jodi: Oh, it was all good. Ryan settled down. Mom settled down. Dad backed off. And everything returned to normal.

Gerard: And their assumption that you would handle it, that it was your job, how did that make you feel?

Jodi: I guess I'd have to say that it made

me feel great. I was just a kid, and here I was with all this authority and responsibility. I think it empowered me. It certainly had an effect on my self-image, and then ultimately of course it influenced my choice of profession. The fact that I was the one who could make Ryan better.

Gerard: You mention responsibility. How did you feel about having responsibility for your brother's welfare? You were just a kid, as you say.

Jodi: I loved Ryan. Helping Ryan was second nature to me. I didn't think twice about it.

Gerard: Has that sense of responsibility for Ryan carried over into your adult life?

Jodi: You mean do I feel responsible for the Ryan who is now an adult? The Ryan who is not in an intimate relationship, not engaged in meaningful work, not speaking to most members of his family? In fact, pretty much thumbing his nose at Adler's basic life tasks? Do I feel responsible for that Ryan?

Gerard: Yes.

Jodi: I didn't expect you to ask me that. Well, maybe I do. Sure. Of course I feel responsible for him. On some level, I suppose.

Gerard: Why do you think you feel that way?

Jodi: Wouldn't you? I mean wouldn't anybody? Under the circumstances?

Gerard: How would you describe the circumstances?

Jodi: Okay, maybe what I feel is not exactly responsible. Let's just say I worry. I'd like to be able to help him, but I can't help him. He won't let me.

Gerard: What do you think is the reason for your worrying?

Jodi: I want him to be happy. I want him to be fulfilled. When he's an old man looking back on his life, I want him to feel that he made good choices, didn't waste his opportunities, had a goal of some sort and followed through and accomplished something.

Gerard: Let's talk about *your* goal, the goal of your worrying.

Jodi: What do you mean?

Gerard: What would happen if you quit worrying about Ryan?

Jodi: You think it's a problem that I worry?

Gerard: What purpose do you think your worrying serves?

Jodi: Does worrying need a purpose?

Gerard: Do you think it helps Ryan when you worry about him?

Jodi: Okay. Touché. I get it. I see your point. Of course it doesn't help *him;* it helps *me.* As long as I worry about him I can feel that I'm at least making an effort, that I haven't abandoned him.

Gerard: Do you think that's what you would feel if you didn't worry? That you'd abandoned him?

Jodi: Probably. Yes.

Gerard: What else would you feel?

Jodi: I guess I'd feel that I'd broken our connection. I'd no longer feel connected to him. Because, think about it, the reality is that I hardly ever see him and have no way of keeping in touch. So how are we connected if I don't worry?

Gerard: So when you worry about Ryan you feel connected to him. And if you stopped worrying, if you lost that feeling of connection, what would happen then?

Jodi: I'd worry about the loss of connection. I guess that sounds ridiculous.

Gerard: Not ridiculous. But there may be better ways than worrying to keep your connection with Ryan alive within yourself.

Jodi: For instance?

Gerard: I'd like you to think about that. Let's call it your homework assignment.

20
HIM

Natasha calls as he's on his way to the gym. She wants him home by seven, she says, and would he bring some wine for dinner. That's Natasha for you. Jodi never had him running last-minute errands. Not that he minds getting the wine; what bothers him more is how she puts it, as if it's expected, as if she's in charge. Where's the give-and-take is what he'd like to know. It's not as if she keeps the house clean or even cooks the dinner. The minute he walks in the door she sets him to work in the kitchen.

He turns off Michigan onto Adams and doubles back to the wine store in Printers Row. The place is crowded, and there's a lineup at the cash register. By the time he's out of there his workout is getting away from him, and he decides to grab a beer instead. It's been far too long since he sat in a bar and drank a beer. In the beginning he didn't mind so much the way she kept tabs

273

on him. Given that she's half his age and oversexed, he found it reassuring. But that sort of thing can't go on indefinitely. And things are different now. Now that she's pregnant and not going anywhere.

He'll stop for a quick one and to hell with it. At least he'll be home in time for dinner. She'll smell it on him and she'll make a fuss, but it won't be as bad as the time he came in at three in the morning after his visit with Jodi. Natasha didn't believe that he'd spent all that time with Harry, though in his own mind the way he told it made a perfectly plausible story: "We stayed at the bar till closing and then we went to an all-nighter for bacon and eggs."

"You've been with Jodi," she said clairvoyantly.

In the end she forced him to admit it. But he'd seen Jodi only briefly, he maintained, and it was before, not after, his meeting with Harry. This at least explained the clothes he'd brought away with him. And he wouldn't have felt the need to hide it from her, he added, if she weren't so damn controlling.

Arriving at the Drake he takes a seat at the bar with a feeling of coming home. He loves the burnished wood and leather, the electric twilight, the glittering rows of bottles and glasses, the drone of voices and jostling for elbow room, the first long pull of the frothy draft that his friend the bartender has set down in front of him. He tunes his antennae to the meeting and greeting going on around him, the sense of release and possibility that happens when people get off work and settle down to the first drink of the day, the drifting ions and pheromones, the waves of talk and laughter, the rising hopes and expectations.

Seated on his stool after such a long absence he succumbs to a tender devotion, a reverence for this welcoming sanctuary with its quaint accoutrements and rituals, its shakers and strainers, goblets, flutes, and snifters, pickled onions and lemon twists, distinctive paper coasters, a different one for every drink, its buzzing congregation, and the secular priest behind the bar performing the time-honored rites. It makes him think of the church he used to attend with his mother, who raised him Roman Catholic, or tried to. He never could get his head around the old man in the sky, but he was smitten from the start with the glamour and mystique of it: the solemn processions, colorful robes, smoking censer, chanting and singing. He loved the fact that something could be blessed and thereby changed in its very nature: the wine, the water, and the people, too. And he sometimes dreamed about the tabernacle, the queer little ornate dwelling house built to hold the enigmatic sacrament. He connected with the mystery and the rapture, and now he inhabits the bar at the Drake in much the same way. Salvation is here, too, here for the taking. We are all mediums for our own basic truths. All we really have in life is the primal force that moves us through our days — our unvarnished, untutored, ever-present, inborn agency. Life force is the holy ghost in each of us.

The indwelling presence was strong in him in his younger years — in his childhood as he learned to distinguish himself from his parents, when he broke free and discovered the world at large, the exhilaration of it, and then as he found his feet in business and felt his power and his blamelessness, and when he first encountered Jodi and through her the substance of communion. He's a lover in love with the world, and when he's in form the world gives back. It's how he wants to live every minute of every day. He wants it all unwrapped. He wants to look the barefaced mystery in the eye, be a participant, immersed — not an observer, a packager, a regretter.

This is not the way some people see it. Jodi, for one. But you can't live your life by other people's rules. And Jodi admires him nonetheless. Admires his success, his ability to realize his promise, walk in the field of his dreams. He likes to be admired by Jodi. Her admiration has buoyed him up and given him heart over the years, and with that has come a certain discipline, enough to temper him a little, keep him steady on his course. He could have made his way without her, but with her he had this precious grease for his gears. Not every man has been loved like that. Even his mother's love was compromised — blighted by her guilt, even a little thwarted by her loyalty to his father.

So much of his life has had Jodi in it. The days lived, the words spoken, the feelings felt, an accumulated history, a quantum of meaning. His life with Jodi is a hoarded treasure, sewn into a pouch and stowed in the hollow of his chest. It isn't her fault that she couldn't save him from himself. What he fears now is that the black hole will open up again. Sometimes he feels its tug. These days the promised land is elusive. He needs to be an opportunist and reel it in where he can. In the dusk of the bar in the afternoon or on a rainy night with the pavement a river of reflections. In a woman's desiring eyes or in her stupendous nakedness. Love after all is indivisible. Loving one more doesn't mean loving another less. Faith is not a construct but something you carry inside you.

He takes off his jacket and drapes it over the back of his stool. There's maybe half an hour before Natasha starts to fret and an hour after that before it's actually dinnertime. He orders a burger with his second pint and wolfs it down in three or four bites, but he takes his time with the draft. He isn't a guzzler like his father. Nor is he a mean-spirited son of a bitch, not even when he puts away more than he should. Sitting down to a beer is a small enough reward for a day's work, a reward well earned and well deserved. He's a good provider. He takes care of business. Also unlike his father. The old man was a real piece of work, verified by the fact that nobody came to his funeral. At least his mother had a few good years after he died.

Remembering Natasha, he pats the phone in his pocket. If she calls he'll try to make her feel good. There's been too much fighting and not enough of the old fun and tenderness. She's basically insecure; that's the problem. She ought to take a lesson from Jodi, who never tried to run his life and didn't pick fights.

By the time she calls, he's finishing off a second burger, and before picking up he washes down the last of it with a slug of beer.

"Sounds like you're in a bar," she says.

"I stopped for a drink on the way home."

"You didn't go to the gym?"

"Didn't have time."

"You've been in the bar since you left work?"

"You know how much I love you," he says.

"That's hardly the point," she says.

"I think it is the point. You're beautiful and I love you and that's what matters."

"If you loved me you'd be here. We're having dinner guests. Did you forget?" Her voice is verging on shrill.

"Try to calm down," he says. "I'm just having a drink."

"Is anybody with you?" she asks.

"No," he says. "I'm alone."

"I suppose you forgot to get the wine."

"Not at all."

"You have the wine?"

"Yes, I have the wine."

"I want you to come home now."

"Fine. If you want me to come home, I'll come home."

"I'm going to wait on the phone while you pay your tab. Have you paid your tab?"

"No. But I'll pay it if that's what you want."

"I want you to pay your tab. I'm going to wait."

"I'm doing it now. I'm paying my tab."

He signals to the bartender, gets out his wallet.

"Tell me when you've paid your tab," she says.

He completes the transaction and drinks what's left in his glass. "Okay," he says. "I've paid my tab and I'm leaving the bar."

"Are you standing up?"

"Yes, I'm standing up." He gets off his stool. "I'm walking to the door."

"You were talking to someone," she says.

"I was talking to the bartender."

"What did you say?"

"I told him to keep the change."

"Have you left the bar yet?"

"Yes, I've left the bar. I'm going to hang up now."

"I want you to come straight home."

"I'm hanging up now."

21
HER

She hasn't left the apartment in eight days. She would not have thought it possible, but all her requirements have easily been met. For most of her daily essentials — groceries, toiletries, DVDs, and the like — she can shop online. The doorman brings up her mail, and the dog walker now comes three times a day — morning, afternoon, and evening. Much of what she needs she already has on hand because she likes to buy in quantity and keep things well stocked. Nonetheless, spending every minute of her time at home is taking its toll. With the loss of the activities in the wider world that she normally counts on for stimulation, ordinary life has taken on a dreamlike quality. There's an awareness of reality fading. And having too little to do makes the autumn days, already compacted, shorter than ever. With so few demarcations and little sense of time extending through places and events, the daylight hours tend to vanish in a snap. The sun comes up, the sun goes down, and not enough happens in between. Her nights, on the other hand, are unaccountably long, in spite of their utter emptiness.

In her solitude she's taken to playing out possible future events in her mind, scenarios that frighten her more the more she dwells on them. She contemplates a raid of the kind she's seen in war movies, with thugs in uniform breaking down the door and dragging her off in the night. She imagines an act of betrayal by one of the people she habitually opens the door to: a client, the doorman, the boy who delivers her groceries. In lucid moments she understands that these worries are irrational. If they're going to come for her they'll come during the day, and Todd will let them in with his key. But it's at night that she feels most afraid. Between sunset and dawn there is no period of time when she feels safe.

The one thing she needs to get her hands on is sleeping pills. The OTC brands don't work, and to get a prescription she would need to see a doctor. She's thought about trying an Internet source, but buying drugs online would be like buying them on the street. Sleeplessness has never been a problem in the past, but lately it's gotten so bad that she's been blanking out and seeing double. She wishes now that she had saved Natasha's eszopiclone. Giving it to Todd accomplished nothing.

There are times when she dozes off, but then she starts to dream and it's all turmoil and confusion. When she wakes up she feels worse than before. Without a good sleeping pill to knock her out it's better not to sleep at all. More and more she's taken to sitting at her computer into the small hours playing game after game of solitaire, or else she carries her bedding to the sofa, where she watches movies. In her former life she used to read herself to sleep, but these days she lacks the concentration to read. It helps to keep a tumbler of vodka beside her and sip from it as the hours creep by. She likes its bitter, raw taste and the way it makes her feel, like a rag doll that's lost its stuffing.

But come morning she's exhausted and still half drunk. To get herself ready for clients she spends a long time in the shower and drinks a full pot of coffee followed by a swill of Listerine. With her security threatened it's vitally important that she not alienate her clients, and she's doing her best to keep up appearances, but her troubles have erupted on her face for all to see: the deathly pallor, worse than before, the swollen eyelids, dark circles, pinched flesh — universal signs of things gone wrong. She's upgraded her relationship with makeup, but blush and concealer can only do so much. None of her clients have said a word, but they must be wondering. With her concentration shattered it isn't easy to follow along during sessions, and on top of that she's been moody and irritable. Most days with most clients she's on the verge of losing it by midsession.

What she's doing now is standing at the window looking out at the view. The mottled sky squats low over the lake, spitting rain like a large animal relieving itself. The water, choppy and sludge colored, makes her think of boiling sewage. This is not her fault. None of this is her fault. She did her best to make it work with Todd. She was tolerant, understanding, and forgiving. She was not grasping or possessive. Unlike the women you see on the *Dr. Phil* show, who fall to pieces when the randy fellow happens to stray. Boo hoo. Women the world over have been putting up with far worse for centuries. Soul mates is a nice idea but rarely borne out in practice. Marriage coaches like Dr. Phil raise the bar too high, teach women to expect too much, and end up breeding discontent. We live alone in our cluttered psyches, possessed by our entrenched beliefs, our fatuous desires, our endless contradictions — and like it or not we have to put up with this in one another. Do you want your man to be a man or do you want to turn him into a pussy? Don't think you can have it both ways. She did not make that mistake with Todd. She gave him plenty of space. He had nothing to complain about. This is not her fault.

Today is Wednesday, the day Klara comes to clean. Klara is a married woman with teenage children who cleans part-time to supplement the family income. She arrives at one o'clock and spends four hours scrubbing, polishing, vacuuming, changing sheets, and doing laundry. Klara's approach is to work on all the rooms simultaneously, which means that steering clear of her is next to impossible, so Jodi has always made a point of being out when Klara arrives. At least that's how it used to be, before she became a shut-in. Today, Klara let herself in as usual and nearly jumped out of her skin when she came across Jodi in the kitchen. It was the first time in months that she and Jodi had actually laid eyes on each other.

"What are you doing here, Mrs. Gilbert?" she asked. "Are you sick?" She is careful to enunciate her words. Her English is good, but she speaks with a strong Hungarian accent.

"I'm fine, thank you," said Jodi. "Please just carry on as if I weren't here. I'll try to keep out of your way."

At the moment Klara is temporarily absent because Jodi has sent her on errands. She gave her a sheaf of checks to deposit in the bank machine and asked her to take out some cash and pick up a bottle of Stolichnaya. She could have asked one of her friends to help her out with errands, but that would involve explanations, and so far her friends don't know about the latest developments. Nor do they need to know. They don't need to know, for instance, that she is not the person she thought she was, the sturdy branch that bends in the wind and doesn't break, the one who laughs things off and has made a profession of helping others to be more resilient, like her. In the past she has always been open with her friends, but that was when she was on top of things. Jodi not coping is something they don't need to witness. Besides, she can barely acknowledge even to herself the vast, unkind thing that is happening to her. Most of the time she's looking only as far ahead as the next hurdle in her day: the client, the shopping list, the searching look on the doorman's face when he hands her the mail, the compromise she makes between eating a proper meal and eating nothing at all.

It hasn't been difficult to keep her friends at bay. The only one making a nuisance of herself is Alison, who has taken to calling her practically on a daily basis. Alison is a good friend; these days she'd have to say her best friend. Certainly the one person who is trying to be there for her. Alison's concern is endearing, and no one could appreciate Alison more than Jodi does, but right now she needs to stay focused and conserve her energy, devote herself to keeping her home intact.

After Klara has returned with the vodka and the cash and the bank receipt, Jodi shuts herself in her office and looks at the blinking light on her telephone. She's been aware of people calling but these days regards the ringing doubtfully, much as she would a barking dog. Every day or two she scrolls through the list of missed calls and listens to selected messages. There are some from Todd, but not the Todd she knows and loves. This is a different Todd, and today this different Todd has called her once, from his cell phone, early in the morning. She plays his message but it's hard to hear with Klara battering at the ramparts — she has

287

the vacuum cleaner going and is knocking it against Jodi's office door as she works on the lintel and paneling. Holding a hand over her spare ear Jodi tries to make out what Todd is saying, something about a nightmare, and he sounds distraught, but she can't really get the gist of it with all the noise, and anyway she doesn't have the patience and debates with herself for less than a second before giving up and hitting erase.

22
HIM

He's in his car driving south on Clark Street, heading to the Walgreens at Clark and Lake to fill his prescription for antifungal lozenges. A cotton ball held in place by a piece of tape covers the spot in the crook of his arm where the needle punctured the skin. He's left behind him, at the doctor's office, a vial of his blood, which is going to be tested for the full spate of STDs, including syphilis, chlamydia, and gonorrhea, as well as HIV. Dr. Ruben refused to comment on the likelihood of the human immunodeficiency virus being the cause of the lesion, which Todd thinks is bigger now than it was before. "Let's wait for the test results," he said. Todd took this as a bad sign, and now he has days to wait, days of worry and foreboding that he'll have to keep to himself. Of course he can't say anything to Natasha, who has already accused him more than once of infidelity. What would happen if she

289

got a whiff of this? The irony is that she really has no cause for her suspicions. He's barely looked at another woman since he's been with her.

It took the doctor two tries to get the needle into the vein, but Todd felt almost nothing. He wasn't thinking about the needle; he was busy with thoughts of HIV, the virus, which he's come to picture as a kind of mutant disco ball, luridly winking and flashing, an image derived from illustrations found on the Internet. He can only wonder what perverse minds have managed to come up with these depictions. With a diameter of four one-millionths of an inch, the virus is beyond invisible, far too tiny to inhabit the greens and pinks and oranges of the illustrations. To detect it at all you need the Rolls-Royce of microscopes, the one that can enlarge a thing to half a million times the size it actually is. Up to a point, being so minuscule, the virus is harmless. Only in large numbers does it pose a threat. As with ants or bees you need a legion of them before they amount to an imposition. But once inside you it sets up house and quietly proliferates, using your body as a factory, harnessing your natural resources to stamp out copies of itself, establishing its power base, choking out your blood, turning you into a science fiction, and there you are — oblivious — walking around as if nothing were the matter, until one day at the dentist the bottom drops out of your life.

Not that it necessarily kills you anymore. Nowadays they keep it under control with an antiretroviral cocktail, but it's still a terrifying prospect. The drugs cost a fortune and there are side effects to contend with and you end up a slave to the medical profession, not to mention the damper it would put on your sex life. *His* sex life. What would Natasha have to say if he started using condoms, especially now that she's pregnant? How could he ever explain that he'd put her at risk, and not only her but the baby too? Even if it turned out well and she and the baby were safe, chances are she would never speak to him again. And then there's Jodi. She, too, would have to be told.

By the time he gets his results the wedding will be just a few days off. First the results, then the wedding, in quick succession, and the truth is that he's dreading the one as much as the other. The way he feels about both upcoming events is that things have gotten away from him. He doesn't know who is in charge of his life these days but it sure as hell isn't him. He's beginning to see himself as little more than a witness, standing on the sidelines while everyone else determines his fate.

As he crosses the river his tires hit the grating on the bridge, and the steady hum of the engine becomes a jarring tremolo. He stops for the red light at Wacker and his hand reaches for his crotch. Damn it all, he meant to ask the doctor about this. It feels like a rash but there are no marks of any kind: no spots or bumps, no welts, no redness, no discoloration. It flares up out of nowhere and feels like an army of centipedes scuttling around on feathery legs under his foreskin. The more he scratches the itchier it gets, but it's impossible to stop scratching. As he pulls across the intersection, one hand on the wheel, he's caught in a frenzy of rocking to and fro. The car weaves and pedestrians turn to stare, some of them smiling. It isn't hard to guess what they're thinking.

He and Natasha could be perfect together if only she didn't keep pushing, trying to force his hand. Like getting pregnant when she did, and the way she's handling the wedding. Every day she invites more people or adds something to the menu or the table setting. Why does she want asparagus spears when she already has mixed greens? She's spent a fortune on flower arrangements so why does she need an ice sculpture? Yesterday she took on two more bridesmaids, making it a total of eight, and who knows if she's going to stop there. Every bridesmaid gets a dress, a corsage, and a pair of shoes. He's also paying for their hair and makeup. He should have taken control from the start, laid down some ground rules, set some limits.

He's not a violent man. He's not his father and never will be. In all his years with Jodi he barely even raised his voice. But Natasha has to learn that she can't push him around, that he won't be pussy-whipped, not by her or any woman. Natasha is bossy and she's also immature and lacks judgment. There was no need for her to go running home to her daddy, as if his relations with Dean weren't bad enough already. And the truth is he barely laid a hand on her. A cuff on the ear can hardly be called abuse, and it wasn't the reason she fell. It caused her to momentarily lose her balance, but that was only because she was taken off guard. It was *her* who assaulted *him,* and yet she was surprised when he struck back. That's a woman for you. Anyway, after she steadied herself she turned to leave the room, and *that's* when she stumbled and fell. Yes, it was unfortunate, but seconds later she was already twisting the story. All this because he'd asked her to show some restraint. "You know I love you, but you're being unreasonable." That's all he said. Nothing more than that. And yet she took that tone with him.

"I can't *un*invite half my bridesmaids."

"You shouldn't have invited so many in the first place."

"You said I could have whatever I want."

"Natasha. Dearest. You're dressing your bridesmaids in Armani."

"Not all of them. Two are wearing Vera Wang."

"Okay. Fine. Have as many bridesmaids as you like. Have ten bridesmaids. Have twenty bridesmaids. Just keep the budget down to three grand. I think that's fair."

"Oh, great. You want us to shop at Target. Or maybe we should go to the Goodwill."

"Shouldn't your father be paying for this? Doesn't the bride's father normally pay for the wedding?"

"Don't, Todd. Just don't go there."

"Why not? Why am I picking up the tab for your deadbeat father? That's something we've never even discussed."

"Now you're being impossible. I don't know why I'm even talking to you."

"He's got to have at least a million stashed

away. He owns his house. What does he even spend money on?"

"Leave my father out of it. You know he hates you."

"Hates me so much that he gets out of paying for the wedding."

"I thought you wanted this wedding. I thought it was important to you."

"This is not a wedding. This is a shopping spree."

"Maybe you don't want to get married."

"You're acting like a child."

"Yeah, well, who knew you were such a cheapskate."

This took place over dinner, and with most of the food still on their plates, she left the table and slammed into the bedroom. He got up and followed her. He couldn't understand why she was acting this way. "Why don't you stop being such a bitch?" he said. She was lying facedown on the bed, and when he said that she leapt up and came at him like a cat, all teeth and nails.

That's when he struck her.

It doesn't help that he hasn't been sleeping, that he wakes up night after night with the same goddamn nightmare. This is entirely new for him. He never has nightmares. He rarely even dreams. Jodi says that everybody dreams, but when he wakes up in the morning, as a rule, he remembers nothing. And this is the nightmare to end all nightmares. Jodi would be impressed. Not only that, she could help him. She'd have a take on it. Jodi works with her clients on their dreams, and she has a way of making sense of them. He really needs to talk to her — about that and other things. The loss of control he's been feeling and the worry about his health and his future. Too much is happening and it's happening too fast.

In the nightmare he's running on a treadmill at the gym. It's an ordinary day and an ordinary workout, but even so he has a sense of approaching doom. And then, abruptly, the scene changes. The gym has disappeared, the treadmill is gone, and there he is like Bugs Bunny, still running, but now suspended over a void, feet paddling in midair, arms spinning like windmills. The sustained motion somehow holds him aloft, and he keeps at it, frantic to save himself, but his muscles are tiring, his strength is giving out, and he knows that he can't keep it up for very much longer, that it's only a matter of time before he drops like a stone.

23
HER

In retrospect she'd like to say that it was all Alison's doing, but she knows that if she hadn't played her part it wouldn't have happened. And it was more than just going along with Alison; she actually fell to fawning on her friend, and she hates herself more for the fawning, just as in eighth grade she hated herself for being teacher's pet. Still, she has to allow that she was under duress. Isolated, vulnerable, run-down, drinking a lot and not eating, trying to hold herself together but in reality falling apart.

Alison's way of talking about it was so offhand that Jodi's alarm bells never sounded. As if it were a basic household repair, like stopping a sprung leak; or a minor surgery, the removal of a troublesome appendix. Get a plumber, find a surgeon, come up with the money, problem solved. It was easy. Alison made it easy. When Jodi finally understood what was on offer, she felt grateful and relieved, so much so that she nearly broke down and cried. It was the perfect moment for the floodgates to open and all the grief and sorrow to come pouring out. But tears rarely fall in Jodi's personal biosphere. The benefits of a good cry are known to her — the release of pent-up emotions, the clearing of static from the system — but as the years go by she finds herself less and less able to let go, becomes more and more accustomed to the brittleness that goes with endurance. The day will come, she imagines, when fine cracks appear in her skin and go about branching and splitting till she comes to resemble the crackle-glaze vase on the mantel.

She's glad now that Alison broke through her hermetic seal. After such a long spell of not cooking and not eating it felt good to get into the kitchen and make dinner for the two of them, engage in routine tasks like slicing and chopping, the process of rendering bulky roots and gourds into tamer domestic forms: a mound of ribbons, a pile of cubes. The kitchen provides the simple satisfaction of exact measures and predictable outcomes, and yet in the business of precision there is also alchemy, something she learned from her pharmacist father. In culinary terms it's the alchemy of applying heat or a whisk or pounding something in a mortar. What's tough and impenetrable becomes yielding and permeable. A viscous liquid ends as a mass of froth. A pinch of dry seeds releases an unexpected, outlandish perfume.

Alison arrives in full makeup and stiletto heels, in spite of it being a quiet dinner at home. She smells like heaven, and her silver bracelets festively clink as she lifts her arms to fix her hair. Jodi has never seen Alison in any other mode. It's like she always has a party or a hot date lined up for later. Alison can make an occasion out of anything.

She accepts a glass of wine and says how worried she's been. "You can't *do* this to me. Last time I saw you, in case you've forgotten, when we left the restaurant you could barely even stand. Would it kill you to pick up the phone and call?"

The scolding is benign and makes Jodi smile. They take their glasses into the living room where the panorama of the sky, ashen and sickly throughout the day, has deepened to a lusty blue-black. Jodi circles the room switching on lamps. She turns up the flame in the fireplace and settles next to Alison on the sofa. On the coffee table in front of them is a plate of canapés that Jodi placed there earlier: slices of toasted baguette topped

299

with a savory olive relish.

Alison knows nothing of Jodi's present dilemma. The last thing they discussed was Natasha's pregnancy and the possibility of Todd and Natasha getting married. Alison doesn't know that — according to Dean — a date has been set for the wedding. She hasn't heard about the eviction notice and is unaware that Jodi has dug herself in like a hobbit. She doesn't know what Barbara Phelps had to say or even that Jodi has been to see a lawyer. Jodi has kept these things to herself in the belief that even Alison, the most indulgent of her friends, is unlikely to support her decision to protect her home by never leaving it.

But she is wrong about Alison. Given her line of work, Alison has witnessed a lot of injustice, from everyday petty tyrannies (girls having to dance in the blast from an air conditioner; girls required to remove even their G-strings on stage) to out-and-out abuses of power (girls entertaining the manager's friends; girls providing special services to officers of the law), and she does not take a philosophical view of such matters, does not hold with playing the game or going with the flow or following the path of least resistance. Alison has a history of sympathizing with the underdog and taking on other people's problems. She is not a vigilante; she knows better than to kick up a fuss and call attention to herself in her place of employment. It's more Alison's style to short-circuit a switch or spike a drink or place an anonymous call to a man's wife or mother. She's even been known to take advantage of an officer's improper behavior by relieving him of his weapon. Jodi has heard that Alison can get out the bigger guns, too, but until tonight she had not formed an image in her mind of what that might mean.

They move from the sofa to the table and tuck into the seafood risotto. Alison talks about Crystal's ex-boyfriend's bad behavior and the restraining order that Crystal is trying to get. She goes on to describe a feud taking place between two of the girls, Brandy and Suki, which has escalated to the point where they're shredding each other's costumes. Jodi listens politely but can't help feeling inwardly distracted. It's her own fault of course that Alison is focusing on other people's problems when she, Jodi, is in such terrible straits. She longs now to open up to her friend, tell her everything, but still she prevaricates. Alison will laugh at her for burrowing in the way she has, making things harder than they need to be, when it can't make any difference in the end.

But then, after dinner — after they've pushed back their chairs and recrossed their legs and switched from wine to coffee — Alison surprises her by saying, "Is Todd going to marry that girl?"

And here's where Jodi understands what Alison is made of, because as the story comes out in all its humiliating detail — especially the part where Jodi becomes a pathetic shut-in — Alison is nodding and agreeing, could not in fact be more approving or supportive.

"You're doing the right thing," she says. "You can't let him get away with it."

"But he *will* get away with it," says Jodi. "Nothing I can do is going to stop him."

"Wrong," says Alison. "We can make this problem go away."

"We can make *this* problem go away?"

"Without a doubt."

"Ha ha," says Jodi. "That would be nice."

"You think I'm joking," says Alison.

"Not joking. But how is it possible? Even the lawyer couldn't help me."

"It's possible," says Alison. "We just need a little time to arrange things."

"Okay," says Jodi.

"How much time do we have?" asks Alison.

"I don't follow you," says Jodi.

"Do we know when they're getting married? Because once that's done, your options are going to seriously drop off."

"You want to know the date of the wedding?"

"Didn't your friend tell you? Dean?"

"The second Saturday in December."

"What's today? Okay. I think we can cope. The one thing we need to be sure of is the will. As long as you're still the beneficiary . . ."

"Well, I am. As far as I know. I mean, he could have changed his will." She hasn't given any thought to Todd's will. The realization that he'll undoubtedly be revising it in favor of his wife and child, if he hasn't already done so, is a new kind of slap in the face.

"He may not have changed it yet," says Alison. "Chances are he hasn't. He's getting married, so why bother, that's what he'll be thinking. Because the second he's married any will he has is going to be null and void." Alison is folding and refolding her napkin, smoothing it out, turning it over, making it into a rectangle and then a square. "The law doesn't give a damn," she says. "The law will keep you jumping through hoops till you've lost everything, including your self-respect. I've seen it happen a million times. Forget the law. I make one call and you get your life back." Thrusting her napkin aside, she turns her attention to the items on the table — salt shaker, candlestick, water glass, coffee cup — lining them up like soldiers.

Jodi gets up and fetches a bottle from the sideboard. "This is a really nice Armagnac," she says. Carefully, her movements concentrated and spare, she pours out the amber liquid and hands her friend a glass.

A revolution is taking place within her, as though a lifetime's experience could be outdistanced in the span of a conversation. Like a molting snake she finds herself shedding her useless defiance, pathetic innocence, and sense of being a noncontender — the butt of a legal joke. The beauty of it is that there is no point at which she has to make a decision. She is not required to decide, for example, if she can overcome her reservations, work herself into enough of a rage, do the deed in cold blood, cope with consequences. Lost in a desert, you drink the tainted water that your friend is offering. Fatally afflicted, you put yourself in the surgeon's hands. The pros and cons no longer count. The options have run out. Survival is what's now on the table.

"Renny is blue-chip," Alison is saying. "He makes a rotten husband but he has a good Rolodex. And he owes me a favor. And could use the money, of course. But don't worry, he'll give you a fair price."

Jodi is captivated by this alternate world in which her problems simply disappear, not just the immediate problem of keeping her home intact, but the prospective problems as well — the problem of putting Natasha in her place, the problem of the endless days ahead and living through them as Todd continues to eat, sleep, and fornicate in another part of town. The world without Todd in it is not just a new concept but a new *kind* of concept, one that even now is forging a fresh neural pathway within her, like a tunneling worm. But the real surprise is Alison. She has always liked Alison but sees now that she has failed to give her proper credit and at this moment is regarding her with virgin eyes.

"It has to be cash," Alison says. "But forget about taking it out of the bank or getting a cash advance on your credit card. Those kinds of transactions can be traced. If they see that you've made a large withdrawal, they'll be on you like a pack of wolves."

Jodi understands that by "they" Alison means the police, the judge, the jury, the prosecutor — the whole law enforcement community. "I don't have much in the bank anyway," she says.

"You will. But why don't you just sell something? Your jewelry. Some of these knickknacks." Their two pairs of eyes light on various objects in the room. The gold Peruvian figurines, the Matisse cut-paper lithograph, the Rajput painting in its gilt frame. "And don't go through an agent. Look for buyers online." She lifts Jodi's hand and peers at the stone in her ring. "Stick with smaller things that are portable. Insist on cash. You'll have to move fast. And get enough to take a trip while you're at it. You'll want to be away when the moment comes."

24
HIM

It's morning. He's sitting at his desk. His
BLT wrappings are in the trash can by his
left foot, along with the cardboard cup from
which he drank his first coffee of the day.
Coffee number two is still on the go. The
caffeine notwithstanding, he's feeling
groggy, just barely awake, and yet keenly
alert to the small animal stirring in his gut.
He's been helping himself to Natasha's
sleeping pills, but they haven't affected this
gnawing, spitting, scratching presence that
never seems to rest and prevents him from
sleeping deeply or for very long. It's a new-
old feeling for him, this sense of the frac-
tious lodger within. At one time, not so long
ago, he naively believed that Natasha could
banish his anxiety forever, as if their love
were a form of enchantment that could keep
him always safe.

Hearing Stephanie come in he looks at his
watch. Stephanie has always put a loose

interpretation on the notion of office hours, but lately she hasn't even bothered with excuses. He resents the presumption on his good nature and generosity. He ought to speak to her, outline his views on punctuality. In a better world he might even give her a warning. The trouble is she could conceivably walk out on him, the way she's been. Distant verging on rude, which no doubt has to do with her loyalty to Jodi.

He can hear her moving around out there — rinsing mugs in the washroom, picking up her voice mail, making a call. Her cherry-gum perfume hits his nostrils with a twang, soon followed by the darker aroma of the coffee she's brewing. Stephanie, never without a coffee at hand, lives in defiance of the coffee break. Every week she goes through two or possibly three bags of a premium Starbucks blend that must be costing him ten dollars a pound, taking the position that she buys and brews it for the office and overlooking the fact that he drinks his entire daily quota of coffee before she arrives in the morning, which leaves only Valerie, the bookkeeper from 202, and Kevin from the printing operation in the basement to join her in a cup, which they are happy to do on a regular basis. He ought to be docking her pay not only for the coffee but for the time she spends gossiping with his tenants.

He makes up his mind to confront her, but when she appears in his doorway, coffee mug in one hand, files and notepad in the other, he takes one look at her churlish expression and decides not to push his luck. Besides, he's distracted by the sweater she's wearing, one he hasn't seen before. The scoop neck reveals more of her collarbone than usual, and her breasts — nipples foremost — assert themselves against the soft weave. The urgent feelings that arise from Stephanie's daily presence in his life can at times leave him groping and bankrupt. On an ongoing basis he fantasizes more about Stephanie than he does about any other woman.

What she says as she traverses the room and sits down facing him across his desk is: "I don't know why you drink that crap from the deli when our office blend is as good as it gets. What are you paying for that — a buck fifty, two bucks a cup? It adds up, you know."

Blood rushes to his head but he holds his tongue and lets the moment pass. "Am I still underwriting Jodi's credit cards?" he asks.

"Of course. Nothing has changed."

"How many are there?"

"Six. Seven. Seven if you count Citgo, which you also use."

"I want you to close out all her cards. Pay them off in full and cancel them."

"Citgo too?"

"Yes. Anything she has access to. Make sure you get them all."

She hesitates, pen poised over paper.

"What?" he says.

"I hope you're going to forewarn her about this."

"She'll find out soon enough."

Stephanie drops her eyes to her notepad and says nothing, but he gets her disapproval, plainly conveyed in the set of her shoulders and tilt of her head. Too bad. Her defiance doesn't affect him as much as she would like it to. Stephanie should tend to her own affairs. He needs to get serious with Jodi, show her that her freeloading days are over, that he's not fooling around, that he means business.

With the meeting at an end, as she gathers up her files, he says, "I hope it goes without saying that what happens in this office is strictly confidential."

He waits for a reply but doesn't get one.

When Stephanie has gone and shut the door behind her he gets up and moves around the room with clenched fists and an odd gait, doing his best to defy an urge that is all but irresistible, a defiance that crumbles in less than a minute, giving way to a fit of scratching, frenzied and hysterical. It's like he has electrodes taped to his balls or a live wire sizzling in his pants. His poor little penis could light up the world. And even in his pain he feels ashamed — that he can't keep still, can't keep his hands off his crotch, as if he were a dirty old man with a case of the crabs. Which is not even the worst of it. The worst of it is that his frenzy is marbled with terror. What if it never goes away? What if it doesn't just persist but worsens and spreads until he can't think or eat or sleep, can't do anything but scratch? What if he has to go to the hospital, and even so what could they do for him there other than bandage his hands or strap him to the bed or put him in an artificial coma?

The other component of his terror is the thought that this would not be happening unless there were a deeper underlying condition, such as the HIV that he no doubt has. He needs to face up to the HIV because he's come to see that it's the only plausible explanation for his lesion. When the immune system fails it's like pipes going dry

— there's an end to the rinsing and lubrication, and things start to grow in the dim, dank places — fungus, for example. In biology, fungus is a kingdom unto itself, a documented land of rot and decay, a place for yeasts and molds and spores and every manner of thing that grows in the dark, a fairy tale gone wrong. *In the Kingdom of Fungi there once lived a little spackle spot named Thrush who made a home for himself in the mouth of . . .*

He goes for the antifungal lozenges in his desk drawer, shakes one out of the packet, puts it in his mouth, and holds it in the pouch of his cheek, but he knows that it's a stopgap at best, that it won't reverse the conditions that enabled Mr. Thrush to set up house in the first place, won't breathe a fighting spirit into his mucous membranes, won't prime the pump of his immune system, won't stop the diabolical itching. Is this his punishment for what he's doing to Jodi? If he were Catholic, if he'd stuck to the path, he could go to confession and ask God's forgiveness. And he would, too, because he's sorry, he really is, but how then would he go on with his life? What changes could he make that would set things right? He can't leave Natasha now, not while she's pregnant, and keeping up two households is not within his means. He's trying to live his life as best he can, wants to do what's right, and yes, he's made mistakes, but you can't say that he's not a good person, that he's without a conscience, that he doesn't try to be the best that he can be. He's a generous man, damn it. He's just not as rich as everyone seems to think he is. And he's a good man, too, a man who doesn't hold grudges or kill insects, a man who spends money on water-saving toilets even though big industries in this country waste more water every day than his toilets will save in a lifetime.

He slows his pacing, comes to a tentative halt, clasps his hands together, holds his breath, waits and endures. The deception is that, if you scratch it, the itch will go away. Isn't that how it normally works? But this is no ordinary itch, and only through resistance will he ride it out and cross the bridge to sanity and peace. There. You see? It's subsiding now to a feeble tremor, the dying vibration of a stringed instrument, the quivering of a leaf, the purring of a kitten. But this is when the deception arises again in force, the notion that it's just a little itch that needs scratching, and the urge to scratch it is overwhelming. He's on his knees now, head bowed, tears splashing onto the granite tile, begging God for the will to endure. And then all at once and without formality it's over, gone as it began, suddenly and unannounced.

He stands up feeling like a ghost, runs a hand through his hair, breathes into his abdomen, circles the room, comes back to his desk, and picks up the phone to call Natasha.

The slump they've fallen into — he's willing to concede that it all comes down to him. He needs to relax and take a longer view. What he tends to overlook these days is his son. His son is of course ever present in the form of his mother's distended abdomen and volatile moods, but what he needs to bear in mind is his-son-the-person, the unique individual with fingers and toes and a God-given (if microscopic) shooter, as he saw with his own eyes in swirling, grainy black-and-white at the radiology clinic. He would have been okay with a daughter — this is not a time to split hairs — but the fact is he has a son, and his son is the future, the forward momentum, the paradox whose birth will put an end to the fighting and commotion. His son, when he arrives, will bring them to their knees.

And Natasha will be different with a baby to look after. Her focus will shift from him to the needy infant. He's looking forward to that, but in the meantime the least he can do is make an effort to be more tolerant and more compliant, because basically she can't help herself. The fact is she's a bubbling sea of hormones with instincts out of control driving her to fight for the best nest and exclusive rights to the male provider. What she's going through may be a form of temporary insanity, but the last thing he wants is to thwart or obstruct her, given that her purpose is also his purpose. He's been premature in asserting his rights as a free agent — he sees that now. What he needs to do is tell her he loves her and ask her to come home.

25
HER

Finding buyers online is easier than she thought it would be. There's a thriving market out there for the items she has to sell; in fact, people are practically lining up for the chance to meet her at the Art Institute or the Crystal Gardens and count out their bills in exchange for her wares. In order to conduct her business she has to leave her home unattended, but it must be done, and as it turns out she enjoys the outings immensely, revels in the icy winds that make her eyes tear up, the smell of food venting out of restaurant kitchens, the sight of strangers milling around in public spaces, starved as she is for any kind of sensory input.

In the beginning there was a problem with authentication. The e-mails people sent in response to her ads included comments like: *I love the ring but how do I know it's real? The painting could be a fake. What if there's a problem? Can I have your number?* But as it turns out there are plenty of people who are not concerned. Maybe they're jewelers or dealers or experts of one kind or another. She doesn't know because she doesn't ask.

Sharing her e-mail address, meeting her customers face-to-face — these are risks she can't avoid, and she compensates by dressing in an old anorak and woolen toque that belong to Todd. The semidisguise completes her sense of drama. While loitering near Magritte's *On the Threshold of Liberty* on the third floor of the modern wing watching for a man with a chevron mustache, or sitting on a bench by the high-arching fountains keeping an eye out for a woman in red leather gloves, she thinks of herself as someone who is playing a role, a character on a stage. The acting is a diversion. All she has to do is collect her money; she doesn't have to think about what the money is for. And when she gets back home she adds it to the growing stash in the black leather Louis Vuitton briefcase — a gift to Todd that he never used — pleased with the way it's adding up.

She expects that Alison will ask for a deposit but ends up giving her the total payment up front. That's how Alison wants it, and Alison is the best friend she has right now. Anyway the money means nothing. It might as well be play money, Monopoly money. The items she has traded for it never enter her mind. Somewhere along the way they lost their hold on her, became uninteresting in themselves, significant only in terms of their purchasing power. She has even lost her regard for the briefcase except as a container for her funds. When she pays Alison she throws in the briefcase without giving it a second thought.

Now that she knows how to get cash, she worries less about the immediate future, a timely development as it turns out, because the day after she closes the deal with Alison, Stephanie calls to say: "I wanted to tell you, Mrs. Gilbert — I thought you should know — that he's canceling your credit cards."

"I see," says Jodi. "Well then. Is he really?"

"Yes. All of them." Stephanie's tone is low and urgent, the way people talk when they're sharing secrets. "I thought I should warn you so, you know, you're not caught off guard. Please don't tell him I called."

Unexpectedly, Jodi finds this funny. It hasn't occurred to Todd that two can play at this game. In any case she has a credit card of her own, ironically one that she's mainly used to buy him gifts over the years.

318

The Louis Vuitton briefcase, for instance, although it was not among her more extravagant offerings. One year on his birthday she bought him a horse and riding lessons. Just an idea of hers. She thought it would give him a break from work, get him outside for some fresh air and exercise. He was keen at first but of course it didn't last.

When she puts the phone down she does a little dance of exultation, but her mood eventually fizzles, and in the end she is left with the pettiness of canceled credit cards beside the magnitude of the scheme that she has set in motion, the unspeakable future event that she has summoned up and paid for. Voices within are telling her to reconsider while there's still time, but she's caught in a sense of destiny unfolding, a reluctance to retrace her steps. It's in the back of her mind that she's crossed a line, that she should seek help, and she thinks of Gerard — she could look him up. But she waves the thought of him away. Gerard is undoubtedly retired and living in Florida or Mexico, and besides, what could he possibly do for her now? She should have stuck with him when she had the chance, allowed her therapy to run its course, come to its natural conclusion.

He was good at his job; there was never

any doubt about that. It was Gerard who opened her eyes about Ryan, brought her to terms with reality, ended her habit of quarreling with facts. Only because of Gerard did she accept in the end that Ryan was going to live his own life in his own way, that his choices were his to make, that what she wanted for him — the material security, the personal advancement — were worthy ambitions but not his ambitions, that her misgivings about him were founded in judgments, that to judge others was to willfully do them harm. Respecting differences, she gathered, went beyond simply making allowances; it meant giving up your blinkered perspective, your assumption that you are necessarily right and others necessarily wrong, that the world would be a better place if everyone thought as you did.

She had to be given credit, and Gerard was lavish with his praise. He applauded her willingness and perspicacity, commended her for challenging herself and implementing change. This was unexpected progress, given that before she'd come to Gerard she hadn't thought she had a problem because in her mind Ryan was the problem.

With this achievement under their belts Jodi and Gerard moved on with renewed energy. They talked endlessly about her childhood, how it felt to be the girl in the middle, the fact that her parents had expected less of her, the way she had defied them by excelling at school and proving herself as both a professional and a homemaker. There was no denying that she had a competitive streak. They talked about the traits she had taken from each of them: from her mother a love of domesticity, from her father a devotion to method and detail. She was more the product of her family of origin than she had ever supposed.

Her sessions were engaging, even enjoyable, but she began to suspect that her insights into her relationship with Ryan were destined to be the apotheosis of her work with Gerard, that there was nothing of any significance left to accomplish. Accordingly, she grew restless, even a little bored, and expressed to Gerard her feeling that she was wasting his time. Privately, she began to fear that she was shallow, tragically lacking in any real depth or substance. It came to the point where she could almost wish she'd had a horrible childhood, an abusive father, an alcoholic mother. What she wouldn't have given on some days for a history of depression or anxiety, an eating disorder, low self-esteem, mood swings, panic attacks. If only she stuttered or compulsively washed her hands. She wasn't even a procrastinator. As the weeks went by, her stasis became the subject of banter. She would arrive for her session and say, "Doctor, I love my life and I'm happy. What should I do?" And Gerard would reply, "Don't worry. I know the cure."

And then came the turning point.

It was not a propitious-seeming day, hardly a day that held out any hope of progress. Outside the consulting room it was spring and there were blossoms on the trees, but inside Jodi was wearing a cardigan over a pullover to fend off the air-conditioning, and Gerard was a little off his game, lacking his usual focus. They'd been jumping from one topic to another, unable to come up with anything of interest, and as the session neared its end they were flagging. She figured they were done. It was time to go home. And then, in a valiant last-ditch effort, Gerard inquired about her dreams.

Jodi: It's just been the usual white noise.
Gerard: Define white noise.
Jodi: You know what I mean. (Annoyed that he would ask her this question

when she'd been using the term all along.)

Gerard: Humor me. Give me an example.

Jodi: Oh, well, like, I'm at a party talking to people I don't know. I catch a glimpse of myself in a mirror and notice that I'm half naked, but I feel nothing about it one way or the other. Then I'm at my parents' house, hunting around for something, but I can't remember what. Even in the dream it didn't seem important. Like that. White noise.

Gerard: (Silence.)

Jodi: Sorry. I *have* been making an effort.

Gerard: I know you have.

Jodi: (Silence.)

Gerard: So that's it then.

Jodi: I guess so.

Gerard: (Silence.)

Jodi: Hang on. I had a dream about Darrell.

Gerard: You had a dream about Darrell?

Jodi: I forgot about it till this very minute.

Gerard: Tell me.

Jodi: Darrell came to visit. And just as

he arrived I was writing down a dream, which was Darrell's dream. It was a dream of Darrell's, but I had dreamed it for him. I had a whole notebook of Darrell's dreams, dating back to his childhood. I'd been dreaming them for him and writing them down.

Gerard: Go on.

Jodi: That's about it. I asked him if he remembered any of the dreams, but he wasn't interested and didn't want to talk about them, and then he left.

Gerard: What were you feeling while this was going on?

Jodi: Spooked. I was feeling spooked.

Gerard: What spooked you?

Jodi: The whole thing. It was creepy.

Gerard: But you subsequently forgot the dream. When I asked you just now about your dreams, you said there had only been white noise.

Jodi: I guess I put it out of my mind.

Gerard: Did you feel anything else? Other than spooked?

Jodi: Not really. No. I was just spooked. Scared, I'd have to say.

Gerard: Of something in particular?

Jodi: Scared on Darrell's behalf, I guess. It's like I had him on life support or something, but he was bloodless, totally disengaged. There was something horrifying about it. That he wouldn't participate in his own dreaming. As if he were absent. As if he didn't exist.

Gerard: And you had been doing this on his behalf.

Jodi: Yes.

Gerard: And you had been doing it because . . . ?

Jodi: Because I loved him.

Gerard: In the dream, did you feel your love for him?

Jodi: Yes. I did.

Gerard: So in the dream you felt scared, and you also felt your love for him.

Jodi: Yes.

They let it idle for a moment, and then Gerard looked at his watch and said, "Let's return to this next week. I'd like you to write the dream down in as much detail as you can and bring it to the next session. That's your homework."

She stood up to go, removed her cardigan and put it in her satchel, took her windbreaker from the coat rack, and thanked Gerard on her way out. She walked to the elevator and pressed the down button. As she waited she looked at the elevator doors, at her feet in their Doc Martens, at the pat-

325

tern on the carpet — a geometric design in blue and orange on such a minuscule scale that the overall color effect was beige. She felt a caustic wind rising up within her, unobstructed, as if her insides were nothing but a barren landscape. She thought of taking the stairs but felt as though she were stuck to the spot, as if the carpet and the soles of her boots had fused together in the manner of a skin graft. And even as she stood there she knew there would be no going back, that the simple uncomplicated times of just moments before were lost to her now. There would be no more sitting around with Gerard wondering what to talk about. No more banter about her perfect childhood. The dream had been retrieved and the memory with it, inevitably, like a bunch of tin cans tied to the back of a wedding car, and she could not now reverse the process — close her mind around the images and reabsorb them into the tissue of forgetting.

The memory had borne its burial well, had returned to her intact, untarnished, fully dimensional, part of her living history, complete with visceral analogues — tastes, smells, sensations — actual voltage. It was a sightless memory, however, clothed in darkness, which she took to mean that the remembered events had taken place at night. Either that or the girl she had been was resolutely shut-eyed, had decided from the outset to curtail the offensive sensory input. Initially, the explosion within had been all pain and alarm, but later on she learned the trick of surrender, came to understand that capitulation was her means of disengaging, her ticket out. Her only hope now was that she might have been complicit, played a part in making it happen, because if so then maybe she could love him still and nothing would have to change. But she was only six when Darrell was twelve, and she didn't see how it could have been her fault.

26
HIM

Natasha is home again, but she has not forgiven him. In many ways things are back to normal — they sit down to dinner, she studies, he cleans up, visitors come and go — but she's taken to undressing in the bathroom and falling asleep before he comes to bed, and she has him on a strict curfew, which strains his goodwill, and she continues to try his patience with incessant talk of centerpieces and seating arrangements, not to mention strollers and car seats, none of which has anything to do with loving each other or loving their son — whose name by the way has become the subject of intense speculation and debate involving all her friends and all the neighbors. She won't be satisfied until she's wrung out every last entry in the boys' half of an encyclopedic volume titled *A Century of Baby Names in English-Speaking Countries.* She refuses to accept that names like

Herschel and Roscoe are not worth discussing, and she keeps both Clarence and Ambrose on an ever-expanding short list. Post-its bearing names like Chauncey and Montgomery are stuck to the bathroom mirror and rearranged as one or another gains or loses precedence. "You can't veto a name just because you don't like it," she tells him absurdly.

There comes a point in the evening — with dinner over and the apartment an overheated closet crawling with stale odors and unwanted guests — when all he can think about is flinging himself out the window. It would help if there were someone he could talk to the way he used to talk to Jodi. But Jodi won't speak to him now, and with his buddies it's mainly bravado, and anyway his time with them has been curtailed. "If you want to see them, Todd, why don't you ask them to dinner?"

He misses coming home at night and walking the dog by the water, an interlude that banished the cares of the day and helped him get down to the business of sleep. In the deep of the night, with the city dozing and muted, he'd walk along the shore and feel himself alone in a wilderness, listen to the water's breath, its snorting and sighing, submit to the immense hollow of the sky, its infinite folds cascading down to the very horizon. On clear nights he could pick out the Big Dipper and the North Star. He used to know Orion and Cassiopeia and Pegasus and so many more, and when there was no moon and it was very dark, he'd look for the Milky Way. As a boy he dreamed of a sea of stars and being in their midst, not in a spaceship but floating free, doing a backstroke through the thick of them, a billion trillion pinpoints of light that crackled and popped against his skin like cool fire.

So much pleasant musing has been crowded out and all but forgotten. The sound he hears in absolute silence, a hissing sound — he thinks of it as atmospheric pressure. As a boy he imagined that everything, absolutely everything made noise, if only he could hear it. In autumn, the leaves turning color, a different sound for turning yellow and turning red. The falling snow in winter. Buds forming on the trees in spring. Clouds drifting. Small birds intent in their flight, their shadows moving on the ground beneath them. He likes to be in tune with things as they are, move through the world in step with its music. When it's working for him he can do and be anything. Some people call it luck.

There's not much point anymore in restricting his drinking to the evening hours, and he's taken to seeking out watering holes at lunchtime. His new find is a sports bar in Humboldt Park, an out-of-the-way haven with old-timers in the front drinking cheap draft and playing dominoes and a worn-out pool table in the back — an establishment where the air has been motionless since 1980, to judge by the smell of it. He likes it more because nobody he knows would ever go there. An elderly Spaniard in a crumpled fedora, the owner, spends his days on a stool at the cash register, while the work of pouring and serving is done by a single waitress. When he first wandered in here last week he thought he'd have a quick one and leave but discarded this plan the minute he caught sight of her. Since then he's been back every day, holding down the table by the jukebox, facing into the room with his back to the wall.

Today he's focused on tracking her movements — covertly but with GPS precision. At any given moment he knows her location, route, speed, and schedule of stops. As she orbits the room she could be deaf and blind for all the notice she takes of him, but the signals she emits peal like church bells calling him to worship.

The way she looks — gaunt with lank hair

331

and hollow cheeks — makes him think of an undernourished child. She has a long torso with a flat chest, jutting hip bones, and a concave belly. Feet like planks but narrow. Eyebrows unplucked. In the hours he's spent here fewer than a dozen words have passed between them. She has a Mediterranean look but speaks without an accent. Her voice is toneless and her words run together, as though she lacks the energy to enunciate. She never looks at him.

"Tell me your name," he says as she waits to take his order. He's been meaning to ask her this and biding his time, taking his cue from her indifference. But he's not a stranger anymore. He's a regular now; she's used to him. When it comes to women he has pretty good horse sense.

"Ilona," she says, her eyes alighting briefly on his face, possibly for the very first time.

He wants to tell her she's sensational, stunning. Everything about her says she doesn't know this. He feels the burden of wasted time, an urgency that doesn't compute but drives him nonetheless. What he'd like to do is lead her into the men's room and lock the door. What he can conceivably do is ask when her shift ends, take her to a good restaurant, and impress her by throwing some money around. All women like money. Any woman will give in to you if you spend enough money on her. Whatever the rule books say, it's money that gets a woman in the mood.

She shifts her weight to her right foot, thrusting out her hip. Her eyes are fixed on something at the front of the room.

"A pint and a shot," he says. It's practically the only thing he's ever said to her. She starts to walk away.

"Ilona," he calls.

She turns and comes back.

He's broken into a sweat. A prickly heat is spreading across his chest and burnishing his forehead. "When I was ten," he says, "I watched my father break my mother's arm. He held it behind her back and twisted till it snapped. It was her left arm. 'So you can still work,' he told her. When he did it he was looking straight at me. I'll never forget the expression on his face. Like he was showing me something, giving a demonstration. Teaching me."

He watches her as he speaks, wipes his brow with his sleeve.

"I vowed that I would never be like him. I've always respected the women in my life. I'm not saying I'm a saint, but I've loved women deeply. When I was old enough I got my mother out of there. Looked after her till the day she died."

He hates himself for this speech. It's nothing but a craven bid for sympathy, a shameless ploy. This is not the first time he's told a woman this story or some version of it. Not that it isn't fundamentally true; there's emotional truth in it anyway. And even before he's done she's moved a half step closer and a light has come into her eyes. It's hard to tell if it's her sympathy that's been aroused or her contempt. But she hasn't yet brought him his first drink of the day, and this has to be working in his favor. He isn't some used-up lush spilling his guts on the floor, some wasted gasbag airing his sour old grievances. Not only is he sober, he's a notch above any other man she's going to meet in this dive. He's relying on his sobriety — along with his calfskin boots, his uptown haircut, and the Rolex Milgauss twinkling on his left wrist — to get his point across.

"I don't know why I'm telling you this," he says.

Again she turns away and again he calls her back.

"I'm desperately trying to get your attention," he tells her. "But I'm sorry. I'm sure you hear sob stories all day long, and you deserve so much better — a man who can

334

forget about himself and focus on you. Pamper you. Bring you flowers and gifts. Massage your feet when you get off work. *Min fröken, you iss all day oon da foots and now iss riilly sore.* Take care of the losers who try to pick you up at work. *Don't vorry, you must telling Boris, ve tekking zis man out of hair, same ve do in Savyetski Sayus.*"

Unexpectedly she laughs, her habitual vacancy giving way to a gratifying sunburst, and after that things between them are subtly different. By the time he's ready to leave she's agreed to meet him for lunch on her day off, which is two days before he gets his test results and five days before his wedding. He would have preferred to take her to dinner, but for now at least, with his curfew in place, dinner is out of the question. Once his son is born he'll work toward making some changes at home. He'll lay down some ground rules and get his life back to normal. Sneaking around is not his style and no way to live. He needs to be his own man again, as he was when he lived with Jodi.

He hasn't been himself in so many ways. Like the way he's been ambushed by scenes from his childhood. His mother making doughnuts on a Saturday morning, standing over the pot of sizzling fat, frying up batch after batch while he sits at the table eating the ones that have cooled. To please his mother he eats more than he wants, keeps on eating after he's full and even when he starts to feel sick. Thinking of this brings mixed feelings, as do all his memories of his mother. The way she'd lie down beside him at bedtime and stroke his forehead till he fell asleep. The way she'd lick her thumb to wipe a speck of something off his cheek, even after he was grown. Her loving touch inflected with the smell of garlic on her hands. The way he liked it and hated it at the same time. He's annoyed that such impressions have lately been flooding his mind, as if a door has opened that was previously shut. He has no interest in these memories, which are pointless and pertain to nothing. Among his other creeping fears is the fear that he's going soft, losing his edge.

27
HER

At any given time at least a dozen conferences of interest to psychologists are going on in cities around the world. This is what immediately came to mind when Alison suggested that she leave town. In her years as a professional she has only ever attended one such event, a conference on communication that took place some years back in Geneva. She remembers how enjoyable it was, how easy to talk to people, the sense of fellowship she felt, the interesting speakers who came from all over the world, the fun of going to dinner with new people in a foreign city. She came back with renewed energy for her clients and made adjustments in the way she interacted with them, taking more notice of their body language and choice of words, echoing these back to them as a way of creating rapport.

It had long been her intention to repeat the conference experience, but somehow she never got around to it. Loyalty to Todd was part of it — who would look after him while she was gone? But that was just a surface concern; the underpinnings were undoubtedly bleaker. Possessiveness. Paranoia. A reluctance to give him more rope than he already had. All familiar sentiments, and although they mostly stayed below the level of daily awareness, they no doubt played a part in keeping her at home.

It came down to a choice between Anger Management in the historic city of Winchester in the south of England and Emotions, Stress, and Aging in sunny Jacksonville, Florida. She was more interested in anger management, which she'd never had the opportunity to study. With a conference under her belt and some additional reading, she could work with clients needing help in this area. But after checking the weather network and talking to her travel agent about price points, she opted for Emotions, Stress, and Aging, consoling herself with the prospect of palm trees and tropical breezes.

Thus it happens that she finds herself in a Jacksonville hotel room coming awake to the insistent humming of the telephone on her bedside table. The room is black, with no light showing anywhere, not even around the drapes or under the door. She rolls onto her side to look at the digital clock with its toxic green numbers. Not yet six. Sunrise at least an hour away.

Since arriving the day before yesterday she hasn't thought about why she's here or what could be going on back home. Forgetting is easy in the world of the conference, which is uncomplicated and undemanding, a world where real life gives way to endless diversions and distractions. The lecture rooms are filled with warm natural light, patio doors open onto gardens of flowering shrubs, and when she steps outside she can lift her face to the sun and catch the scent of the ocean. The most she ever has to do is sit comfortably in a padded chair and listen to interesting presentations, join the throng in the restaurant for lunch, dress for dinner on the town. She shares no history with anyone here. Her background and circumstances are off the radar. For all anyone knows she could have dropped down from outer space or materialized out of thin air.

The ringing telephone does not belong in this picture. She closes her eyes and waits for it to stop. When the room is again silent, she lets out her breath in a slow, deliberate stream that's like a sigh and wills herself back to sleep, but deep sleep is evasive now, so busy is her dreaming mind, so filled with strange and disturbing scenes — milling people, bright lights, someone running. It can't be more than a few minutes before the phone starts up again. Its low urgent sound in her dreams is someone sobbing before it fully wakes her. Blinking needlessly in the dark she gets out of bed and gropes her way to the bathroom.

Later, when she's eating breakfast in the hotel restaurant with a group of colleagues, someone approaches from behind and touches her shoulder. It's one of the conference heads, a friendly woman who has made a point of introducing herself to everyone, sometimes repeatedly.

"There's a call for you," she says. "You can take it in the lobby."

28
HIM

For the past three and a half days his mind has been churning out Ilona-shaped thoughts, and the Ilona-shaped thoughts have been forming Ilona-shaped patterns, like metal filings in a magnetic field. The three and a half days were a Friday, a Saturday, a Sunday, and a Monday morning, days when he neglected to tell Natasha that he loved her, took her shopping with bad grace, refused to help around the house, got through a twelve-pack of tall boys, and masturbated every time he took a shower. Over these few short days the unsuspecting Ilona has reached a pinnacle of erotic allure in his engorged imagination. The focus of outrageous projections, she has achieved the status of a female counterpart, his match in every way, a positive to his negative and a negative to his positive, the piece of the jigsaw that renders his life complete. Even he can discern the sick liability of his musings, but only in lucid moments, which he resolutely shakes off.

The restaurant on South Dearborn, where Ilona agreed to meet him, is intimate and stylish. He foresees the two of them locking eyes as she raises a glass to her lips, pictures her chewing on small morsels of costly flesh. She's never tasted a fresh oyster, has no notion of what a really good bottle of wine can do for a person, of this he is confident, just as he knows that, once indoctrinated, she'll become insatiable, addicted to all that he has to offer. Even as he emerges from his office and turns toward the parking lot, he swaggers. It doesn't occur to him that she could stand him up, that conceivably she already has a man in her life, that she might have seen through him, come to her senses, changed her mind. On the contrary, he has an idea that he's heading for the assignation of his life, the rendezvous that's going to turn everything around. Though she doesn't yet know it, Ilona is the chosen one, the one who will save him from the mess that he's so haplessly fallen into. Ilona — skinny, undiscovered, wary like a cat, credulous like a child, with little sense of her own beauty and power — is the answer to all his problems. He jingles his car keys and laughs out loud, expelling a cloud of mist into the wintry air. Already he's counting down the minutes, making of his actions a deliberate choreography. He slides into his car and starts the engine, flicks on his wipers and waits for them to clear away the frost, drives to the curb, and curses the oncoming traffic. Checks his teeth in the rearview mirror. Puts on his right blinker. Pops a lozenge into his mouth.

He's feeling remarkably well, better than he has in weeks. His lesion has all but disappeared, the itching attacks have subsided, and he's worrying less about his test results. He was really frightened at first, beside himself for a day or two, but now he's regained his composure. Gunning the engine he hits the power knob on the radio and catches the opening bars of "Unchained Melody." There's no resisting the sea of longing invoked by the plaintive music and Bobby Hatfield's fluid tenor. He thinks of a girl he knew in high school, revisits the smell of her hair, the citronella tang of the cheap gel that drove him wild. Maybe it's her he longs for; who's to say? He's aware of boundaries blurring and fading, the boundaries that separate past and present, those that distinguish Ilona from Natasha from Jodi from the girl in high school. And then the song ends and he's back in his car driving north toward Roosevelt.

He sticks with the curbside lane and brakes for a stoplight. The car just ahead is a Ferrari, streamlined and low to the ground, exciting and seductive. He's gripped by a fervent desire to own the very car, an ardent wish to be magically transported to its driver's seat, to take his place behind its wheel. His Porsche — which he has always doted on — strikes him as conservative, sedate, even priggish, the choice of a man who has lost his passion. How could this have happened? When did he change?

It's nearly time now. Only seconds are left. If only he knew it he wouldn't waste them on resolutions that can never come to pass — the notion of trading in his car, disposing of deadwood, getting himself free. He believed that Natasha had made him young again, but now he understands. The women who start to think they own you and the obligations that can break a man. You have to keep moving in life. You have to move fast so they can't pin you down.

When the first impact comes he thinks it's a rock. Someone has thrown a rock through his driver's-side window. The sound explodes in his left ear, and fragments of glass spray the side of his face.

"What the fuck," he says aloud.

He touches his cheek as he turns his head to look. Seeing the small round hole with its halo of shattered glass, he thinks he must have been shot, though he feels no pain. His eyes telescope and the car idling beside him at the traffic light blazes into his field of vision. He registers the open window, the head in the woolen cap, the penetrating gaze, the flare of the gun. He doesn't know the man, but no questions arise in his mind.

It isn't true what they're going to say — that he didn't see it coming, never knew what hit him. Still, it happens very fast. Delinquent images burst on his mental screen; this is all the dying he has time for. Paradoxically, in the heightened moment when his unborn son should matter most, the child he doesn't know and will never meet means less to him than all the others. His doting mother and even his aberrant father. Cliff and Harry, his best buddies. Natasha, who appears to him as a child, holding her daddy's hand; Natasha and Dean, both of them survivors. Even more compelling is the image of Ilona waiting at the restaurant, her disappointment building by the minute, with no one to save her from it. And Jodi as she was on the day he came home from the country, prone and splayed under the open sky. Beautiful, singular Jodi. If he had the choice to stay he would do it for her. But there are no choices left to him now. Time hangs suspended, and yet it's about to end. Death should be a seduction, not a rape. Given one more minute he could do so much. Even the guilty are allowed to make a phone call, send a message. How alive he feels, how brightly he shines, like a lit fuse, a firecracker about to go off. What he wouldn't give for a minute more, just one ordinary minute tacked crudely onto the end of his life.

■ ■ ■ ■

PART TWO:
HER

■ ■ ■ ■

"This is Jodi Brett," she says, holding the phone as if it were a dead rodent.

The voice of a despot comes back at her, as pronounced and menacing as if it were booming from a speaker in the lobby. He's calling from the police, he says. He's afraid he has bad news. He wonders if she's sitting down.

In fact, she is standing primly upright, spine erect, feet together, hips at a precise right angle to the reception desk, staring sightlessly into the glare of the hotel's glass entrance doors. She doesn't see what difference it makes if she is sitting or standing and feels impatient with the show of concern. If he cared about her welfare as he pretends, he wouldn't have been calling her at all hours of the night, ruining her sleep.

She makes an attempt to cut through his equivocation. "I'm in the middle of breakfast. What is it you have to say to me?"

Still he won't come to the point. "I understand you're attending a conference down there." His voice is thick and polished. She can see the words rolling off his tongue, each one a fat slug that crawls into her ear.

"Yes," she says. "Is that a problem?"

"Ms. Brett," he says. "It's of the utmost urgency that you return home at once."

Now comes the sound of Todd's name, large and soft as it leaves his slurry lips, and now a vertiginous image of milk pouring out of a bucket, an image that conveys nothing but is nonetheless dense with nausea and a reeling sensation. By the time her eyelids flutter open, her head is resting on a cushion, and a crowd of faces bobs above her. She feels lost and bewildered as a great many mouths cluck and murmur with concern. But when she's taken by the arms and brought to standing, she quickly comes to her senses, and once again she is face-to-face with the crushing facts. Fact number one: Todd is dead. Which she struggles to assimilate even as she realizes that, fact number two: Her guilt is so transparent that the Chicago police have already hunted her down. There is little doubt in her mind that when she steps off the plane at O'Hare the force will be there waiting for her. She'll be placed under arrest, possibly handcuffed, and taken away to a lockup in some godforsaken sector of the city, wherever it is they have jails.

Given these certainties, she finds it surprising that she doesn't feel inclined to run. Rent a car, drive away, find a border to cross, fade into anonymity. She has the instincts of a homing pigeon. Even though nothing but danger awaits her, she can't abandon all that she knows and loves. At most she'd like to wait a few days, enjoy another glass of wine at the restaurant on the beach, savor the tropical heat and the scented air for a while longer. This is a prospect that greatly appeals to her, but it won't come to pass. They would only plague her with phone calls, or worse, send someone to escort her home.

After reassuring the detective, who's been waiting on the line, and after seeking out the conference head to say there's been a death in the family, and after the conference head has extended condolences and promised to look into a partial refund, Jodi goes to her room to reschedule her flight, forewarn the pet sitter, and pack her things.

As the plane touches down, drifting snowflakes catch the lights on the runway and animate the night sky. She's still in the halter dress and wedge sandals that she put on in the distant morning, but she's had the foresight to carry a trench coat with her. Over the course of the flight she's downed her allotment of vodka tonics, and her mood has cycled silently through sorrow, despair, and defiance. Now, stepping onto the gangway, pulling her valise behind her, she clings to a fragile bravado. She was not detained while the other passengers disembarked; no men in uniform have so far made an appearance. She understands that it's just a matter of time, but this at least is going better than expected, and after picking up her luggage without incident, a breath of hope stirs faintly in the smog of her misery.

Wearing her coat but with legs still bare she exits the airport into the frigid night and joins the lineup for a taxi. The drive home is uneventful. She enters her building and crosses the lobby, rides the elevator to her floor, takes her key out of her purse. There's a single sharp bark from behind the closed door, and then she's assaulted by eighty pounds of undiluted joy. The pet sitter, on the other hand, takes one look at her and bursts into tears, distraught over news of the tragedy. She pays the girl and sends her on her way. It feels good to be safely home, and she's encouraged by her luck.

With the improvement in her spirits her mind becomes more lucid. She begins to grasp that the failure of the police to waylay her can only mean that her situation is not as dire as she supposed, that getting her home from the conference was merely routine, a matter of procedure. She celebrates with a fresh vodka tonic and feels like eating for the first time since breakfast. The sitter has left some deli meat in the fridge and she uses it to make herself a sandwich, adding pickles and hot mustard. With food in her system her mood levels out. She changes into jeans and brews a pot of coffee. She finds herself intensely curious about the manner of Todd's death. Even on the plane she couldn't stop conjecturing, running the phone call through her mind, trying to remember the exact words the policeman used to break the news. *There's been a death . . . there's been a homicide . . . foul play is involved . . . I'm sorry to inform you that foul play is involved . . . I'm afraid there's no doubt . . . the evidence leaves no doubt.* There was nothing specific, nothing that can help resolve her fever of speculation. But as she moves around the apartment setting things aright, she spies this morning's *Tribune* on the coffee table.

The story is bigger than she anticipated,

starting on the front page and flowing over to an inside spread. She didn't foresee the murder of a small-time property developer as being of any special interest to the public at large, but reporters are using it to get on their hobbyhorses, spinning out copy about the drug trade and the firearm crisis. There's a lot of madcap speculation — for instance, that the killing was an opportunistic attack by gun-happy, amphetamine-crazed teen-agers. Another theory involves the mob. Conjectures aside, the facts of the case are plainly stated.

A man was gunned down in his car yesterday afternoon as he waited at a stoplight in Chicago's South Loop. The victim has been identified as Todd Jeremy Gilbert, 46, a local businessman. He was shot in the head at approximately 12:45 PM at the corner of Michigan and Roosevelt. According to eyewitnesses, a vehicle pulled up beside him and one or more gunmen opened fire. Police are seeking a description of the vehicle in question. After the shooting took place, the victim's car rolled into the intersection, bumped against a curb, and came to a stop. The driver was found slumped over the wheel. No bystanders were harmed.

She thinks about the lunch-hour traffic, the seclusion afforded by the two cars, the factors that remain as question marks. "One or more gunmen," the article says. Even their number is a point of speculation. But there would have been two men, one to drive and one to shoot, and no more because a third would have been superfluous, and there was only so much money to go around. Whether or not one of them was Renny, she can't say. She has the impression that Renny keeps his hands clean, and Alison spoke of recruits. Either way her mental image of the men is vague. She has never met Renny, has never even seen his picture.

She is struck by the timing at play. A car is idling at a stoplight and shots are fired from its window. In spite of the public setting — a major intersection during the lunch-hour rush — the car disappears before anyone can register what's happened. This is evident because, otherwise, the police would have a description of it. She thinks about it. The prompt escape could only come about if the light turned green precisely as the killing took place. They must have waited for it. With the seconds fleeing by and their weapon at the ready, they waited for the very instant when the light would turn and they could take off across the intersection.

She needs to walk through it step by step, to imaginatively reconstruct the phenomenal, shattering event that she is still unable to accept. She pictures him leaving the office, walking to the parking lot, getting into the Porsche, and heading north on Michigan. He's in the right-hand lane when he stops at the light. He has to be in the right-hand lane because the shooter would be in the passenger seat of the car adjacent. Close to his mark and sure of his aim. Not taking any chances.

Let's say that Todd and the perpetrators, idling side by side, are first in line at the traffic light. Todd is oblivious. He has no inkling that he's become a mark, no clue that he's in danger. The two men, meanwhile, do not have an exact plan. They're really just ad-libbing, waiting for the auspicious moment, the ripe opportunity. If necessary, they'll get out of their car and stalk their prey on foot, but in the best-case scenario it won't come down to that. The sooner they get this over and done with, the sooner they can go back home and collect their pay.

It's by sheer chance, a chance determined solely by the flow of traffic, that he is caught by the red light, and it's also by chance that the spot next to him becomes vacant. Once in place beside him, they see their opportunity. Taking stock, they identify the need for an escape route. As soon as the deed is done they will have to move, and so they watch and they wait. They watch the traffic and the pedestrians crossing in front of them and wait for the flow to subside. They watch the green light directing the flow and wait for it to change to orange. They watch the left-turning cars move into the intersection, and still they wait, like the half-mad, risk-taking mercenaries they are. Finally, the one who is not driving, the designated shooter, takes aim, extending his weapon through the open passenger window.

How many shots did he fire? The news story doesn't specify, but the wording of it, the notion that "one or more gunmen opened fire," implies a volley. Did the first of the bullets hit home? Or did he have a moment to realize his peril, consider what was happening and why? She finds now that she wants very much for him to have seen it coming. This is her wish. That he registered the truth, understood it as her doing, saw that he'd brought it on himself. And yet she doubts that he would think of her because as far as he knew it wasn't in her nature to cross him. The Jodi he held in his heart was not someone who could do this.

Uncharacteristically, she gets ready for bed without setting the house straight first. Her dishes are in the sink unwashed, her suitcase in the foyer unopened. Sleep is a default mode brought on by her spent circuitry, but once the first layer of exhaustion has been sloughed off she finds herself back on the surface with her eyes open. Ambient light reveals the dark shapes of furniture and the orientation of windows and doors, but these fail to coalesce into anything she can recognize. The day, the place, the circumstances of her life all evade her, as if her mind were a glass of water that's been poured out. She waits, and when her faculties return she identifies the breach as a complication of jet lag, compounded by her wish that she could go back in time and reconsider her choices.

The sense of security and optimism she felt after reading the article in the paper — neither the car nor the perpetrators had been identified — is now displaced by the belated realization that being the victim's ex-spouse automatically makes her the prime suspect, and that it will only be worse if she's named in the will. The fact that this did not occur to her before — while she was plotting and scheming with Alison, hawking her household goods, fleeing to the tropics — she finds astonishing. It's as if she's been in some kind of trance, a self-induced hypnotic state, a stupor of wishful thinking. She panicked when the call came through in Florida, but that was nothing. *That* you could sleep off or drown in drink. *This,* what she feels now, is vicious and barbed, like circulation returning to dead limbs, like someone has shaken her up and made her blood fizz.

Todd was a child in so many ways, in Freudian terms a case of arrested psycho-sexual development, a phallus-fixated five-year-old preoccupied with sexual ascendancy, still in love with his mother, displacing his desire onto all women, the embodiment of the Oedipus complex. Freud has never inspired her, but he really knew how to crucify a person. Let's just say that Todd was not one for self-reflection and did not typically factor his own shortcomings into his worldview. Though in all fairness he also overlooked what was indefensible in others. He was a forgiving man. But that in no way absolves him. She would like to believe that in death he'll be forced to face up to things, that even now he's reflecting on his wrongdoings, whether in purgatory or elsewhere. But she can't dismiss the feeling that he has somehow managed to escape, has finagled things so he gets off scot-free, like always.

When the knock comes in the morning she's drinking coffee and reading the paper. Today's story, downsized to a single column, provides no new information. Still damp from her shower, wearing a terry robe and white cotton socks, she's thinking that once she's finished her coffee, which she hopes will take care of her headache, she'll go back to bed and catch up on the sleep she missed last night while lying awake with her mind racing. There are no clients due and she has no obligations since according to her schedule she's still in Florida. She doesn't know who's knocking, but it has to be the doorman or one of her neighbors. Anyone else would have to buzz her from the lobby. Or so she assumes, forgetting that policemen have special privileges and go where they please.

The detective, in his mid to late thirties, is a stocky man with a square face and eyes the color of soil, topped by eyebrows like dashes, straight and true. Under his coat, which is hanging open, he's wearing a brown suit, a light blue shirt, and a tie with a bold, uncomplicated diagonal stripe. Even before she takes note of his wedding band she has him pegged as a family man — a man with three or four children under the age of twelve and a wife who likes the security he doubtless provides.

"Miss Jodi Brett?" he asks.

She nods.

He takes out his wallet, flips it open, and holds it at eye level so she can see his ID.

"Detective Sergeant John Skinner. Mind if I come in?"

She stands aside and he steps into the foyer, closing the door behind him.

"Sorry to intrude at such an early hour," he says. A reference to her bathrobe. "If I may, I'd like to offer my condolences. I'm aware of how deeply affected you were when we gave you the news. It's unfortunate that it had to happen that way — over the phone, I mean. We'd been in touch with the Jacksonville force, but there was some kind of mix-up."

"Was it you I spoke to?" she asks.

"No, ma'am. That was Constable Davey. But he did inform me as to your considerable distress."

She has the fleeting, wily thought that fainting the way she did has garnered her some sympathy and may conceivably be the reason for this excessive politeness. She invites him in and leads the way to the living room, which at the moment is spectacularly lit by the morning sun. Gravitating to the view, he says, "You must get a lot of enjoyment out of this."

"We do," she says. "Or we did." She falters and then collects herself. "I love the view and so did Todd. It's pretty much the reason we took this place, which isn't as big as some we were —" She lets the sentence drop, suddenly embarrassed by her privilege, thinking of the poky little house that would be all he could afford on his policeman's salary, especially with a family of five or six.

"Can I offer you coffee?" she asks.

"Well now. If it wouldn't be too much bother."

"No bother. I have some made."

"Black will be fine," he says.

When she's back with a mug of coffee she hands it to him and excuses herself. "If you'll give me a minute, I'll just get into some clothes."

Escaping into the bedroom gives her a brief but much-needed respite. Her hands are clammy; her hairline is damp; she feels grubby in spite of having showered. If she had stopped to imagine a visit from the police it would have been nothing like this. To begin with there would have been two of them — don't they normally travel in pairs? — and they would have been hard on her case, capitalizing on her state of undress to keep her off balance, using the conversational ball as a weapon. That, at least, would have drawn out her mettle and roused her defenses. Whereas this — a lone detective with an overly diffident manner — what can it mean?

She returns to the living room in pressed trousers and a fresh shirt. She's applied some color to her cheeks and tamed back her hair. The detective, who is standing at the window looking out, turns when she enters. She has made no sound, but he's caught her in his peripheral vision. They both sit down, her on the sofa, him on a facing wing chair.

"I know the news has come as a blow," he begins. "In a perfect world we would give you time to recover before barging in on you, but we need to jump on this without delay. We have very little to go on, and with every hour that passes the trail gets colder. I'm sure you can appreciate what we're up against."

He raises his hands, palms up, a plea for

363

understanding.

"Without knowing it yourself," he continues, "you may have information that will help us in our investigation. Details of the victim's lifestyle, an account of his movements in the days and weeks leading up to the crime. These can be critical in piecing together what actually happened. Something he said or did, which you may have ignored at the time, could turn out to be an important piece of the puzzle. I can't emphasize enough how valuable you could be in helping us solve this case. You are extremely important to us, and I want you to think of yourself in just that way."

She finds, to her dismay, that she can't look him in the eye. Her guilt must be utterly transparent to a man like this, a stalwart man with a big backlog of experience. Why else would he torment her with all this guff about her value and importance?

"I'm sorry but I've forgotten your name," she says.

He repeats his name — Detective Sergeant Skinner — but even as he says it she's forgetting it again, still thinking of him as the family man.

"About this business of prying into your affairs," he says. "Believe me, I wish there were another way. Someone dies, you barely have time to register the fact, and here we are grilling you, asking you to dredge up memories that can only be painful to you at such a time."

His voice has a quiet, lilting quality that gets on her nerves. He's poised, complacent, sure of himself, a cat grooming his prey. She looks at his squared-off fingers with their clean nails, at the virtuous stripe of his tie, at the lobes of his ears, which curve deftly into the sides of his head with no superfluous flap.

"This part of the job is hard on everyone," he says. "We don't like it any more than you do. We try to go as easy as we can, but people are apt to take offense, and you really can't blame them."

She feels hot and cold at the same time: head hot, extremities cold. Any second now she's going to burst out laughing. She gets up from the sofa and rummages in the credenza for the pack of Marlboros that she knows is there. She doesn't smoke, but right now it seems like a good idea.

"Can I offer you one?" she asks the family man, holding out the package.

He declines. She finds a book of matches and lights one for herself. She last smoked a cigarette twenty or more years ago, when she was still in school, but she inhales deeply nonetheless. Not surprisingly the room spins. She waits it out and then returns to her seat, cigarette in one hand and in the other her souvenir ashtray from Mont St. Michel, which she keeps because it's cheerful.

"About your relationship with the deceased," he is saying through the haze of smoke. "If you would just clear that up for me."

She wants to tell him the truth, that the deceased was someone she barely knew — or not the man she thought he was, anyway. She says instead that she and he had lived together for twenty years. He pounces on this and bleeds it of every conceivable drop of suggestion, asking her why they never married, whether or not it mattered to her, how she felt about him leaving, if she'd seen it coming. He's ghoulishly curious about their failure to produce any children; in his world it has to mean something. He wants to know if she's acquainted with Todd's fiancée, the woman he was living with at the time of his death. When she thinks he's come to the end he circles back and begins again. What circumstances led to his departure? Did she subsequently have any contact with him? Has she consulted a lawyer? Does she know that at the time of his death he was a father-to-be?

On and on he goes, working his way through ever more intrusive questions, leaning forward in his chair now, grave and intent. He learns about her practice, that she works part-time from home, that she went to Florida to attend a conference. "It's too bad, ma'am, that you had to come all the way back from Florida," he says. "You manage to escape from the cold, and then something like this has to happen. What kind of conference was it? — if you don't mind my asking."

She sucks on the stub of her cigarette, squinting against the smoke, eyes watering. The head rush brought on by the first intake of nicotine and carbon monoxide has been replaced now by a tightening in her chest. "It was a conference on stress and aging," she says. "For mental-health professionals."

"Was there a special reason for you to be there?" he asks. "Were you invited to speak, for instance?"

"I wasn't a speaker," she says.

"Do you attend such events on a regular basis?"

"Not on a *regular* basis."

"How often then?"

"I don't know. When something comes up that's important to my work."

"When did you last attend a conference, prior to the one in Florida?"

"I'd have to think about that."

"Take your time."

"There was a conference in Geneva, oh, maybe two or three years ago. I guess it's been a while." In spite of herself she laughs apologetically.

"In what way was the conference in Geneva important to your work?"

"The theme was communication. That's a key area for any counseling psychologist."

"So the last conference you attended, prior to the one in Florida, was on communication, and it took place in Geneva either two or three years ago. Have I got that right?"

"It could have been four years ago."

"So then. Can we say four years?"

She knows what he's getting at. That she happened to be out of town at a conference on this particular occasion is a little too convenient, a little too pat. In spite of the story in the paper with its angle on drug-crazed teens and organized crime, this detective knows exactly what he's dealing with, and the big tip-off is her airtight, impregnable alibi, which is now working against her and which in any case she didn't need because no one was going to suspect her of taking part in a drive-by shooting. That it was a hired kill would be obvious to a ten-year-old.

"Oh hell, how should I know?" she snaps. "Maybe it was *five* years ago. How can you expect me to remember something like that at a time like this?"

"Now, ma'am, try to calm yourself," he says in his unperturbed way. "I know how difficult this must be for you, but as I said before, it sometimes happens that a seemingly trivial piece of information turns out to be an important clue. Nothing can be neglected. I'm sorry to put you through this, I truly am, but getting the case wrapped up is in your best interests too."

She finds the room so airless and stifling that she fears she might keel over. She thinks of getting up to open a window but instead takes a copy of *Architectural Digest* from the stack of magazines on the coffee table and uses it to fan herself. Meanwhile, the detective moves on to ever more forward questions. *What is your income? What was the income of the deceased? Did he give you any money after he left? What is the total worth of his estate? Are you familiar with the terms of his will?* And still he's not done. Not until he's asked about her parents and her friends and taken down their names.

But not Alison's name. This she has with-
held.

When he gets to his feet at last, he turns
once again to the view and comments on
the cloud formation over the lake. "Cirro-
stratus," he says. "Snow on the way."

She looks out at the white haze. Now he
wants to linger and talk about the weather.
Next he'll invite himself to lunch. She
moves deliberately toward the foyer, leaving
him little choice but to follow. On his way
out the door he hands her his card and says,
"Call me for any reason. As I said, we're
counting on your help. Crimes get solved
because people tell us things. Call me even
if you think it's not important. Let me
decide. You have my number right here."

She keeps an eye on the obituary pages of
the *Tribune* and in due course comes across
the announcement. It's brief, just a few
lines, ending with the particulars of the
funeral. There's nothing about the way he
died, and she, Jodi, is not mentioned. Natasha, who no doubt wrote the piece, has
positioned herself and her fetus as the chief
mourners. "Todd Jeremy Gilbert, 46, entrepreneur, is survived by his loving wife-to-be
and their unborn son." Jodi's own twenty
years with him, her care and attention, devo-

tion and forbearance, have not qualified for the public record, while he himself is dismissed in his own obituary as an "entrepreneur." Natasha must know his story: that he rose from humble beginnings, met with success under his own steam and through his own mettle. Todd was the ultimate self-made man. If there's a time and place to give him credit, surely this is it.

Whether or not she will attend the funeral is yet to be decided. She's been keeping her clients at bay, sleeping a lot, and mostly staying home. Maybe during her period of confinement she got used to not going out, and maybe, too, she needs a chance to catch up with herself. She's having memory lapses, forgetting for long moments at a time that he ever left her. Even his death is not firmly established in her mind. Parts of her seem unaware of it — or maybe just refuse to believe it. On one occasion, as she navigates the mists between waking and sleeping, she makes up her mind to call him and ask him outright if he's dead or alive. "Tell me the truth," she means to say. "I need to know."

More than once she dreams that he's come back to life. For the most part it's all very prosaic. They're sitting down to dinner and she says, "I thought you were dead," and he says, "I was dead but I'm not any-more." Or she's riding the elevator with a stranger and the stranger turns out to be him. And always there's a sense of relief. Something was horribly wrong, but now all is well and life can return to normal. It's this intermittent backsliding that finally makes up her mind about the funeral. Although she's apprehensive about appear-ing in public as the discarded wife and as much as she'd like to preserve her pride, she needs to have closure. She needs to teach herself that he's dead.

His death might be easier to swallow if it hadn't been so grisly. The way it happened has affected her deeply. When her friends call she talks to them about it obsessively — the obscene public execution — and as time goes on her fascination with the particulars tends to grow rather than abate. She feels compelled to eviscerate every sordid detail, never tires of poking and prodding the tat-tered corpse. Her feeling is that it should add up to more than it does. It should amount to something meaningful, some unholy grail or inverted power that she can use to shield herself, but the scandalous facts remain inert and somehow negligible as compared with the overriding reality of his absence. Unable to share the truth of her situation she's forced to fall back on conventional statements such as, "I can't believe it happened" and "It doesn't seem possible."

The family man has been to see her parents, has been plying them with questions. She takes comfort in their proprietary outrage, their annoyance that her honesty and decency should be in doubt, their objection to picking through the details of her private life. As always, her parents talk to her simultaneously, her father upstairs in the bedroom, her mother on the kitchen extension. They know of course what Todd was up to before he died and don't quite say that he had it coming, but clearly that's what's on their minds. She finds it endearing that they've done this about-face on her behalf, setting themselves so thoroughly against him.

The family man has also been visiting her friends, and they too are on her side.

Corinne says, "Most murders are committed by someone the victim knew, and ninety percent of the time it's the spouse or the ex, so they *have* to check up on you. Don't worry, it's just routine."

Ellen says, "I'm sure you wanted to kill him and God knows you *ought* to have killed him. Look at it this way: Somebody else did it for you."

June says, "I told the detective that you didn't do it."

The friend she most wants to speak to is Alison, but Alison is not returning her calls. She doesn't know quite what to make of this. There's no reason she can think of why Alison would be on the outs with her. It can't be a money issue: Alison has her money. She wasn't sure about handing over the full payment in advance, but Alison promised to dole it out to Renny in fitting installments. "No worries," she said. "I'll give him a down payment of half, or maybe not even — enough to enlist his recruits — and the balance when he gets the job done." Maybe Alison is just being cautious. It could be that she wants to avoid contact till things settle down. But if that's the case she could have said so in the first place.

The day before the funeral she drives to Oak Street, which features valet parking and the best shops, to look for a black skirt suit, a black overcoat, and a black hat. She knows that dressing in black for a funeral is not obligatory, but she wants to go this extra distance, let people know what kind of person she is, show them that in spite of Todd's latest indiscretion she has enough class to see him off with proper respect. When she's back home unwrapping her parcels, a call comes in from Cliff York.

"How are you holding up?" he asks.

The call is unexpected. Cliff was a fixture in Todd's life, but it was rare for her to see him or hear from him. It occurs to her now that Todd's death must be quite a blow to Cliff.

"I'm doing okay," she says. "I guess this is bad for you, too."

"It's just kind of unbelievable," he says. "A lot of us are taking it pretty hard."

By "a lot of us" she knows he means the construction crew, which includes men who share years of history with Cliff and Todd both.

"I know," she says. "It doesn't seem possible."

"I guess we're all still in shock," he says. "But listen, I wanted to check in with you about the funeral. I hope you're planning to come, and I know some of the guys are thinking about you, and — well, if I could just say something on Todd's behalf, he made some mistakes and did some stupid things, got himself into a mess of trouble, and I don't want to make excuses for him, but the way it happened, things just kind of spun out of control. He was up to his neck before he knew what hit him. I hope you don't think it's out of line for me to say so, but he spoke very highly of you right to the end. He really did, you know. I think he felt kind of lost, that things had gotten away from him. I think if he'd seen a chance to get back with you and get things back to normal, he would have jumped at it."

As Cliff is saying this she's thinking about the eviction letter. Cliff probably doesn't know about that. Why would Todd tell him what's really going on when partial truths could get him sympathy? But anyway it's nice of Cliff to call. He really just wants her to know that he's on her side, she can see that, and she's grateful for the effort he's making.

"I'm glad you called, Cliff," she says. "I *am* planning to be at the funeral, so I guess I'll see you there."

But Cliff has something else on his mind. He wants to talk business.

"I don't like to add to your burden, but I just want to say that the timing couldn't be worse. The apartment house — another couple of weeks and it would have been done. It's that close. And now the work has stopped, and I hate to think how long it'll be on hold if we don't do something about it. So I was thinking that — maybe after the funeral — you wouldn't mind getting together. We could talk it over, look at some of the details, deal with the outstanding accounts, maybe find a way to carry on."

She understands that this is the real reason for Cliff's call. Not that he didn't mean everything he said, but uppermost in his mind is that Todd owes him money and the project is stalled.

"I wish I could help," she says, "but I'm in much the same position as you are. Maybe you should talk to Natasha."

He's silent for a couple of beats, but then he comes back strong. "Todd didn't write you out of his will if that's what you're thinking. He meant to provide for Natasha and the baby, of course, but he was going to wait until after the wedding. He thought it made more sense, the way the law works. But no. You're safe there. As far as that goes, Natasha is out of the picture."

The funeral takes place at the Montrose Cemetery and Crematorium on the northwest side. June and Corinne have teamed up as Jodi's escorts. When they buzz her from the lobby she's standing in front of the foyer mirror assessing the effect of her jet-black pillbox hat. Embellished with nothing but a puff of black netting, the hat is discreet — very funereal, very widow, very Jackie Kennedy. She's wearing no makeup to speak of and her bloodless, waxy complexion for once appears fitting and seemly.

She, June, and Corinne enter the chapel together, and heads turn. They seat themselves midway up the aisle. The coffin, resting on a plinth by the altar, is mercifully closed. She may be struggling to accept the fact that he's dead, but she has no interest in seeing the evidence.

Sheltered between her two friends, she's feeling pleased that she decided to come, pleased that the chapel is filling up, pleased on Todd's behalf that people are gathering in force to say their good-byes. The crowd, the setting, the trappings remind her of every funeral she's ever attended, and she takes comfort in the congruity: the people coming together for a solemn common purpose, the pensive yet theatrical atmosphere, the flowers in their stiff arrangements, the mawkish scent of old wood, the daylight straining through colored glass, the dank chill, the self-important rustling of the crowd, and the hush that falls as the pastor steps up to the pulpit. Even the sermon is familiar, not tailored in any meaningful way to the identity of the deceased. Once dead we're all alike, recruited into a common human denominator presided over by a scriptural template.

Because death is the end of troubles, trials, pain, sorrow, and fear.

Then shall the dust return to the earth as it was and the spirit shall return unto God who gave it.

Naked came I out of my mother's womb and naked shall I return thither. The Lord gave, and the Lord hath taken away. Blessed be the name of the Lord.

She is less gratified when the sermon veers toward Todd's position as bridegroom and father-to-be, the all-important provider snatched away on the eve of matrimony. But the preacher has scant comfort to offer the bereaved bride.

In all things give thanks. Gratitude looks beneath the surface. It is a deep and abiding acknowledgment that goodness exists, even behind the worst that life brings.

The exodus when the service is over happens according to protocol, with the front rows of occupants peeling off first, followed by subsequent rows in stately, sober procession. Jodi has never encountered the adult edition of Natasha, but the girl grown up is not hard to spot as she moves past with chin raised and eyes averted. Aside from being taller and out of pigtails she looks much the same; her features had that swollen, sensual cast even in childhood. She's attended by a cluster of friends, girls of her own age who surround her protectively. There's no sign of Dean, not that Jodi was expecting to see him.

The corpse remains where it is, soon to be taken away and cremated. Outside, people are milling around exchanging greetings. Everyone feels the relief of the bracing air, the social crush, and the imminent escape to the parking lot. Harry LeGroot stands before her and with no trace of embarrassment offers his condolences. Others line up behind him. Todd's real-estate agent, a small man who talks too fast. Cliff and Heather York, Cliff looking dapper in his double-breasted suit. Various tradesmen who know her as Todd's wife. All of them say how terrible it is and how sorry they are. Stephanie appears, flanked by tenants, asking what will happen to the office building. She says there are bills to be paid, that she isn't authorized to sign checks. She wonders if she ought to stay on and try to deal with things. She's worried about her pay.

All this solicitation does Jodi good. It was the right decision to come here and show her face. There's a sense that something fitting and proper is happening. Through Todd's death her rightful position as his wife and heir has been restored. Embracing her newfound authority, the authority bestowed on her by the crowd and the occasion, she tells Stephanie that she will look into matters and get back to her. Jodi is grateful to Stephanie for tipping her off about the canceled credit cards, sparing her the indignity of finding herself in a shop unable to pay for her purchases. Stephanie didn't need to stick her neck out like that.

The postmortem takes place on the way home in the car. Corinne kicks it off by saying that Todd would have been pleased with the turnout. "The place was packed. There were even people standing at the back."

"A lot of people I didn't recognize," says Jodi. "Probably guys he's worked with. Maybe a few nosy parkers who read about it in the paper."

"Some of it must have been family," says June.

"Todd didn't have any family," says Jodi.

"None at all?"

"Maybe a cousin or two somewhere. No one he knew."

"What about *your* family?"

"I persuaded them not to come. It wasn't that hard."

"Do you think Natasha made the arrangements?" asks Corinne.

"Had to be Natasha. It was all a bit tawdry if you ask me. I was kind of embarrassed for Todd."

"What was wrong with it?"

"It was obviously done on the cheap. You know. She had a closed coffin so she wouldn't have to pay for embalming. Opted for cremation to save money on the coffin. Todd didn't want to be cremated; he wanted to be buried. He might have liked a proper Catholic mass as well."

"I didn't know Todd was a Catholic," says June.

"He wasn't a *practicing* Catholic. But he was *raised* Catholic."

"I guess the coffin was a rental job," says Corinne. "I think that's how it's done for cremations."

"It was definitely a rental job," says Jodi.

"I wonder if he was there," says June. "You know how they say that people show up at their own funeral. Drift around the room to check attendance and listen to what's being said about them."

"He would have been desperate to upgrade it," says Jodi.

"I guess Natasha will get the ashes," says Corinne.

"She's welcome to them," says Jodi.

"Did you speak to her at all?"

"No. Thankfully. She kept her distance."

"She knew enough to steer clear of you."

"What could she possibly have to say to me now that she has nothing to gloat about?"

"It's great that things worked out in your favor," says Corinne. "As far as the will goes, I mean. I'm so happy for you, Jodi. After all you've been through, you really deserve this."

"God works in mysterious ways," says June.

After the funeral, life picks up its normal rhythms. She's back to her morning dog walks, her workouts, her clients, and dinner with friends. But her habitual poise and self-assurance are gone. She no longer inhabits her world with any degree of composure, and over the passing days she comes to feel appalled by what she's gone and done, unable to grasp how it could have happened. Every morning when she wakes up there's a time delay before she remembers, a peaceful second or two before it hits her, and it always hits her in the same way: like a news flash. Time passes but the facts refuse to settle and recede.

She feels that in killing him off she killed off parts of herself as well. But at heart she knows that those parts perished long ago — the parts that were guileless and trusting, whole-hearted and devout. Places where life once flowed, having lost their blood supply, became dead spots in her psychic tissue, succumbed to a form of necrosis that also invaded the thing that was neither her nor him but the ground between them, the relationship itself. You'd think that she, a psychologist, would have put a stop to it, found a way to save herself, to save the two of them, but the process was subtle, insidious, all but imperceptible. It happened the way your face changes as you age: Every day you look in the mirror and every day you fail to notice the difference.

She never saw the point in fighting with a man who was not going to reform. Acceptance is supposed to be a good thing — *Grant me the serenity to accept the things I cannot change.* Also compromise, as every couples therapist will tell you. But the cost was high — the damping of expectation, the dwindling of spirit, the resignation that comes to replace enthusiasm, the cynicism that supplants hope. The moldering that goes unnoticed and unchecked.

There are practical problems, too. For one

thing she must now provide for herself entirely, taking up the slack where income is concerned. Her practice generates enough to cover household costs, and for everything else she can continue to sell off her trinkets, but sooner or later she'll run out of trinkets and the bills will overtake her. She may be Todd's acknowledged heir, but she is far from home free. As much as she would like to, she can't shake the feeling that the walls are closing in on her. The family man is hard at work looking for evidence that will bring her down, talking to everyone she knows, pursuing her like a well-trained bloodhound. Her friends have been calling to tell her as much. Like her, they find him unnervingly methodical, perversely polite. June, Corinne, and Ellen agree on this. There's been no word from Alison, but this doesn't mean that Alison has been over-looked. The family man has ways of finding things out. He even showed up at the funeral; she noticed him after the service, standing alone at the edge of the crowd. He smiled when he caught her eye, just to let her know that he hadn't forgotten her, that he was watching her, that he'd be back to see her with more questions or the same questions. In case she thought she was off the hook.

Remembering her promise to Stephanie she calls Harry LeGroot to ask for details of Todd's estate. He suggests they meet for lunch. She doesn't look forward to it, but once they're seated at Blackie's he begins the process of winning her over. He's sorry about the eviction letter; he had no choice but to follow his client's instructions. He understands that Todd was not an easy man to live with. He, Harry, was forever urging Todd to settle down and spend more time at home. Philandering is for men with ugly wives or boring relationships, whereas Jodi is beautiful and accomplished. There was no need for Todd to carry on the way he did. He had a wild streak that couldn't be tempered. Todd was a maverick, a dissident, a man in pursuit of an illusive and ill-defined ideal. Whatever he managed to achieve or attain or accumulate was never going to be enough.

This is Harry talking and Jodi gradually surrenders. Harry is charming, persuasive, and knowledgeable. His twin specialties are real estate and family law, two areas where she greatly needs assistance. Harry is not only on her side, he's optimistic about her prospects. Still, she needs to get ready for a battle. Although she is named in the will as executor and sole beneficiary, and although the will is legal and proper, Natasha Kovacs will doubtless stake a claim on behalf of herself and her unborn child. She will argue that the deceased meant to change his will after he married her. And her claim will have merit. But Harry has seen this kind of thing before, and there's no trusting a young woman who takes up with an older man. God knows he's a cynic — fired in the kiln of too many youthful wives — but it wouldn't surprise him to learn that Natasha had lovers aside from the deceased.

"We shall see," says Harry.

Even in the event that Todd's paternity is verified, he adds, there's really nothing to worry about. She, Jodi, can afford to be generous. A settlement for child support would not make much of a dent in her assets.

Harry is eager to proceed on her behalf. He will file a probate claim. He will see about power of attorney. He will start to prepare his case. And according to Jodi's wishes he will get in touch with Stephanie and arrange to retain her on behalf of the estate.

Every day she waits for the family man's return, catches herself waiting in spite of her resolve to put him out of her mind. But his next move is unexpected. When the knock comes — in the early afternoon as she's writing out a shopping list — and she succumbs to the inevitable by opening the door, the man standing there is not him but a colleague he's sent in his place, a colleague as thin as a rail who can't be more than thirty, but who nonetheless shows her his ID and tells her that he is Detective Somebody-or-Other. The man has the eyes of a psychopath, a nearly colorless blue with pupils like pinpricks and white half-moons riding beneath the irises. He pushes past her, moving uninvited into her living room. Like everyone else he gravitates to the view, which gives her a moment to take stock of the back of him in his black jeans and nylon bomber jacket. Skinny legs, skinny ass, sloped shoulders, big head. But he doesn't stand there for long.

"Miz Brett," he says. "Jodi."

He's agitated, twitchy. He circles the room, picking things up and putting them down. The ashtray from Mont St. Michel, a millefiori paperweight, a stack of DVDs. He flips through her copy of *American Psychologist*. Not looking up he says, "About the murder of your. Ex. Just a few things we. Need to discuss." His speech is fitful, as if he can't focus on what he wants to say. His voice is a scratchy contralto that sticks in his throat. His eyeballs move restlessly in the flat planes of his face, beacons to warn the unsuspecting.

She invites him to sit, pointing to the easy chair most recently occupied by the family man. He alights briefly on the chair arm and then resumes his pacing. His agitation is unsettling. Maybe that's the point. Placing herself on the sofa, she says in a spirit of protest, "Another detective was here last week. I answered a *lot* of questions."

"I'd hate to disturb you for no. Good reason," he says. He appraises her with studied insolence, gathering in the leopard-print pumps, manicured nails, pretty pair of molehills, little pointed chin. When his eyes once again meet hers, he continues. "This new piece of information that we happened to. Come across. I don't think you mentioned it to my colleague. Detective Skinner. We were just. Wondering. You know."

He moves to the window and turns his back to it, faces into the room. "Can you verify that the deceased. Mr. Todd Jeremy Gilbert. Your ex. At the time of his death had initiated eviction proceedings against you? Was in the process of legally evicting you? From this property. This apartment. Of which he was the sole and rightful.

Owner. Can you verify that, Miz Brett? Jodi?"

He talks so fast that his speech is slurred, and yet he halts abruptly after each of his odd clumps of words, filling in the pauses by shifting his weight, looking around the room, fingering the surfaces near at hand. Backlit by the sky, he's standing in a blaze of light that all but blinds her. She can't make out his features, can't see his eyes. How has he managed to do this? Put her at a disadvantage on her own stomping grounds. She ought to get up and adjust the drapes or move to a different chair. One of those Marlboros would be good right now.

"Yes," she says. "He was trying to evict me."

"But you weren't planning to leave. You didn't want to leave and you knew that you didn't have to leave because you had. Other ideas. You were making your own. Plans. If he wasn't around to file an order. With the sheriff, say. Then there wouldn't *be* an eviction. Would there, Miz Brett? Jodi. And here you are. Still here. Which proves your point."

"It's your point," she says.

He continues. "And not only would there be. No eviction. You would stand to inherit. As long as he was out of the way before his marriage to Miz Kovacs. Before he got around to. Changing his will. Timing was everything. Before he could evict you. Before he could marry the other. Woman."

Her guilt is hanging on her like that moldy Dior gown she bought last year at auction. He may think that she's a spoiled bitch who would sooner do murder than give up her little indulgences, but the fact is she has a highly developed sense of economy. Contrary to the impression he's no doubt formed of her, she was not spawned in a wealthy home and did not grow up in luxury. In the early years with Todd, when he had no money, she was the one who managed, found ways to cut corners. She even made a point of learning how to cook. Psycho cop might be surprised to know this about her. He ought to try her spicy pork sauté with pickled cabbage. Or her home-made gnocchi with truffle sauce.

He's waiting for her to speak, but she says nothing. Her default mode when bullied or badgered is silence. The second you open your mouth to defend yourself, they've got you. Got you on the run. She knows this intuitively, has always known it.

He believes in her guilt, she understands that, and would like to formalize his belief by placing her under arrest. But if he were planning to arrest her he wouldn't be wasting his time with all this bluster. What he doesn't get is that she's not going to crack. If he thinks she's an easy target he should think again. She is not the confessional type. Instead of churning her up or breaking her down, the interrogation is making her numb. The more he talks the number she gets.

"Let me tell you something," he says. "You can't inherit from the man you. Murdered. Maybe you didn't know that. Miz Brett. Jodi."

She has the sensation that he's far away, on the other side of a gorge, a malevolent child throwing sticks and stones. His aim is good but his missiles lose force across the distance and end up falling at her feet. Maybe he senses this. He's on the move again, coming away from the window to stand in front of her. She can see his face clearly now — his eyes floating high in their sockets, his lips twitching in tender disdain.

"Whatever you do you should stay put," he says. "You'll be seeing us again in the very near. Future."

With this parting shot he slouches to the door and lets himself out. She waits a moment and then stands up and tries to breathe. As far as she can tell no oxygen is passing through her lungs.

■ ■ ■ ■

In the following days she's suspended in a tyranny of waiting. Time is pressurized, a force of unbearable impact; it seems that she's grabbed and squeezed by every ruthless second. Food has no taste and she eventually stops eating. Her daily workout saps what little energy she has, and so she gives that up too. Even alcohol has lost its appeal, though she continues to use it as a medicinal drip, grateful for its sedative effects. Unable to look after herself she turns her attention to the dog, making him special meals and taking him on long rambling walks. As if to make up for her apathy, his appetites are keener than ever.

She's impressed by the fact that life goes on around her undiminished, that people have the wherewithal to give each day their best shot, inhabit their lives with a show of spirit. She respects them for it. They have their problems, she knows, as everyone does, but somehow they manage to keep themselves going. Compared to her, even her clients are doing well. They at least have left themselves openings for forward movement and future alternatives. If Miss Piggy enjoys her secret life, if the judge has divided loyalties, if the prodigal son and Mary Mary refuse to play the game, if Cinderella craves attention, if Sad Sack can't accept his limitations, if Bergman won't give up her dream and Jane Doe won't give up her marriage — they are still, each of them, making a better job of things than she is.

All that she knows or imagines about prison clatters around in her head, a kaleidoscope of vulgar prospects and showy threats. Isolated, with no one to confide in, she's given up on herself, fallen prey to a ruinous doomsday mentality. The trial will be a public spectacle; every detail of her life with Todd will be fodder for public consumption. And afterward, when the uproar has died down and people have moved on, long after that, she will still be locked up, trading her mashed potatoes for lipstick or aspirin and doing unspeakable things in the interest of self-preservation.

When the family man arrives again at her door, she greets him with a drink in hand and a ferment of reaction. The taste of her stomach is in her mouth, as if she were in a plummeting elevator. She surrenders to an unbecoming sort of cowering subservience, but that at least is tempered by a trickle of annoyance. She's surprised that some part of her can still resist.

"Forgive the intrusion," he says, stepping into the foyer.

Dusk is falling and her living room is a well of shadow. She switches on a table lamp and turns up the gas flame. They take the seats they occupied before — her on the sofa, him in the wing chair — as if that first visit was a rehearsal and now they've come to the real thing.

"Can I offer you a drink, Detective? I'm sorry but I can't remember your name." She began on the iced vodka at lunchtime, and although her mind is perfectly clear, her words collide as they tumble out of her mouth.

"Skinner," he says. "I'll have to pass on the drink, thanks, much as I'd like to join you."

She'd forgotten about his inane civility. He's come to arrest her but he's going to do it politely.

"I don't imagine the past little while has been easy for you," he says. "Please believe me when I say that we don't want to add to your distress. I know that my colleague has been here to see you as well, and I'm sorry we've had to put you through these repeated interviews. But, as you know, our first priority as always is to find the guilty party and make an arrest."

He's leading up to it now — the moment when he'll put her in handcuffs and take her away. It's what he's here for, though given his apparent sympathy, maybe he'll forgo the handcuffs and deprive her neighbors of the spectacle. It's a good thing she has a few drinks under her belt. Her intestines are roiling but she'd feel much worse if she were sober. The thing to do is top up her glass while she still has the chance.

"The point is that we have our case and it's a pretty solid one," he says. "We hit some stumbling blocks at first. It was hard to believe that something like this could happen without there being someone who could ID the car. But it came together in the end."

He doesn't say how it came together and she doesn't ask. When she stands up and slinks toward the kitchen, he raises his voice to cover first the distance between them and then the sound of the ice cubes as they clatter into the bucket. In the end he's practically shouting.

"Normally, of course, the victim's family and friends are relieved when we make an arrest. But sometimes the news is unwelcome, even disturbing. It all depends on the identity of the suspect. In this case, as it happens, the suspect is someone who was very close to the victim."

She can't believe the way he's beating around the bush. How can you be a policeman if you can't even make an arrest? Standing at the bar top she throws back what's left in her glass before refilling it and wonders how it will be to wake up in prison with a hangover.

"The thing is," he says, "I don't want to have you reading about it in the papers without forewarning you." He lowers his voice abruptly as she returns to her place on the sofa, fresh drink in hand. "I understand that you've known Dean Kovacs for a long time."

"Who?" she asks.

He clears his throat. One eyebrow shoots up. "Dean Kovacs. Isn't he an old friend?"

"What does Dean have to do with it?"

"That's what I'm trying to tell you. We've placed him under arrest."

"You're not saying you've arrested Dean Kovacs."

"I'm sorry. I knew it would come as a blow. If you don't mind my saying so, ma'am, you're looking very pale."

"Dean didn't kill Todd," she says.

"You're right, of course, in that he didn't pull the trigger. But he hired the men who did. It might help if you drank some coffee.

How about a glass of water?"

"Dean," she says. "You think Dean killed Todd."

"If you don't mind, Miss Brett, I'll just get you a glass of water. Please don't try to stand up."

She feels now as if she's been staring into the sun. She saw herself as different from all those others who commit crimes, in a league of her own, subject to a higher justice, but the truth is she's been burning out her retinas in a staggering feat of vanity and pride. Her thoughts have been simplistic and self-serving, the musings of a child in a narcissistic, preempathic phase of development. She made assumptions, far too many of them. Assumed, for example, that she was at the center of it, with the possibilities and probabilities orbiting her and her alone. Assumed that the game she was playing had a rule book, that she was operating in a known field where only certain outcomes were permissible.

She, Jodi, happens to like Dean Kovacs. He's a nice enough man, if a little misguided. She certainly has nothing against him. She may be a touch off-kilter these days, slightly out of whack, but she's not without her principles, not depraved. To see an innocent man destroyed for her own wrongdoing is not something she bargained on, not something she can live with.

Damn Dean. Damn him. What did he say or do to bring this on himself, what flag has he been waving to attract this kind of attention from the police? The family man would tell her nothing. "I can't give you any details just yet, I'm afraid, Ms. Brett. I'm very sorry but I just can't release that information. Not at the moment." She hates this. This ludicrous turn of events that's ruining everything. Trust Dean to come blundering into her private affairs. He never did have much sense, Dean. He's a meddler and a blowhard. She could almost allow him to rot in jail. Almost, almost.

She puts on a jacket and takes the dog to the water, where they walk along a stretch of beach in the onrushing gloom. The sky is a heaving, turbulent mass with dark clouds billowing up from the horizon. A bitter wind tosses the water and streaks along the shore. The mood that overtakes her is familiar, a sense of being adrift in an empty existence. This is Jodi's hollow core, her unfortunate place of fundamental truth, a domain that she conceals beneath her mantle of optimism and buries in the rounds of daily life. Here lives Jodi, the Jodi who knows that we thrive and prosper only to the degree that we can manipulate our personal circumstance. This Jodi is rarely seen. But Alison saw and exploited this Jodi. So few things are what they seem to be.

Her home, when she returns to it, strikes her as the lair of some repellent animal. Klara was in just the other day and gave the place her usual going-over, but what's been left undone is magnified in Jodi's fermenting imagination. It's the stench that hits her first, the coffee grounds and overripe fruit, and then, wherever she looks there is filth — grime in the drains, mold between the tiles. She sets to work with a bucket and rags, steel wool, a toothbrush. Uses disinfectant to scour the tiles and the drains and the trash receptacles. She moves through the rooms collecting objects — photographs, table lamps, candlesticks, carvings, doorstops, and bookends — which she places centrally for cleaning on sheets of newspaper. She understands even as she labors that her home is basically pristine, that her sense of a mission is something she's contrived, to do with the illusion of taking control and making things right.

By the time she's ready for bed her mind is made up. In the morning she'll turn herself in. It'll be easy. All she has to do is give the family man a call — she still has his card — and tell him about her arrangement with Alison. Whatever happens after that will be up to the police and the lawyers and the judge and the jury. They will do with her as they see fit. Justice will be in their hands and she will be off the hook, no longer responsible. She conceives this plan in a flurry of inevitability. This is what it's come down to, and she can almost feel glad about it, almost relieved. At least she'll be free of all the doubt and fear. And in the meantime she can look forward to the family man's reaction. That alone will be worth it, catching him out in all his polished conceit.

But her sleep is fitful and during the night her agitation ignites and spreads. By morning a fire rages in her chest and throat, her head is in the jaws of a vise, and her muscles are in shreds. In spite of the sweat pouring out of her, a chill wind is rippling through her bloodstream. She alternates between huddling under the bedclothes and heaving them aside, until at last she is forced out of bed by the dog's breath on her face and the little yips he gives when he needs attention. With a clammy hand she picks up the phone and cancels her morning clients. She calls the pet sitter, who agrees to come by and take Freud off her hands, and then she calls the dog walker to say that the dog will be staying with the pet sitter. Making the calls exhausts her. When she wakes up again it's dark outside and the dog is gone. She's covered in sweat, tangled in her damp sheets. It's an effort to get to her feet. She makes her way to the bathroom, swallows a sip of water, stands over the toilet bowl, throws up a small amount of bile. Gets back into bed on the other side.

Time passes. She notes that it's light outside and then dark again. She recalls hearing the phone and someone buzzing from the lobby. She wonders if it's the weekend, but that may have come and gone. She moves back to her own side of the bed, which is now dry, and wishes that someone would bring her a glass of ginger ale or an orange Popsicle. That's what her mother used to give her when she was sick in bed as a child, though she was never sick for very long. The girl she used to be was resilient. Back then, she believed that only good things would happen to her in life. That was the promise, and when Todd came along, he was the proof. Here was a man with dreams and the will to make them real. In the beginning they were so very taken with each other, so confident of their place in the scheme of things. She didn't know then that life has a way of backing you into a corner. You make your choices when you're far too young to understand their implications, and with each choice you make the field of possibility narrows. You choose a career and other careers are lost to you. You choose a mate and commit to loving no other.

When she dozes she dreams of strangers, unknown men and women telling her things that she can't hear or doesn't understand. She gets up, toasts a piece of bread, butters it, drops it into the garbage disposal, goes back to bed. Now she's in Florida giving a lecture on eating disorders. Someone has died from an overdose of sleeping pills. Alison is pregnant and she, Jodi, is somehow responsible. She trudges through blackness, swims upstream, falls into a pit and struggles to get out. She and Todd are living in their old digs, the little apartment where they were happy when they were first together. She's sorting through an array of household goods, putting items into boxes one by one, but there are too many things and the movers are banging on the door. The scene changes and Todd is saying that he's going to marry Miss Piggy. He hopes she doesn't mind. When she wakes up she feels utterly alone. The taste in her mouth makes her think of mice.

As she suspected all along, there are definitely insects living in her hair. She tosses her head, but the tiny creatures hang on tight, happy in the splendid nest they've made of her damp locks and greasy scalp. They must love that — the oil and the sweat, the rancid smell of it. A perfect place to lay their scummy eggs and raise their revolting young. A breeding ground beyond compare.

On the fifth day of her illness Klara finds her lying on top of the bedclothes like a blown leaf, curled and weightless. She's on her right side with her head and shoulders turned to the left — thrown back against the bunched duvet — wearing an oversize T-shirt that's twisted around her torso.

Klara stands in the doorway, vacillating between a state of alarm and the thought that her employer has merely had a late night. She's tempted to simply shut the door and get on with the cleaning. The woman has always been pale and thin, a poor specimen in Klara's opinion. But even in the half-light Klara can see that something isn't right. Mrs. Gilbert's skin has a bluish tint, and her sunken eyes are beyond the preserve of even a very bad hangover.

"Mrs. Gilbert? You are feeling okay?"

She steps into the room and stands at the foot of the bed. Something has happened to Mrs. Gilbert's hair. Her long, beautiful hair is gone, chopped off as if by a hatchet. The pitiful mess that remains is plastered in clumps to her scalp. This above all else strikes at Klara's core. She leans over the bed and takes hold of Jodi's wrist.

"Mrs. Gilbert," she says. "Please. Wake up."

She gives the wrist a firm shake. The eyes open and a shudder passes through the wraithlike form. Klara lets go and crosses herself. She hurries out of the room to look for the phone.

Later, after the ambulance has come and gone, Klara goes into the bathroom and finds the missing hair — a soft, dark mass mounded on the floor. Flung into a corner are the pinking shears that did the damage.

She's sitting up in bed, resting back against a wedge of pillows. Clear pale daylight pours through the window, heightening every detail of the small room: the laundry mark a black smudge on her turned-back sheet, the soft weave of her blue blanket, the mint-colored walls showing patches of discoloration, on her bedside locker the spreading poinsettia, on the window ledge the speckled lilies whose sweet, rotting smell has been invading her dreams.

Her bedpan is gone and so are the IV tubes. Yesterday, before breakfast, she made her first solo trip to the washroom. There she found her toothbrush, hairbrush, and assorted toiletries in a zippered bag beside the sink. She doesn't know who fetched them for her or who brought the plant or the flowers. People have been coming and going all the while. In the beginning she was barely aware of them. She'd wake up and see someone standing by her bed or sitting in the chair in the corner, and then she'd drop off and be gone again.

One of the nurses, the one with the gappy teeth, has just been in to take her temperature and give her a scolding. "You do know, Miss Brett, that when you first came in we thought we might lose you. Why did you let yourself get so dehydrated? You ought to know that with flu you need to drink plenty of fluids. You should have told someone you were sick. Your friends are all very concerned. Any one of them would have been happy to look in on you, bring you some juice, help you wash your hair."

It's still a shock to look at herself in the

mirror. She has no memory of wielding the shears and no sense of the thoughts that might have been going through her head. What she does recall is the satisfaction she felt at seeing her hair on the floor, knowing it was separate, not a part of her anymore, no longer attached. All her memories from the days of her illness are disjointed like this. But one thing she does know is that a lot of people were trying to get in touch with her. She remembers ringing, buzzing, and knocking, messages and conversations. In particular a conversation with Dr. Ruben — him saying how sorry he was about Todd, how he hated to disturb her at such a time, how he had something to tell her, something that would at least give her one less thing to worry about.

What is it that she doesn't need to worry about? She tries to remember. It's playing at the edge of her mind like the fragment of a tune. And there's Dr. Ruben in her mind's eye in his white coat with his slight stoop, the words coming out of his mouth. "Test results." That's what he called to tell her. Todd's test results have come back negative. A message from beyond the grave. Todd died a healthy man and left his women uninfected. One less thing to worry about.

Mercifully, the nurse has gone away and

left her in peace. She needs to close her eyes and think about the visit from Harry Le-Groot, who came by after lunch to bring her the news.

"So. You're back in the world," Harry said, sitting on the edge of her bed smelling of the outside world — tobacco, fresh air, damp wool — his face ruddy, his hair a sleek silver pelt. He told her about the call he'd received from Stephanie, who'd been alerted by Klara, who had tried to get in touch with Todd. "As far as Klara knew, Todd was alive and well. I guess she missed the story in the papers, and apparently you didn't get around to filling her in." He found this odd, judging from the way he was looking at her, but he didn't prod her any further. Nor did he ask about her hair. The main reason for his visit, he said, was to tell her that the gunmen had been found.

"The gunmen," he repeated, responding to her blank stare. "The perps. There are two of them. They're being held pending their bail hearing."

She didn't like the way he was speaking to her — patiently, carefully, telling her this in the gentlest possible way. It could only mean that the men had talked, that all the dots had been connected.

"They corroborated what we already

knew," Harry said. "That Dean Kovacs hired them and paid them to do this thing."

What was he saying? And why was he smiling? He appeared to be enjoying her confusion. Maybe he wanted to trick her into confessing. Of course. That's why he'd come to the hospital when he could have waited a day or two and seen her at his office. Catch her out while she was still drugged and disoriented. But she'd been planning to confess — that had been her intention all along — and she would have done so already if not for her illness. He didn't have to trick her to get at the truth.

But Harry was on a roll now, warming to his subject, speaking with gusto as he told her that the men were local hoods with rap sheets as long as her arm who had identified Dean as the one who had hired them, but that nobody needed to take their word for it because there was plenty of evidence to back them up.

"Phone calls. Bank transactions. Kovacs was a fool. He left a paper trail a mile long."

Harry went on to say that they were stubbornly pleading their innocence, these two saps, maintaining loudly and energetically that they hadn't followed through. Had they been hired by Dean to do the job? Yes. Had they actually done it? No. When he told her this he laughed and slapped his knee. It never failed to amuse him, he said, the lies that criminals would tell in their desperation to clear themselves. Even when they'd been caught red-handed they'd say anything, absolutely anything.

As she regains her physical strength, her mental acuity also makes a comeback. At first she has no idea how to think about it, the reprieve that she's been granted, the technicality that has given her back her life. Technicality is the word for it, too. She is not one to attribute things like this to a higher power looking out for her. She doesn't disbelieve in God, but there's no reason to think that God would intervene on her behalf and not on Dean's. If God were the judge he would have to find them equally guilty.

She remembers now her phone conversations with Dean. All that rage and fury. She thought nothing of it at the time. It seemed to her that he merely wanted to vent. He was Todd's oldest friend after all — how could she take him seriously? As it turns out, however, there are depths to Dean that she never fathomed. Clearly, she underrated him. But then, as someone who has no children, she must be forgiven for overlooking the parental imperative, the compulsion to safeguard one's offspring at whatever cost. And not being a man, she can never fully grasp the kind of macho posturing that Dean was engaged in, which no doubt played a part in leading him astray, in prompting him to carry things too far.

She inclines toward the view that Dean's men really are the culprits, that their plea of innocence amounts to just what Harry says — a desperate attempt to clear themselves. And what does that say about Alison? It could be that Alison was not to be trusted, had no intention of honoring their deal. Or maybe she just caved in at the sight of all that money. It's also possible that Alison did pay Renny and that Renny was the shirker. On the other hand, Alison and Renny may have both followed through and done what they were paid to do. Or they may at least have meant to follow through. Jodi would prefer to think the best of them. She is not inclined to doubt either Alison's sincerity or Renny's zeal for his work. Still, all she can do is speculate, because the truth will never be known, and besides, in a case like this the truth is relative, complex, tainted. The only thing she knows for sure, the one thing she can count on, is that she won't be getting a refund. If she wants to know why Alison is avoiding her, well, that may be her answer.

Once home from the hospital, after a day or two has passed, when she can muster the strength to face down the blinking light on her telephone, she finds among her messages one from her brother Ryan. Typically, Ryan has been out of touch and knows nothing of recent events, is just checking in, happens to be thinking about her, and will call again. That's Ryan for you. She's sorry to have missed him, but she has long since learned to keep Ryan in perspective and not tie herself in knots over his comings and goings. Thanks, of course, to Gerard Hartmann.

Odd how life can hand you these unexpected gifts. She went to Gerard in the first place as part of her training but can't dispute the fact that during her work with him she peered through the lens of her own eye and discovered important things about herself, for instance her terrific ability to shut out what she didn't want to see, forget what she didn't want to know, put a thing out of her mind and never think about it again. In short, to live life as if certain events had never come to pass.

Every shrink knows that it's not the event

itself but how you respond to it that tells the story. Take ten assorted individuals, expose them all to the same life trial, and they will each suffuse it with exquisite personal detail and meaning. Jodi is the one who never thought about it again. Not once. Not ever. What happened to Jodi in the distant place of her childhood qualifies without a doubt as well and truly forgotten, left behind, defunct, as good as eradicated. Or so she might believe if she hadn't studied psychology. In the end she had to accept that even if you forget that's not the same as if it never happened. The slate is not entirely wiped clean; you can't reclaim the person you were beforehand; your state of innocence is not there to be retrieved. The experience you've had may be unwanted, may amount to nothing but damage and waste, but experience has substance, is factual, authoritative, lives on in your past and affects your present, whatever you attempt to do about it. That pickle jar you threw away all those years ago may have gone to the landfill, but it still exists out there. It may be broken, even crushed, but it hasn't disappeared. It may be forgotten, but forgetting is just a habit.

In this analogy the landfill is the unconscious mind. Not the collective unconscious but the personal unconscious — your own individual, private, idiosyncratic unconscious wherein every object is inscribed with your name and stamped with your number, the unconscious from whence objects can fly at you unannounced — as one flew at her that day while she waited for the elevator after telling Gerard her dream about Darrell. To her credit, and it says a lot about her presence of mind, she did not overlook the value of the event as an object lesson in psychology. Indeed, she got it in a breathtaking flash: The unconscious mind is not just a theory in a book, not some trumped-up paradigm or overblown fancy, but as real as the nose on your face, as real as a pickle jar. According to Jung, everything in the unconscious seeks outward expression; an inner situation that is not made conscious will manifest in outward events as fate. The Greek philosopher Heraclitus made a similar proposition when he said that character is destiny.

How pleased Gerard would be to learn that her dream had ignited this valuable childhood memory. Here at last was something he could get between his teeth, and he had been edging for it, had sensed that something was waiting in the wings, had forged ahead with patience and purpose as if anticipating this very moment, the falling of this very ax. She wondered what cues he might have picked up, and she would have liked to ask, but as it turned out she never did take Gerard into her confidence, decided against it. Instead, she held the secret close and failed to ever mention it, preferring in the end to keep it in a shut box and starve it of oxygen. This was a choice that she considered to be very much her prerogative and even in her best interests. Her training told her that such things need to be aired, but in the balance she was still the same person, her childhood still a source of happy memories. In life's lunchbox there is no such thing as a hundred percent, and ninety-nine percent is downright providential. The only thing she needed to do was deal with the one percent blight, find a way to contain it.

Abruptly, she ended all contact with her older brother, and ever since, over the span of decades, has avoided him entirely, steeled herself against his lobbies and appeals, set him aside without mercy. He knows the reason why; there was never any need to explain. What he did to her was short-lived — a juvenile blunder, a pubescent tic — but some things must not be forgiven.

Nor would she ever forgive *herself.* Her

parents knew nothing, she was sure of that; they would not have put up with such behavior in a child of theirs, and she never could shift any blame onto them. It was she who should have stopped him before he got to Ryan — and she knew without a doubt that he had. Ryan's nightmares began literally overnight. His tantrums were spectacular and without precedent. He'd been such a pliable child. Maybe the adolescent Darrell had considered the younger sibling to be less of a security risk. Maybe he was merely exploiting his options. Quite possibly there was nothing going on in his head and it all came down to glands. Whatever the case, the deed was done and the grown-up Ryan, like Jodi, was out of touch with Darrell and left his name out of every conversation.

Her unspoken pact with Ryan is that neither of them will ever revisit the landmarks, unearth the relics, dig up the ground of things gone wrong. Her measure of Ryan's early years and what Ryan himself may or may not remember — this is out of bounds, effectively null and void, a history forsaken, a past disavowed. Forgetting is just a habit but it brings peace of mind, and above all Ryan must have peace of mind, must be kept safe, permitted to layer fresh experience over the silence.

As for herself, every morning on waking she gives thanks to the God she doesn't disbelieve in. Although she can't credit him with saving her, she needs this outlet for her gratitude. Her freedom is a gift beyond reckoning: that she can still awake each day in her beautiful home, walk barefoot on the thick wool carpets, open the silk-and-linen drapes to the sweep of the horizon, drink a latte made with French roast, go on a ramble with the dog. She is keenly aware — never forgets, even for a moment — that she forfeited all this. Her gratitude is like a hard candy that won't dissolve in her mouth.

She is grateful for Harry, too, who is working hard on her behalf. A court date is set for probate, and he has papers for her to sign. He tells her that Natasha is suing but that he's ninety percent sure she will settle out of court. With her baby due in the spring and the trial coming up, Natasha has more than enough on her plate. In any case she, Jodi, can afford to be generous. There will be plenty of money to go around once the apartment house and the office building are sold. Stephanie will be helping with that, and by the time Stephanie is no longer needed, Jodi will be in a position to offer her a decent termination package. Financially it's Cliff who will be hardest hit since Todd was far and away his best client. But Cliff is good at what he does, and new clients will come along.

She recognizes changes in herself. There's been a softening, a coming down to earth, and along with that a greater sense of kinship with her clients. Having understood that she, too, has been willful and greedy and blind and stuck, that she's been swimming in the soup with them all along, she can only be grateful for their loyalty and kindness. They've been putting up with her lapses, asking after her health. The judge brought her flowers and Bergman baked her a pie. Truly.

But the really surprising thing is that all of them, right down to the wayward Mary Mary, are showing less resistance and making more of an effort to work with her. A certain flow has infected them, a readiness and ease. A willingness to take responsibility and move forward is showing itself in their collective attitude, and everything begins with attitude, meaning outlook, belief, the story you tell yourself, as Adler has said. It's apparent that the changes in her are affecting her clients in turn, and she is now forced to consider that human nature is possibly more yielding than she once supposed. That her hideous fall from grace should end up making her less of a skeptic is a paradox that doesn't escape her.

It's odd to think, with Todd gone, that a son of his will inhabit the world in years to come. Would she recognize the boy if she passed him in the street? Will Todd's features be layered, ghostlike, over his son's countenance, or will there at least be a sign — a mannerism, something in his posture? She wonders if the boy's mother will tell him the truth about his family, take him to visit his grandpa in the state penitentiary. In Natasha's position, Jodi might be tempted to bury the whole egregious mess, never refer to it, invent some fiction to explain Dean's absence, or better still just forget about Dean, as if he too had died, since forgiving him would be impossible.

Anyway, the story is really about the two men, the boyhood friends, one dead and one as good as dead. A young woman like Natasha has no need to drag their unfinished business behind her, burden herself with their defective karma. If she has any sense she'll find herself another husband, someone to give Todd's son a new name. People make too much of blood ties anyway. But Natasha is probably one of those sticklers for the truth, the way people are these

days. Tell the child where he comes from —
he has a right to know. Whereas Jodi has no
problem with the blurring of facts. There
are benefits to be had, and anyway some
things are best left unexamined. No need to
stare reality in the face if there's a kinder,
gentler way. No need for all that grim urgency.

ABOUT THE AUTHOR

A. S. A. Harrison is the author of four nonfiction books. *The Silent Wife* is her debut novel and she was at work on a new psychological thriller when she died in 2013. Harrison was married to the visual artist John Massey and lived in Toronto.